THE DEVIL'S HEART

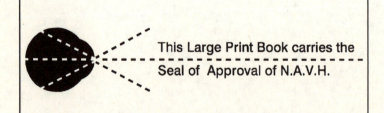

This Large Print Book carries the
Seal of Approval of N.A.V.H.

THE CHATTAN CURSE, BOOK 2

THE DEVIL'S HEART

CATHY MAXWELL

THORNDIKE PRESS
A part of Gale, Cengage Learning

GALE
CENGAGE Learning®

Detroit • New York • San Francisco • New Haven, Conn • Waterville, Maine • London

LIBRARY OF CONGRESS CATALOGING-IN-PUBLICATION DATA

Maxwell, Cathy.
  The devil's heart : the Chattan Curse / by Cathy Maxwell. — Large Print edition.
    pages cm. — (Thorndike Press Large Print Romance)
  ISBN 978-1-4104-6016-5 (hardcover) — ISBN 1-4104-6016-9 (hardcover) 1. Scotland—Fiction. 2. Large type books. I. Title.
PS3563.A8996D48 2013
813'.54—dc23   2013011356

Published in 2013 by arrangement with Avon, an imprint of HarperCollins Publishers.

Printed in the United States of America
1 2 3 4 5 6 7 17 16 15 14 13

The dedication for this book was offered as a silent auction prize to the benefit of Blessed Sacrament–Huguenot School in Powhatan, Virginia. The following dedication is from the school's generous supporters who won the prize:

To two of the most important people in our lives —
Suzanne Miller
and
Doris Estes
You are amazing mothers.
Thank you for being both strong and inspirational.

Love,
Jacques and Lisa Gits

Chapter One

1814
The last days of December
The Road to Loch Awe, Scotland

Margaret moved deeper into the forest. The air was colder here but she sensed the chill rather than felt it. Such was the nature of dreams, and she knew she dreamed.

The path she followed was not easy. The forest floor was deep with damp, rotting leaves. The roots of ancient trees threatened to trip her. Heavy, gnarled limbs loomed overhead as if reaching out to claw her back. She carried a short sword in her hand.

She had come to battle the Macnachtan.

She knew they were close.

She did not know what to expect.

A faint green light appeared just around the curve in the path. Margaret paused. She tightened her hold on the sword. The time of reckoning had arrived. She must not lose her courage.

She stepped forward, the fear in her heart pounding in her ears.

At the bend in the road was a huge tree, an oak, with a trunk wider than the span of a man's arms. She paused, knowing that her enemy was about to be revealed — and then the heavens opened.

Rain poured down, rain that changed to falling corpses. Dead, lifeless bodies, falling upon her from the oak's mighty branches —

Lady Margaret Chattan came awake with a gasp. She had raised her hands above her head as if she could ward off the bodies — and she held them there, waiting . . . waiting for nothing.

For a long second, she stared around the confines of the rolling coach, needing a moment to recognize her surroundings, to realize she was safe. Confused, stunned by the horror of the dream, and more than slightly embarrassed, she lowered her arms.

"Are you all right, my lady?"

Margaret turned toward the speaker, her abigail, Smith, who had been hired especially for this trip.

Smith was a prim, self-contained sort who wasn't any more certain of her new employer than Margaret was of her. For most

8

of the trip, she'd sat on the coach seat facing Margaret's. She'd always had a piece of needlework close at hand and an air of judgment on her round face.

She was knitting now. Her needles hadn't even paused as she made her inquiry. It was almost as if she assumed Margaret would exhibit extreme behavior.

"I had a dream," Margaret answered in a voice that encouraged no inquiries.

Smith had replaced Higgins, who had been Margaret's closest confidante. She and Higgins had been together for over ten years. Higgins had recently married one of the household footmen and was now expecting. Therefore, she was unable to accompany Margaret on this trip.

If Higgins had been here, Margaret could have told her about the dream. Higgins had never sold information or gossiped, which had made her worth her weight in gold. Smith was different. The woman was gallingly curious about Margaret's every action, and Margaret knew she annoyed the maid by being so tight-lipped about their purpose in Scotland.

Margaret sat up on the tufted velvet seat and lifted the flap over the coach window, needing to assure herself they were on a mountain road and not in the forest of her dream.

Winter had finally arrived in the Highlands. Over the past two gray and dismal days of traveling, they had encountered light snow, sleet, rain and, for one rare moment, the sun, proving what everyone claimed about the unpredictability of Scottish weather to be quite true.

Both she and Smith wore heavy woolen dresses and cloaks. They each had a fur-lined lap blanket over their knees, and neither had taken off her gloves. Smith even wore them as she knitted.

The wind seemed to whip at the window. At this particular juncture of the winding mountain road there were no trees to stop it. No gnarled limbs or rotting leaves. As far as Margaret could tell, they seemed to be the only living creatures in the world. There were no crofters' huts, or a herd of sheep wandering over the rocky moorland, or a bird in the cloud-laden sky.

She let the flap fall back over the window. "Thomas says we should reach Loch Awe before nightfall." She tried to keep her voice nonchalant, to hide the doubt and uneasiness inside her.

The task that lay ahead called for a warrior, not a confused, "pampered" miss who didn't feel she had any purpose in her life and was all too aware of her miserable failings.

But she couldn't let any of that show. She never could.

After all, she was Lady Margaret Chattan. Society thought her perfect, complete, whole. She was an acclaimed beauty and on all the best social lists, although she rarely went out. They thought her aloofness was due to her being imperial, discerning. They respected her for it. They speculated on whom she would someday marry and offered potential matches.

Little did they know she did not go out because she was not worthy of any honorable man. She was not what they thought her.

Not even her brothers Neal and Harry, the people who knew her best, were aware of how she had degraded herself — and God willing, they never would. It was her secret, one only Higgins knew. In the rarefied air of the highest ranks of London society an unmarried woman's virginity was her badge of honor. Margaret had tossed hers aside for something as foolish as believing she'd been in love. Of course, she'd been very young when she'd done so, but she'd known what was at stake.

For a period of time, she'd carried on as if nothing was the matter, but it was hard living a lie and easier on her conscience to retreat from society. The curse offered the justification. She'd told her brothers she would not marry knowing that she could pass the curse on to her children. They'd understood. They knew the danger of love.

And now, to save them, the curse was calling her out.

The Chattan Curse. *When a Chattan male falls in love, he dies.*

A Scottish witch of the Macnachtan clan had placed the curse upon them almost two hundred years earlier when Margaret's ancestors had left Scotland for England. And it had not been some bit of nonsense or hocus-pocus. The curse had claimed her father's life, her grandfather's, and their fathers' before them. Knowledge of the curse and the dangers of love had always been a part of her life.

Unfortunately, and against all wisdom, both of her brothers had fallen in love and were the curse's next victims unless she could stop it. Her oldest brother, Neal, Lord Lyon, had been too weak to walk when Margaret had left London. And Harry, well, Harry had surprised her.

He'd traveled ahead of her to Scotland in

search of a Scottish witch who could break the curse. Instead, in that short period of time, *he'd* fallen in love and his left arm was already numb, one of the first signs of the curse taking hold.

She was their only hope. For this reason, she was on her way to Loch Awe, the family seat of the Macnachtans.

Smith interrupted Margaret's thoughts. "I won't be telling fibs, my lady, I'm tired of travel. It's hard to believe we left London only six days ago. I feel as I've been around the world twice and back."

Margaret was tired of travel as well. However, she felt herself bristle at the servant's complaint. This was no pleasure trip but one of life and death.

If Harry's suspicions were correct, Margaret could be the key to breaking the Chattan Curse. She was the first daughter to have been born since the curse existed, and Harry believed her birth might not have been just happenstance.

In Glenfinnan, once the home of Margaret's ancestors, Harry had discovered a book of recipes once owned by Fenella Macnachtan, the witch who had placed the curse upon them. The book rested on the seat beside Margaret now. She'd read it front to back thrice over.

13

At first it appeared to be the sort of book one chatelaine passed down to another. The leather binding was cracked and worn with age. The records were handwritten and covered everything from how to make unproductive hens lay eggs to the refining of soap. But there were other entries as well, notes that read like spells. There was one for the lovelorn who wished to reclaim a lost love, with the word "Charles" written in the margin.

Charles, Margaret's Chattan ancestor who was the first to die from Fenella's spell.

Harry believed that Rose of the Macnachtan, the lass Charles had jilted to marry an English-woman, had written that inscription. She'd taken her life over Charles's betrayal by jumping off the tower of her family's keep.

He believed there were no more answers to be found in Glenfinnan and that they must go to the scene of Rose's death — and he believed only Margaret could do it.

She prayed Harry was right but she had doubts, especially with Neal so dangerously ill.

What if she was traveling in the wrong direction? What if Harry was wrong and there was nothing that she or *anyone* could do to break the curse's terrible power?

14

Right now, Neal's unborn son would feel the weight of it. And if history were any indication, Harry, too, would sire a son before he died.

"If only I had a sign," she murmured. Some indication that she was on the right path. Something that could give her hope.

"Something that would bolster my fragile courage."

She hadn't realized she'd spoken aloud until Smith piped up, "I'm sorry, my lady, what did you say?"

Margaret waved her question away with the hand that had been resting on the book. "Nothing. I'm just musing." Wishing was more like it. Or praying.

A small meow caught her attention. Owl, the strange little cat she'd found clinging to the undercarriage of the coach, poked her head out from under the far edge of Margaret's blanket where she'd been curled up taking a nap. She now stretched in that indolent, satisfied manner of all cats as she eased herself out from under the cover. She climbed into Margaret's lap.

Margaret had never had a cat for a pet. Her mother had not liked them.

However, Owl had captivated Margaret from the moment she'd laid eyes on the animal.

Beneath the mud from the road, Margaret had discovered white fur as slick as silk. But it was Owl's ears that had charmed Margaret. They were folded over, an aberration of Owl's birth, giving a flat, owlish shape to her head, an image that was enhanced by her wide eyes. Margaret had never seen such large, expressive eyes on a cat. Sometimes, they had an almost human quality. She'd heard that many white cats were blind or deaf, but that wasn't the case with Owl. This strange little puss had the uncanny ability to give Margaret, who by her own admission could be overly tense, a sense of peace.

The cat began kneading her paws into the blanket over Margaret's legs as if settling herself in. The sound of purring filled the coach and Margaret felt her worries begin to fade, especially as she ran her gloved hand over the cat's fur. The stakes were literally life and death, but a sense of certainty filled her.

She *was* on the right path. Harry believed it and so must she. From here going forward, she must act on faith —

"Are you certain you are not coming down with an ailment, my lady?" Smith suggested. Her knitting needles had stopped moving and she eyed Margaret with great concern. "Perhaps we should return to England?"

"I informed you when I hired you that we would be making a hard journey."

"Yes, my lady," Smith answered. There was a pause. The maid seemed to be considering something and then said with an appearance of genuine concern, "I fear this trip is having an unusual effect on you, my lady."

"How so?"

The maid frowned at Owl, who was blissfully enjoying Margaret's attention. "Well," she started as if finding the topic more difficult than she had imagined, "You had that dream that seemed to have startled you, and I, well, I fear it weighs heavy upon you."

Margaret felt herself laugh. Yes, the dream had been frightening, but she was fine now. Bold, even. "It was a dream, nothing more."

Smith's frown deepened. "Dreams can mean the mind and body are not well."

"I feel in excellent health," Margaret answered. And she did.

The corners of Smith's mouth tightened and she once again eyed Owl with grave concern. Smith might not be a cat person. Like Margaret's mother.

Another mark against Smith.

Margaret knew she and the maid would be parting company the very second they returned to London. Until then, she'd have to tolerate the woman.

Owl lifted her chin up, silently begging for a scratch there, and Margaret was happy to oblige.

Smith grew more agitated.

She set her knitting aside, not bothering to fold her handiwork or give a care over losing stitches off her needle.

For a long second, she sat tense and nervous, and then, as if she could bear it no longer, she said, "My lady, I *must speak* and I pray you pardon me for being so forward."

"Forward?"

"I don't want you to think I don't know my station."

"I will think nothing of the sort. Speak. Higgins and I rarely stood on ceremony."

A fear that she was dooming herself crossed Smith's face, but when she spoke, the words practically exploded from her. *"There is no cat."*

The charge seemed to hang in the air.

Margaret wasn't certain she'd heard the maid correctly or understood her meaning. "Are you talking of Owl? Of course, there's a cat. She is right here."

Smith glanced at where Margaret's fingers scratched the purring cat beneath the chin. Her gaze shifted back to meet Margaret's. "No, 'Owl' as you call him —"

"Owl is a *her.*"

A flash of provocation crossed Smith's face. "I beg pardon, my lady. Owl, as you call *her,*" the maid corrected, "is not there. You are playing with the air. Your fingers are moving but you are not touching anything. Now I want you to understand, my lady," she hastened to add, "I have had my share of eccentric employers. Your secret is safe with me, but I believe you should know that *I* know there is no cat."

For a moment, Margaret didn't know what to say. If she'd had any second thoughts about terminating Smith once they returned to London, they were gone from her mind. She'd never let a servant go before. Her brother Neal's holdings were vast and there was usually another position somewhere to place a retainer who was less than satisfactory.

But Smith's outrageous charge would earn her a dismissal.

Instead of answering the abigail, Margaret reached up and knocked on the door that separated the interior of the coach from the driver's box. Beside her, Owl stretched, spreading her toes to show her claws before settling back into a ball, seemingly uncaring of the turmoil her sweet presence had caused.

The door drew back. "Yes, my lady?" the coachman, Balfour, asked.

"Stop the coach. Stop it immediately."

Thomas, the driver, had overheard the command and slowed the horses to a halt. The minute they came to a standstill, Margaret opened the door and climbed out. She held Owl on her shoulder like a baby. She did not worry about shedding on her blue merino dress. The cat had never shed. Not one white hair had ever been left on her clothing or blankets.

Along with Thomas and Balfour, her party included four outriders insisted upon by Neal for her protection. These men had been riding a short distance ahead, but seeing the coach stop, they now circled back to join them.

Also among her traveling companions was Rowan, an odd Indian man who served as her brother Harry's valet. Harry had insisted Rowan travel with her to Loch Awe. Margaret was not comfortable with the decision. The quiet Indian's presence had always been a bit unsettling to her. He always seemed to be watching, evaluating, and she sensed he saw far more than what made her comfortable.

Balfour and Rowan climbed down. Thomas stayed up in the box to hold the horses, who stretched and snorted their pleasure at receiving a break. Their breath came out in snorts of cold, foggy air.

"Yes, my lady," Balfour said. "What is the matter?"

"Smith is telling me that she doesn't see a cat. A cat that has been constantly by my side for the last two days of this trip. She has made a ridiculous statement and I want you to tell her that you do see the cat, Balfour."

The maid had not followed Margaret out of the coach. She sat close to the doorway, her head bowed, her brows drawn together in concern.

There was a beat of silence.

Margaret had known Balfour most of her life. She had an easy companionship with the older man. She expected him to answer in the affirmative. After all, he'd been beside her when she'd pulled Owl out from under the coach.

"I see a cat," Balfour replied . . . as if reaching a decision to agree with her.

Margaret did not appreciate the hesitation. "You don't sound certain," she challenged.

"With all respect, my lady, you said for me to tell Mrs. Smith I saw a cat. I said what you expected me to say."

"I didn't mean for you to *repeat* what I said," Margaret snapped. "I want you to tell Smith the truth. There is a cat."

"Do you *wish* the truth, my lady?"

"*Of course,* I wish the truth."

The older man sighed and then admitted, "I don't see a cat. I never have, not even when you pulled it from underneath the coach."

Margaret rocked back a step, stunned.

Was this a jest?

Well, they'd picked the wrong time to play a game. She had too many matters of great importance on her mind to enjoy this. Some servants knew of the Chattan Curse but most did not.

Still, this sort of playfulness was out of the ordinary. And neither Smith nor Balfour was the playful sort.

Aware that the servants all watched carefully, Margaret didn't know what to say.

The cat was right there in her arms. Margaret could feel Owl's warmth, the weight of her body, the beat of her small heart.

She set Owl down.

The cat gave a small meow and then trotted to the side of the road to disappear into the brown grass and gorse to see to her private business in her usual fastidious manner.

Margaret watched the cat move away, but was conscious that everyone else's eyes were upon her.

They did not see a cat.

And their expressions were ones of concern and worry.

Her gaze turned to Rowan. Solemn amber brown eyes met hers. He alone did not appear worried.

And Harry had insisted she trust him.

"Smith, hand me my cape," Margaret ordered.

The abigail dutifully complied, handing Margaret the red cloak trimmed around the hood with sable.

"Rowan, walk with me a bit," Margaret said, throwing the cape over her shoulders. She set off without waiting for him to obey. Of course, he obliged her, falling into step slightly behind her. Impatiently, she said, "Walk *with* me. I am not going to crane my neck to have a discussion with you."

Fear made her voice a touch shrill. Walking would calm her and help her think.

Owl emerged from the brush and fell into pace with them. The cat was as loyal as a dog, following, then plunging into the grass, only to emerge up the road and wait for them.

When they were away from the others, she said,

"You were standing beside me when I pulled Owl out from beneath the coach. You saw her, didn't you?"

"I accept there is a cat, my lady." His English was well-spoken with the faintest hint of an Eastern accent.

She frowned at this answer. "Did you see the cat or not?"

He didn't answer immediately. She turned, confronting him, expecting an answer.

A muscle tightened in his jaw. He nodded as if confirming something to himself and then said, "The colonel saw a cat." The colonel was her brother Harry, who held that rank in the Horse Guard.

"He did?"

"A white cat that he described as having folded-over ears and large eyes."

A surge of relief shot through her. "That is Owl. That's the cat I see."

"Then there is a cat," Rowan answered.

"But did *you* see her?"

There was a beat of silence. "No, my lady. I have not had the honor."

Owl waited for them up the road. Seeing that they were talking, she sat on her haunches, her unblinking gaze upon Margaret.

"I'd asked for a sign," Margaret whispered.

"A sign of what, my lady?"

"That we are on the right course. There is so much at stake, Rowan, and so little time left."

The valet conceded her words with a nod.

"This doesn't make sense," she said, more to herself than to him. "I hold the cat. She responds to me. She purrs and presses her nose against my hand for me to pay attention to her. Her nose is wet, cold."

"There are many things in this world that don't make sense, my lady."

"Such as?"

"A curse?" he reminded her with a faint smile.

"How I wish it did not exist," she murmured. "How different my life would be." She looked up the road where it curved as it went around the mountain. "If Owl is part of this curse, what role could a cat play?"

"In my culture, we believe souls can reincarnate themselves in many forms. Do you understand?"

"Explain."

"Colonel Chattan and his wife both saw the cat. The colonel's wife said the cat arrived in her house at the same time she discovered the book. No one else has seen the cat, until now. In my country, we believe what you call the soul never dies. We believe we can return or reincarnate ourselves into people or animals."

"An animal does not have a soul. At least that is what the church claims."

"And do you believe that is true?"

At that moment, Owl turned her attention from Margaret. She gave a delighted sound and pounced on something only she could see in the grass. Her tail swished with excitement. She glanced over at Margaret as if to include her in the hunt, and it almost seemed as if the cat smiled her pleasure.

"Whose reincarnated soul do you believe Owl is?" she asked Rowan. The question sounded unbelievable.

The valet smiled, a silent approval of her change in thinking, and then offered apologetically, "We don't know. Colonel Chattan believes there are only two possibilities. Could she be Fenella? Or Rose? Then again, she could be someone completely different."

"Why did he not tell me this himself?"

"The cat was not there at the time. And if he had told you of Owl, would you have believed him?"

Margaret's silence said she would not have.

"Have you read Fenella's book of spells?" Rowan asked.

"Repeatedly. Harry believes it may hold a secret to ending the curse, but I've found nothing."

"Because you have not opened your mind to all the true meanings of the spells," Rowan explained gently. "There is a spell in it for bringing a soul back to life."

Margaret frowned. Had she read one? Would she have noticed if she had? Everything was happening too quickly. It was hard for her to grasp it all.

She looked back in the direction where Owl had disappeared into the grass. "It's madness to believe an animal can have a human spirit. It's madness to think I am the only one who can see the cat. Why? What could her presence mean?"

The wind seemed to have turned colder. Or was it fear that made her cross her arms in protection? She thought of her dream, of the bodies falling, of the menacing forest —

There was no forest here, only rocky mountain slopes.

"You do not have to continue on, my lady," Rowan said. "Colonel Chattan wanted me to be certain you understood

27

you have the choice to turn back. He does not hold you accountable for anything."

"He's my brother. He's going to die unless something is done. Both of my brothers will. I must go on." She faced Rowan. "You just told me that this cat could be a mystical force, whether for good or evil, and I'm the only one who sees her. Harry *is* right. I could be the key to ending this. I must go to Loch Awe."

Margaret raised her hand, a signal for the coach. They did not hesitate but drove for her.

"Climb aboard, Rowan," she ordered, opening the passenger door herself.

"What of the cat?" he asked. Owl was still hunting through the grass.

"We leave her here," Margaret said. *"Hurry."*

As he climbed up onto the box, Margaret took her place, slamming the door shut behind her. Smith sat in the far corner of the coach watching Margaret's every move with wide eyes, her knitting needles back in her hands.

"Leave," Margaret ordered her driver. "Take us from here quickly."

There was a snap of the whip. The horses moved forward. The wheels turned.

Margaret leaned out of the coach window.

Owl appeared on the side of the road, a wiggling mouse in her mouth. The cat stared after the coach, not letting go of her prey.

Pulling herself inside, Margaret leaned against the seat, her hands tightened into fists — and then she noticed the book.

She picked it up and began flipping through the pages, searching for some clue that might have something to do with reincarnation.

But in truth, her heart felt as if it was breaking.

She hadn't wanted to leave Owl behind. In a short period of time, the cat had come to mean a great deal to her. Perhaps too much.

Margaret had thought herself at peace in her loneliness. She *chose* to be alone. Love was not an emotion to be trusted. And, when love meant death, what other choice was there?

Whoever, or whatever, had created Owl now preyed upon Margaret's loneliness, and she could not allow that.

Still, it hurt to abandon the pet.

She leaned to look out the coach window again. Owl was still on the road, a small white dot behind them.

They traveled around the curve in the

road, and Margaret's view of Owl was gone.

The violence of the storm caught Margaret's small party unawares. They'd been on the road less than half an hour after leaving Owl when the weather had changed dramatically.

It started with the wind, which came roaring at them with a force stronger than any known and slammed against the coach so hard the vehicle rocked back and forth. Nor did it relent. Time and time again, the wind assailed them.

Thomas tried to keep the horses moving. The outriders flanked the coach, needing to stay close for their own protection. Progress slowed almost to a halt.

A white-faced Smith took to praying aloud and Margaret was silently echoing her words. She held Fenella's book tightly with both arms, wishing there was a spell in it to change the weather.

Had Owl done this? Should she have left the cat?

Such thoughts were madness.

"It's the Highlands," Balfour shouted to Margaret through the door between them. "They say the weather changes in a blink."

"Pull over then," she ordered.

"We will once we find some shelter," Balfour answered. "We are on the downward side of the mountain." He shut the door.

"I'm not feeling so well, my lady," Smith confessed. "How much longer will this go on?"

"Not long," Margaret attempted to reassure her. "Lie down. You will feel better—"

The coach shook as if a huge hand of wind and fury had taken hold of it.

For a heart-wrenching second, Margaret could swear the coach was being lifted from the ground.

There were shouts from the men. The horses screamed.

The coach bounced with a mighty jolt and then listed dangerously to one side. The wheels had gone off the road and there was nothing to stop them from tumbling down the mountain slope.

Margaret realized they were doomed, and in the next moment, all thought in her brain was replaced with terror as the coach began rolling over and over down the mountain. Both women were tossed around in the coach, bouncing like marbles thrown into a container. Smith screamed and would not stop.

Margaret's head hit the edge of the door beneath the coach's window and the world went blessedly black.

How long Margaret had been unconscious, she did not know. The first thing she saw when she opened her eyes was Smith's face. The maid's lifeless eyes were still wide open in terror.

The ground was cold and hard. Broken pieces of the coach surrounded their bodies. There were trees here. Oaks and beeches.

Every bone in Margaret's body felt as if it had been broken. The pain was intolerable.

She wondered where Balfour, Rowan and the others were. Here and there was a moan, or was that the wind? That angry, violent wind had turned calm. Listening a moment longer, Margaret realized there was no stirring or movement of life.

In her line of sight, she could see Fenella's book. It lay within reach of her fingers. The book held the answer. *She must not lose it.*

She strained to reach for it. Her arms would not obey. They couldn't.

Margaret did not believe in tears. They served no purpose, but she began to cry now, silent tears that felt hot against her cold cheeks. She didn't cry for herself. No, she wept for her brothers' wives and the sons they would bear who would be marked with the curse. She wept for Balfour, Thomas, Rowan and the outriders, even for Smith, good people who did not deserve to die.

Soon, she would join them in death, here at the base of this mountain —

A purring caught her attention. *Owl.*

The sound came from her right side. She could not turn her head to look.

The cat nudged her cheek, and then gave it a lick as if to wipe away the tears. She felt Owl's breath upon her skin. The cat nestled itself into the space between Margaret's chin and shoulder. The purring grew louder and Margaret thanked God she would not die alone. In this moment, she didn't care if the cat was Rose or Fenella or the devil. Margaret would accept comfort wherever she could find it.

Warmth replaced coldness. The purring vibrated through Margaret's being, easing the tension and the fear. Almost blissfully, she slipped once again from consciousness to meet her fate . . .

CHAPTER TWO

There were some days when the only thing that could make a man feel better and take the edge off life was to plow a hard fist into another man's face.

For Heath Macnachtan, 16th chief of Macnachtan, raggedy clan that they were, today was just such a day.

He had just returned from Glasgow after a very dissatisfactory visit with his late brother's solicitor. The news was not good. The Macnachtans were paupers in spite of everything Heath had done to clear the debts over the past year since he'd taken over as laird. He'd poured every shilling he owned and had used every ounce of ingenuity he possessed to setting his family's books to right — and it had not been enough.

Now the family was in danger of losing the one thing that held them together as a clan — Marybone, the stone manor house that served as the seat of the Macnachtan and was the roof over his head.

He knew his sisters waited for his return, anxious for news of his discussion with the solicitor. He wasn't eager for the interview.

Was it any wonder then that he would want to bolster his courage after a long ride with a stop at the Goldeneye, a rabbit warren of a pub beneath the shelter of some pines along Loch Awe's shores? And perhaps between a nip of whisky and a pint or two of good ale he might realize a solution to his problems.

It was possible. Not probable . . . but the world always looked better to a man after he'd quenched his thirst.

Heath stooped as he walked through the Goldeneye's door. As he took off his heavy woolen cloak, a remnant of his naval career, and hung it on a peg in the hall, he heard the companionable sound of male laughter coming from the taproom.

The sound made him smile until he walked into the low-ceilinged room and discovered that the laughter was directed at his cousin Rowlly Macnachtan who also served as his land factor.

Augie Campbell was making great sport of shoving Rowlly's elbow every time he lifted his tankard up to his lips. It was apparently not the first time he'd done it.

Rowlly's shirt was covered with ale.

"I don't understand why you can't take a drink, Macnachtan," Augie complained. "That's the third pint I've brought for you. You should be more careful. Nate," he said to the Goldeneye's owner, "pour us another."

Augie was a bully. He was twice the size of Rowlly and carried three times the weight. His eyes were red-rimmed. Apparently he was not having a good week, either, and had decided to take it out on Heath's cousin. A good number of Campbells stood around the pub grinning like fools, obviously enjoying Rowlly being ridiculed.

Rowlly held his dripping tankard away from him, his every muscle was tense, but he had a good head on his shoulders. If he chose to battle, it would not be a fair fight. Augie would roll him up like a ball and toss him in the air.

Heath had no such disadvantage. He could look Augie in the eye, and he might not be as brawny as the Campbell but he was smarter and quicker.

Before anyone registered his presence, Heath crossed the taproom in two steps, grabbed Augie by the back of his thick neck, and brought his head down on the hard wood surface of the bar with a resounding, and satisfactory, *thwack.*

For a second, there was stunned silence.

Augie moved first.

He placed one heavy hand on the bar and then another. He pushed himself up. He faced Heath, his expression one of comic surprise. He started to growl, but then his eyes crossed and he fell to the floor with a thud.

"Good to see you, Laird," Rowlly said with generous understatement. "Stopped by for a pint on your way back from Glasgow?"

"I am thirsty," Heath said, matching Rowlly's dry tone.

"I don't believe you will be having a drink now," Rowlly answered, and he was right.

Augie was not well liked by his clansmen, but he was one of them. Campbell pride was now on the line.

"I'll take a pint, Nate," Heath said to the landlord, even as he felt the Campbells surge forward. He then turned and buried his fist in the abundant gut of the first man coming at him — and it felt good. He'd needed a fight and a fight he was receiving.

Rowlly took the fresh pint Nate had poured and threw it in the face of his nearest attacker. In spite of his size, he was a good fighter when the stakes were even. He now proved his mettle.

Nate turned to pour fresh pints. "You will be paying for damages, Laird?" He filled another tankard.

Heath avoided a response by picking up Jamie Hightower, the blacksmith's son and one of Augie's mates, and throwing him over the bar. Jamie fell upon the keg that Nate had tapped. The barrel broke under his weight and ale went spilling everywhere.

A roar of outrage came from the pub patrons who had not entered the fray but who now had just cause.

It was a good time to leave.

Heath grabbed both the freshly poured tankard the dumbfounded Nate still held and Rowlly's collar. Two more of Augie's clansmen had entered from other rooms, ready to join the brawl. Augie himself was starting to rouse, no doubt brought to his senses by the fresh ale on the floor.

Gulping down his pint, Heath shoved Rowlly out into the hall and then threw the empty tankard at the Campbells following him. It hit one over the eye. He hollered. The others shoved past him.

Rowlly and Heath charged out the front door, running for Admiral, Heath's horse tied at a post. "Hurry," Rowlly shouted, but he needn't have bothered. Heath was right on his heels. It had been a long time since

Heath had moved so fast.

The cousins mounted Admiral just as the Campbells came pouring out of the pub. Heath put heels to horse and they were off and safe. There was no one who could out-race Admiral; the long-legged draft horse had the spirit of a Thoroughbred when given his lead.

They dashed toward the open road. The wind against Heath's sweaty face felt good. His hands stung and he'd have a bruise beneath one eye, but in this moment he was *alive.*

Months of struggles and sadness fell away. He'd find them again; they were not lost completely. But for right now, the tension that had become his constant ally had been dispersed.

When he was certain they weren't being followed, Heath brought Admiral to a walk. The horse was fair winded. After a few minutes, Heath turned off the road into a forest before reining the horse to a halt. Rowlly slid off Admiral's rump and raised his fist in triumph.

"We gave them something to think about, didn't we?" He still smelled of the ale Augie had poured over him. "They will think twice before they pull that nonsense on a Mac-nachtan."

"How did you find yourself in that situation?" Heath wanted to know. He would have assumed that with him gone to Glasgow for a few days, Rowlly would be so busy he'd not have time to drink in the Goldeneye.

Instead of answering the question, Rowlly said, "It was like old times when you and Brodie and I used to regularly teach those lads their manners. In those days, no Campbell would have been disrespectful to a Macnachtan, but you showed them today that they'd best still think twice. Where did you learn to jab like that?" He punched the air with his fist, demonstrating what he meant.

"I've had to use my hands a time or two," Heath said, walking Admiral.

"Not in the King's Navy?" Rowlly said with teasing mockery. "I thought you had a bevy of sailors to command wherever you went."

"Once they respect you," Heath agreed. "Until then, there are hard lessons to learn."

"Well, we tried to raise you right, Laird. And we did indeed. It will be a long day before Augie lives this one down. He doesn't receive his comeuppance often enough. By the by, how did the meeting in Glasgow go?"

Heath frowned. "Not good. I've been

40

advised to sell the land."

"Can you?"

His cousin's response surprised him. "Should I?" he countered. "I could. It is not entailed. Not even our grandfather thought it important, so neither did Father or Brodie. I can hear the three of them now, why entail what you will not sell?"

"And are they right?" Rowlly said as he started to pay attention to the damage the ale had done to his clothes.

Heath's own clothes were in need of repair as well. He'd torn the seams of his sleeves in the fight. His sisters would not be pleased —

He'd forgotten his cloak. "Damn it all," he swore.

"What?"

"My cloak. It is either still on a peg by the Goldeneye's door or Augie is wearing it."

"Augie's wearing it," Rowlly assured him. "He won't let that opportunity pass by but you can take it from him again."

"He'll probably piss on it."

"That he will," Rowlly agreed with a grin.

"Damn," Heath repeated, and cursed himself as well. At eight and twenty, he was too old to be brawling. His knuckles hurt, as did his right shoulder. Age was not kind.

"Did the solicitor have any suggestions for

us?" Rowlly asked.

"Other than selling? No. He even had a buyer for me."

"Who?"

"Owen Campbell."

Rowlly made a deprecating noise. "That is not news. How many times has he offered to buy Marybone? Now I understand why you were such a fighter in there. And here I was thinking you were protecting my honor."

"I was. Augie deserved a lesson. However, the Macnachtan and Campbells have always been allies of sorts. I have nothing against them," Heath said as he picked up Admiral's reins. "Even Owen."

Rowlly reached a hand up to rub the horse's muzzle and asked, "Are you going to sell?"

"You'd be out of a position if I did that," Heath answered.

"We all would . . . although you and the girls would be fine."

Heath frowned and focused on adjusting his saddle's girth. Rowlly was right. Selling would mean good things for his immediate family.

"I mean, now that their mourning is past, you will need to find husbands for them," Rowlly said. "Not that you couldn't find good men for them, but not men of their station — not without dowries."

"What of loyalty, Rowlly? What of a chief's responsibilities to his clansmen? If I sell to Owen, I know what he will do. The man is after money. He's a younger son of a duke's younger son and he is ambitious. If he buys Macnachtan lands, he'll clear them like a good number of our 'noble' gentry have. They've turned out people who have given generations of loyalty and replaced them with sheep. Owen will send our clansmen packing without even so much as a fare-thee-well and to go where? There is no place for them."

"Well, if Swepston is fired up over the modern changes you've made, including choosing new crops, he'll be mad as the devil if that land was sold."

"Now there is a tempting thought *in favor* of selling," Heath replied. Swepston was Heath's crown of thorns. The crofter re-sisted any inkling of change. He was a charismatic figure who lauded the old ways, the "ancient ones," he called them, and his personality was such that he'd recruited a number of people to his opinion. Heath had stopped counting the number of his clans-men who now wore small bags of herbs and who-knew-what around their necks on

Swepston's say-so.

"I don't care if he believes himself some Druid," Heath said, "as long as he leaves new equipment alone and lets us work in peace." Heath couldn't prove it but he thought Swepston was behind the disappearance of the barley seed purchased for crop rotation.

"The land *does* belong to the laird," Rowlly said. "You could do the same as Owen Campbell if you had a mind to instead of going bloody broke filling all of their bellies. I know a bit about sheep."

"I'll not do that, Rowlly. Not even to Swepston."

Rowlly fell into a somber silence then and Heath did nothing to change his mood. The situation was not good and no amount of positive spirits would change it.

He prepared to mount, gathering up the reins until he realized exactly where he was. This stretch of the woods was familiar. Very familiar.

When he'd first returned to Loch Awe, he'd come this way every day.

He knew he needed to return home. His sisters waited, but suddenly the pull was too great to ignore.

"Stay here with Admiral," he ordered

Rowlly, and began walking deeper into the woods.

Rowlly did not obey. "Laird, *Heath,* wait. Where are you going? *Och,* not there. Not again. Why are you doing this? Why are you going there now? Leave it alone."

Heath ignored his cousin. It had been a few months since he'd visited this place, and right now, he needed to return.

It was almost as if Brodie was calling him.

"All right, *I'll* come with you," Rowlly said, almost as if it was some threat. "Come along, Admiral, let's save him from torturing himself."

"It is not torture," Heath answered tightly, shoving aside thorny bushes and bare branches. The forest was thick here, even in winter. There was no path. Few people came this way.

His footsteps made no sound on the floor of damp leaves. A smattering of snow was still on the ground. All was peaceful. Dark.

Heath had been first officer aboard the HMS *Boyne* when he'd received word of his brother's death. As the heir and only male relative, Heath had been expected to return to Marybone, and it was then he'd learned Brodie had been murdered. The news had shocked him even more than the news of his brother's death. He himself could be an arrogant son of a bitch, but Brodie had been a good and fair man. Who would want to kill him?

There wasn't even anyone who stood to gain anything from Brodie's death — save for himself.

And he would have never harmed Brodie. He had loved his brother. He'd respected him.

"You must let it go," Rowlly was saying. "If we could have caught the killer, we would have done so by now. It's been over a year —"

"I *know* how long it has been."

There was a long pause, and then Rowlly said, "We did hunt for the man who did that to him, Heath. We left no stone unturned."

Heath didn't answer.

He had his doubts.

Rowlly fell silent then. A brooding silence.

Through the tangle of undergrowth and trees, Heath reached the giant oak. Mistletoe grew from its trunk. The tree's bare limbs were as thick and strong as a man's arms. They reached out as if stretching for every corner of the forest. A crofter had found Brodie's lifeless body pinned to its trunk by three arrows shot from a crossbow.

A solemn stillness seemed to circle this one place.

Heath approached the tree. Every time he came here, his gut tightened and he knew he would have no peace until the man, or men, who had done this to Brodie was brought to justice.

His brother's blood still stained the tree. It was as if it would not leave. Heath placed his hand over the largest of those stains. The arrow entry holes had grown over, but the stains remained.

Rowlly stood beside Admiral, watching.

"Why would someone do this?" Heath asked. "We Macnachtan are a poor lot. We are fisherman, crofters, woodsmen . . . not murderers." He looked to Rowlly. "Would Swepston have done this?"

"No. He may buck your authority but he had complete respect for Brodie. They saw things alike. Brodie wouldn't have modernized the way you have. He honored the old ways." Rowlly took a step forward. "None of us would have killed him. He was our laird. It had to have been someone else. Someone from the outside."

"A thief?" Heath frowned at the stain. "What did Brodie have to steal?" He turned to his cousin. "There was a time when I began to suspect a Campbell. After all, everyone knows Owen has coveted our land for a good three years. But Owen was away in London at the time of the murder. I could learn of no one else who might gain from Brodie's death. Can you think of anyone?"

"As I've told you before, Laird, I cannot."

"*Could* it be one of us?" Heath had to ask one more time. The question haunted him.

Rowlly straightened. "Are you accusing me?"

Heath paused a moment, and then said, "I don't know." He hesitated, realized what he was implying and said, "No, I don't suspect you. Of course, there are times I am suspicious of everyone."

"And that *is* madness. Do you also distrust your sisters? Or Dara?" He referred to Brodie's wife. Dara and Brodie had always been a couple, ever since the first moment they'd met in her father's church.

Heath took a step away from the tree. Ignoring Rowlly, he murmured, "I don't understand why Brodie was here, in this place. It is so out of the way."

"I don't know why he was here, either," Rowlly said. "Especially at nine in the evening. This part of the forest would have been darker than Hades."

"The better to ambush him." Heath tried to picture himself in his brother's mind. Why had Brodie left his warm hearth and willing wife to traipse around in the night?

"He had to have been meeting someone," Heath insisted. "It couldn't have been random."

And the fact that his killer still roamed free chewed at Heath's soul. If he accomplished nothing else in this world, he would discover the murderer —

Heath heard a sound behind him.

He turned, readying his fists, thinking Augie and his ilk had tracked them here — but then lowered his hands at the sight of a magnificent stag not more than twenty feet away from them. The regal animal had to be close to seven feet tall. He held his antlers proudly as if wearing a crown.

"Have you seen the likes?" Rowlly said, his voice the barest whisper.

For a long moment, men and beast eyed each other. Heath wished he had a gun. They needed meat for the table.

Then again, this animal was too bold and courageous to be taken down. There was pride in him, just as there was pride in Heath.

At that moment, a piece of flimsy material drifted down from the sky, floating into the clearing. Startled, the stag went bounding off.

Heath swore and moved forward to catch

the material. He was surprised to discover it was a woman's petticoat, one made of the finest stuff.

"What is it?" Rowlly asked.

"Smallclothes," Heath answered, holding up the petticoat with its expensive trim of lace and ribbons. "For the ladies."

"I've never seen anything like that," Rowlly declared, a dull red coming to his cheeks. "But I've heard of them."

Heath walked in the direction he thought the clothing had come from and noticed more clothes snagged on the trees and winter brush. "There is more clothing here," he said. "All women's clothes. If it hadn't been for the stag, I wouldn't have noticed them."

He started collecting the clothing but as he moved away, Admiral snorted and stamped his mighty hooves as if warning him. Heath frowned. He glanced in the direction of the trail of clothing and then back to his horse.

A sense of disquiet settled over Heath. He pushed it away.

"Tie him up," he ordered Rowlly. "I want to explore this."

"I'm coming with you," Rowlly said, and hurried to secure Admiral.

The horse didn't put up any more fuss,

instead following them with grave eyes.

Heath recognized London tailoring when he saw it. These clothes were expensive, too expensive for wandering around the Highlands. Too soon, clothing gave way to broken pieces of a coach that led to the lifeless bodies of men and horses.

Rowlly swore under his breath.

The accident was a grisly sight.

Heath was no stranger to death. He'd seen men blown to pieces by cannon fire, but he'd not witnessed anything like this. The bodies were broken as if they had been thrown to the ground and seemed more damaged than just a coaching accident would warrant.

Scanning the forest, Heath saw the direction the coach had fallen. They must have been coming from the north, traveling on the mountain road.

"Was there a storm yesterday?" Heath asked.

"A bit of one. Nothing bad," Rowlly managed to answer. "A fair amount of wind."

"Wind shouldn't have been a problem for a coach this large," Heath answered. "We'll need a crew of men to clean this up. Could the road have washed out?"

"I'll check on it," Rowlly said. He hung back as if overwhelmed by so much carnage.

51

"We will need to see to decent burials for all those who have lost their lives."

"Aye, it will be grim business." Heath began counting the bodies. Several wore a nobleman's livery. One of the men was an Indian in English clothes.

Heath noticed he was breathing. He knelt beside the man. "Here is one who is alive." He felt for a pulse. "Just barely though. Fetch Admiral and we'll carry him to Marybone."

While Rowlly went for the horse, Heath used leather reins he found on the ground to lash together a makeshift sled, using the roof of the coach for the base. He and Rowlly lifted the Indian onto the sled. Admiral was not pleased at his new duty, but he'd do as Heath wished.

"Let's leave," Rowlly asked. He was growing more green around the gills.

"Not yet. Where are the women?" Heath still held the petticoat. He expanded his search of the area and found a woman of middling years dead in the brush. She was not the sort to wear such a fine petticoat.

Heath kept searching.

And then he found *her.*

She lay in a copse of stately pines. The late afternoon sun didn't penetrate this place, giving it the feeling of being in another world. The forest floor was cushioned with their needles and the air carried their scent. She was on her back, her hands folded at her waist, her eyes closed, her face so serene, she could have been sleeping . . . and she was very beautiful.

Black hair curled around her shoulders. Her lips were red, her complexion flawless.

Heath recognized her immediately.

He heard Rowlly draw in his breath. "What is something like *her* doing here?"

"That is a good question. Lady Margaret Chattan rarely strays from London."

"Chattan?" Rowlly immediately recognized the name, and he spit on the ground as any good Macnachtan would. "I thought they had only males."

"They did, until *she* was born." Heath stepped forward.

In London, they called her the Unattainable and she was rumored to be worth three times her weight in gold.

He'd seen her once in the city. She'd been followed by a flock of male admirers who trailed in her wake like lap dogs. The crowds on the street craned their necks for a better look as if she were the queen herself.

Heath had been struck by the blueness of her eyes and the perfection of her figure. Hers was a face no man could ever forget.

They fought over her, they begged for her favors, they worshipped her — and yet they said her heart had never been claimed.

That day, almost five years ago, Heath had gazed upon her and told his fellow officers he had the feeling that one day their paths would cross again. They had assured him he was deluding himself. A beauty of that caliber would not waste herself upon a Scot, especially a Highlander. They'd enjoyed much sport over his infatuation.

But Heath's belief had not been so outlandish. She was a Chattan; he a Macnachtan. Their histories were entwined by legend.

And now she was dead and here in his wood.

So young, so lovely . . . and without a mark on her.

The other bodies were battered almost beyond recognition. Her skin was clear and pink — and then he realized the truth.

She was alive. She had survived.

CHAPTER THREE

Margaret feared she would not wake up. She struggled to bring herself out of the darkness, but her eyes refused to open.

It was the smell of baking bread that finally alerted her senses.

She had slept hard and well. The bed was comfortable, the sheets fresh. But the time had come to leave this place.

The time had come to wake.

She struggled for consciousness . . .

Margaret opened her eyes.

The light was blinding and she quickly closed them again. Her lungs hurt. She had to pull deep to gain a decent breath and her arms and legs felt as if they were weighed down with lead.

Someone gasped, the sound close at hand, followed by footsteps. A door opened.

"She's awake," a girl's voice exclaimed with the lilt of a Scots accent. She sounded

very young. "Miss Anice, Miss Laren, my lady, she's awake."

Panic forced Margaret to lie very still. She did not recognize the names.

Where was she?

And then the memories came.

Her mind was remarkably clear. Only moments ago, she and Smith had been tossed around the coach like dice being shaken in a cup. She had been thrown into the air and landed on rock —

Margaret remembered the pain. She recalled lying in the mud and snow, her body broken.

And Smith was dead.

What of the others?

"When did she wake?" a woman's voice came from the hall.

"Just this moment," the girl reported. "I sat there, as you told me to, and her eyes opened."

More Scottish voices, their accents musical — and Margaret became aware of *why* she was in Scotland.

In her mind, the accident had happened only moments ago. She could still smell the blood, the fear, the scents of wet wool and rotting winter leaves. She could see the bodies, the death.

But she was far away from that right now.

She wasn't even wearing the same clothes.

They entered the room and she sensed their presences as they approached the bed. She could open her eyes, and she would, once she knew she was safe.

"She's not awake," a woman's disappointed voice said.

The girl spoke. "I saw her open her eyes. Just this moment."

A woman's voice from the other side of the bed said, "I'm certain you did, Cora. Remember what Mr. Hawson said, Anice. Patients in a coma can give the appearance of rousing. Perhaps she isn't ready."

The one called Anice said, "Why do you suppose Lady Margaret Chattan is here, Laren? It's so far from London, from anything that would interest her."

They knew who she was. But who were they?

"Father said that the Chattans would come up here from time to time," Laren answered. "You know, always wanting us to right their curse."

There was a beat of silence and then Anice asked, "Do you believe in it?"

"The curse?" Laren laughed. "Of course not."

"What is the curse?" Cora asked. She must be very young, Margaret concluded, because of the honesty of her question.

"They claim an ancestor of ours placed a curse upon them that the males all die when they fall in love," Anice answered.

"And it is nonsense," Laren said. "A wives' tale."

"What is a wives' tale?" the child questioned.

"Just what Laren said," Anice said. "A bit of nonsense. Run along now and fetch Dara. She needs to know our guest is awaking."

Listening to them, Margaret's heart had gone cold with realization. They were the Macnachtan.

"It's terrible about the accident," Anice said. "I'm glad she isn't awake yet. Dara was saying she didn't know how we would let Lady Margaret know that almost all of her party was dead. Everyone but that Indian gentleman, and we still don't know if he will live."

Rowan was alive. She *wasn't* alone. *Thanks be to God.*

And she wasn't here without a purpose.

Bravely, Margaret opened her eyes.

This time, the light didn't bother her as much and she could see she was in a rather plain bedroom with cream-colored walls and green draperies. The bed she lay in was a simple four-poster one. The coverlet over her was a quilt.

The weak winter light of an overcast day filled the room. Margaret estimated it must be sometime after mid-morning.

But what interested her were the two women.

They were both lovely and around the age of twenty. They didn't appear to show the anger one reserved for an enemy. Instead, they viewed her with compassion in their eyes.

And still she did not dare trust them.

The one to Margaret's right, the one called Anice, had curly brown hair that she wore styled on top of her head. Laren had straight hair more blonde than brown. They shared inquisitive blue eyes, pert noses, and full lips.

Anice was obviously more meticulous about her appearance. She'd tied a green ribbon through her curls and wore a ribbon of the same color around her neck. Her dress was of the same homespun brown as her sister's except that she had added rosettes fashioned out of ribbon around the bodice. If she'd made those herself, she was clever with a needle.

Laren appeared more reserved. She wore her hair in a long braid and her hands showed that she was no stranger to work.

"You *are* awake," Anice said, sounding genuinely pleased. "And look at you. You don't appear the worse for wear." She leaned forward with a smile.

Margaret started to speak, to warn them to stay away from her. She opened her mouth but no words came out. Her tongue felt thick, her throat dry.

"You must be starved and thirsty," Laren said, reaching for a pot of tea that sat on a bedside table. There was also a mound of cloths that appeared to have been used for her care, a basin and pitcher, and a candlestick with the candle burned down to the stub.

"The tea is not hot," Laren warned, pouring a cup and offering it to her, "but perhaps that is best. We need to put something nourishing in you."

She was right, but Margaret feared moving her arms. She remembered the terrible pain of them breaking and of her hips and her legs . . .

"Let me plump the pillow," Anice offered, and placed a gentle hand under Margaret's shoulder to help her sit up.

"I can't," Margaret managed to say, her voice as dry as a rusty hinge.

"Yes, you can," Anice encouraged her. "I'll

help." Again, she placed her hand under Margaret's shoulder.

This time, Margaret let Anice lift her — and was shocked by the absence of pain.

She frowned and looked to her left arm, the one she had used to attempt to reach for the book in that horrible moment after the crash. She was able to lift it without even a twinge of discomfort.

Margaret stared at her fingers and stretched them. They moved easily.

"My lady, are you all right?" Anice asked. Both girls watched her actions with interest.

Margaret frowned up, needing a moment for the question to make sense in her confused mind. *All right? Nothing was right.* She *knew* what had happened. It was vivid in her mind. She'd experienced the pain, felt her bones breaking —

"I must see Rowan," Margaret croaked out. Rowan would explain all of this to her.

"Yes, my lady," Laren answered, "but first, have a drink of this." She placed the teacup against Margaret's lips. The brew was strong and lukewarm. The first sip made Margaret feel as if her throat was opening.

"Don't drink too quickly," Laren warned, but Margaret could not stop once she started. Her body needed the liquid. She drained the cup dry.

"More," she ordered.

Laren complied. A third cup followed the second.

Margaret fell back on the pillow. She looked to the young women. "What did you do with the others?"

Brows furrowed. Anice spoke. "They've received a Christian burial."

"Thank you," Margaret murmured, heartbroken by the deaths of Balfour and Thomas. Even of Smith. Their deaths cried for vengeance, and she swore silently she would deliver it. "How long have I been in this bed?" she asked.

"We found you three days ago," Laren answered. "Actually, our brother found you. His name is Heath Macnachtan —"

"He's the laird," Anice interjected. "He's very important."

"And he *saved* you," Laren reiterated.

But Margaret barely heard their praise of their brother. Instead, she was stunned to realize *three days had passed*? Three days for the witch Fenella to gather her power.

"Rowan," Margaret said. "Please take me to him."

"Yes, my lady," Anice replied. "But do you believe you should move?"

"Take me to him," Margaret repeated, her tone allowing no room for refusal. She sat up, relieved that her body did not protest. She pulled her nightdress down over her legs, needing a moment to steady herself.

There was a simple oak linen press on the opposite wall, and beside it were several bags that she recognized as her own from the coach. There was also the coachman's whip, leaning against the press.

Seeing the direction she was looking, Anice explained, "The linen press holds most of your clothing. Your things were spread all through the woods, but we think we have most of it. Heath had a party comb the forest thoroughly."

"Heath?"

"Our brother," Anice said. "Laird Macnachtan. We just told you about him. He is the one who found you. We believe your accident happened just after you crossed the border to our lands."

Fenella had wanted to stop her from reaching Loch Awe?

Or was it that Fenella wanted her in Macnachtan hands?

Margaret pushed up from the bed, not certain what to think. She was surrounded by her enemies, and yet Laren and Anice reached out as if ready to catch her in case she fell. She was relieved that her legs held her weight, albeit unsteadily at first. "A robe?" she said.

Laren crossed to the linen press and pulled out Margaret's blue robe. She helped Margaret into the soft fabric and started to tie it at her waist but Margaret caught her hands. "I'll do it." She chose her actions because these girls should not be waiting upon her, but also she didn't want to appear weak to them.

"Where's Rowan?" Margaret's voice was still hoarse.

"This way, my lady," Laren answered, and moved toward the door. Anice hovered behind Margaret as if anxious that she would fall.

Laren was about to reach for the handle when the door opened and a tall, regal woman entered the room. Seeing them about to go out, she stopped, blocking their path.

This woman was obviously not related to the sisters. Her hair was the color of a shining copper kettle and her almond-shaped eyes reminded Margaret of Oriental jade.

While the Macnachtan sisters were trim, solid women, much like herself, the air of grace about his newcomer was tangible in her shoulders and high cheekbones. She could have been a Slavic princess or cast in the role of a fairy queen upon the stage.

"Our guest is up," she said, her melodic accent coupled with a warmth of tone that made her voice distinctive. "Lady Margaret, welcome to Marybone, the Macnachtan family home. I am Dara, the dowager Lady Macnachtan."

A widow. A very young one.

Margaret tried to smile. They all seemed anxious to please her, and she was just as anxious to be on guard. "Thank you," she murmured. This whole experience after the violent accident was too strange.

"Lady Margaret wished to see the Indian gentleman," Anice explained. There was a hint of distance in her voice . . . as if she did not completely like her sister-in-marriage.

"Oh, well, this way then, my lady," Lady Macnachtan said, taking charge.

As she went out the door, Laren stepped aside to let her pass and even Anice seemed to move back a step.

The hallway was as plain as the bedroom had been. Margaret noticed the unevenness of the paint as if there had once been pictures gracing the walls that were now gone. There were no furnishings or carpet, and the cold wood floor was scuffed and marked with age. Back in London, she would never go barefoot, but there was no maid to see to her needs here. Smith was dead, and Margaret was humbled by that fact.

Doors to three other bedrooms lined the hall. Stairs led down to the ground floor and up to the second floor. Lady Macnachtan began climbing the stairs. They were very steep.

Margaret gripped the handrail. Climbing was a bit of a challenge for her but she persevered, conscious that Laren and Anice were watching her every move.

The second floor hall was narrow and as shabby as the downstairs hallway. This would be where the nursery or servants' rooms were located.

Lady Macnachtan opened the door closest to the stairs. She went inside and stepped aside in a silent invitation for Margaret to enter.

For a second, Margaret was tempted to hang back, uncertain what to expect. She gathered her courage and went in. The bed was only a few steps from the door, and the sight of the stoic Rowan made her bring her fist to her mouth to keep from crying out.

He was only a shadow of himself. If they had pulled the covers up over his head, no one would have known he was there.

His dusky skin was a pallid gray. Bruises

misshaped his face. His broken arms had been set with boards wrapped with linens. His fingers were swollen from breaks in them as well.

This was what she should have looked like.

And yet she was whole and well.

Margaret fell to her knees beside the bed. Her eyes burned with unshed tears. She reached for Rowan's hand.

"The doctor has encouraged us *not* to touch him," Lady Macnachtan warned. "He believes the less the patient is moved, the better he will heal."

Pulling back her hand, Margaret felt the terrible, dark coldness of fear.

These women might appear normal, but there was something terribly wrong. *Dangerously* wrong.

And she was unnerved.

She needed to be alone. She needed to think. *She needed to find Fenella's book.* That thought was crystal clear. The book would be her protection. It would have answers. Harry was certain this was true, and right now, she had nothing else.

"You found everything from the accident?" she asked.

It was Anice who answered. "Yes, my lady. It is all either in the wardrobe or in the bags beside it. Everything is in your room."

The book would be there. If they had found her body, then they would have seen the book. She'd looked at the book as she'd been dying.

And yet, here she was.

Owl had been with her. Owl had saved her.

The impossibilities threatened Margaret's sanity. She had to focus on what was real and concrete. She feared she could not trust her own mind . . . and she knew no one would believe her story if she told it. No one save this man. Rowan was a witness, and he might die for it.

"I will return," she whispered to him. "I will save us."

There was no reaction.

But she had one. A trembling started inside her.

She left the room before she betrayed herself, the Macnachtan following her.

"His name is Rowan," she said as she went down the stairs. "He's very dear to me. Please, whatever expense it costs to care for him, I shall cover it."

"Yes, my lady," one of them said. Margaret didn't know which, and she didn't care. She had the grotesque feeling that she was caught in a world she didn't understand. A world that might not be what it appeared — just as in her nightmare she'd experienced in the coach before the accident.

Margaret practically ran to the haven of her bedroom.

The Macnachtan women thought her actions peculiar. She could see questions in the lift of their brows. She didn't care.

"I am exhausted," Margaret heard herself say. "I need to rest."

"Of course, you do," Lady Macnachtan said. "Have you eaten anything?" She didn't expect Margaret to answer but looked to Laren and Anice.

"She's only had some cool tea," Laren reported.

"I'm not hungry," Margaret said. And that was true. She was too wary to think about food now. She must place her hands on Fenella's book.

"You need to eat," Lady Macnachtan insisted. "Anice and Laren, does Heath know our guest is awake?"

"Not unless you sent Cora after him," Anice answered.

"I sent her to the kitchen to help her mother," Lady Macnachtan said. "So Heath doesn't know yet."

"We shall go tell him," Laren said. There was a hint of frustration in her voice . . . an annoyance. "Come, Anice."

Anice turned to Margaret before she left the room. "We are happy that you are well. Please, rest."

Margaret nodded, but crossed her arms.

"Yes, rest would be good," Lady Macnachtan echoed. "In the meantime, I know Cook has made a broth that will be nourishing and help your spirits. I'll see that a tray is brought up to you."

"Thank you," Margaret murmured, and they all blessedly left the room, closing the door behind them.

Margaret almost collapsed. It had taken all she possessed to appear calm and at ease when she felt anything but those two emotions.

There was something wrong, from her robust health to the Macnachtans' willingness to comfort her. Laren and Anice seemed open and pleasant, but there was something about Lady Macnachtan that she could not trust. Margaret was very good at guarding her own thoughts and actions and she recognized the trait in others.

She crossed over to the window. Her room overlooked the back of the house. There was a small garden marked off with a border of trees.

A door below her window opened and she overheard Laren's and Anice's voices although she could not make out what they were saying to each other. She stepped back from the window lest they catch sight of her, but they were too interested in where they were going.

She watched them follow a path off to the side of the house that led through the trees toward stables built of stone, wood and plaster. There were other outbuildings, but the stables were clearly the family's pride.

A goodly number of people congregated in the stable yard, milling around as if waiting for something to take place. She wondered what was going on.

And then she noticed the figure of a tall, hatless man. Everyone at the stables seemed to be listening to or milling around him. He had dark hair and wore his coat open.

Margaret could not make out his features but she had the unsettling feeling of recognition.

Even from this distance, there was an air of command about him. She could tell by the way he sliced his hand in the air that he was not happy. His people stepped back and some hung their heads.

This must be the Macnachtan. The laird.

The link between her ancestors and Fenella.

His sisters had said he had discovered the

coach accident. Heath Macnachtan.

As she watched, Laren and Anice set out to warn their brother Margaret was awake. Soon they would return to check on her and she'd lose this precious opportunity to find Fenella's book.

Margaret set to work, frantically searching her baggage for the book.

Someone had organized her possessions. Hair ornaments were in one place, jewelry in another. Some of the items were Smith's, and Margaret regretted she hadn't been kinder to the older woman.

Stockings and petticoats had been freshly laundered and folded. It took time to accomplish these tasks. Margaret frowned at the layers of cleaned clothes, a bit unsettled that someone had gone through her belongings.

The first important item she found was the pistol her brother Harry had given her before she'd left him in Glenfinnan. He had taught Margaret how to shoot, so he'd trusted her to use the weapon if necessary.

Margaret found the gun in her portmanteau, which had been with her inside the coach. She held the weapon in her hand, feeling its weight, and then pulled out the ammunition bag.

The leather was water stained, an obvious

sign of the storm she and Rowan had experienced, but the powder inside was not caked. Certainly, moisture would impact the powder, but to what degree? Harry had told stories of his men using powder that had been damp. The powder in the bag seemed dry now.

The gun gave her a sense of confidence. She was no longer entirely at the Macnachtans' mercy.

Margaret returned to her search. She tried to be orderly, but the longer she looked, the more she panicked. She could not find the book. Everything that she'd had with her on the trip was here *except* for the book.

Her suspicions of the Macnachtan motives had been correct. *They had taken Fenella's book.* They were keeping it for themselves.

Anger exploded in her mind. Her brothers' lives depended upon her. Without the book, she was powerless.

She had come here on a mission to save her family, and so she would.

Margaret dressed quickly. She didn't bother with her hair but reached for her fur-trimmed cape and threw it over her shoulders. She then loaded the gun, tucking the ammunition bag into a pocket inside her cloak.

There was a knock at the door.

"What is it?" Margaret asked.

"I have a tray for you, my lady," the young girl who had been watching for her to wake said. "It's a bowl of broth and a bit of good bread."

"I'm not hungry," Margaret said. And it was true. She didn't need food. She was sustained by generations of righteous anger. "Return the tray to the kitchen," she ordered.

"Yes, my lady."

Margaret waited a moment and then walked to the door. The hallway was empty.

The gun in her hand, she left the room. The time had come to confront Laird Macnachtan, and he *would* give her back the book.

The gun would help her see that he did.

CHAPTER FOUR

Whisky was the devil's curse.

And just as Heath Macnachtan stepped into the mucky pit of the pigpen, he wished he'd not indulged himself in it so much the night before. He was unshaven, having been woken from a sound sleep to chase pigs, and heartily annoyed, especially since he wasn't the only one who had over-indulged.

His second cousin Irwin started every morning with a dram or two or ten. The man didn't understand his responsibilities. True, at four and thirty, he had the simple mind of a ten-year-old child, but how difficult was it to remember to shut the pigpen every evening?

This was the third time in the past two months he had forgotten.

Usually, Heath could be patient with Irwin, but not this morning when his own brain pounded with dissipation.

It was the English Chattan's fault. Her

presence made him feel as if a noose was tightening around his neck. The noose that had been placed there by Brodie's death.

She symbolized the outside world, the one he had been forced to set aside.

God, he missed the sea. He missed salt air. He missed freedom. The uniform he'd worn had stood for something.

Now he had nothing. He represented nothing. His realm was made up of these mountains and these irascible, lazy, disloyal, and infuriatingly opinionated people known as Highlanders. And he could no longer escape that he was one of them.

Brodie and his father must be laughing in heaven.

Marybone, the family seat, had been built almost a hundred years ago. The family had taken the gray stone from what had once been known as Macnachtan Keep to build the house and stables. The house was a sturdy four-story home that was drafty in the winter and an oven in the summer.

In truth, the house was considered one of the region's important landmarks, although Heath concluded that was because of the stables. That building had stalls for twenty horses and room for vehicles of all sizes, which his father had purchased even though they were rarely used. Most of those vehicles

Heath had sold to pay debts.

The majority of the stalls were now empty save for the bold Admiral and the mares Heath's sisters and sister-in-law had to ride. Admiral performed double service as both Heath's mount and the plow horse when one was needed.

The mares were of genuinely good stock. Brodie had dreamed of breeding fine Thoroughbreds and had sunk a considerable amount of money he didn't have into the endeavor.

Behind the stables were several outbuildings for geese, goats and a cow.

The pigpen was a new addition. Always before they'd let the pigs roam free, which was why, Heath was certain, they'd lost their herd. It was too easy for the Campbells to nab one whenever they had a taste for ham. Heath was determined to see the practice stopped, and Irwin seemed equally determined to let it continue.

Heath and several others, including Rowlly and his wife, Janet, had spent a good hour searching for the young pigs that they intended to slaughter come spring. The bloody beasts had not been easy to find, while all Irwin would do was sit and boozily cry to his mother, Nila.

"Don't you blame this on my son," she

declared as Heath dumped the squirming pig Rowlly had passed to him into the pen to join the others.

Heath shut the gate and slid the board in place to keep it closed before addressing her. He needed that much time to tame his temper, and decided it was hopeless. He'd lost his sense of humor the moment he'd seen the open gate and empty pen. "And who *should* I blame, Nila?"

The others in the yard, the crofters who had aided in the search and the stable lads all stopped to listen close.

"You expect too much of him," Nila said. "He can't be responsible."

"It is a gate," Heath said. "You open it; you close it." He demonstrated while Nila's frown deepened, which was unfortunate. She had the looks of a troll with a wrinkled face and huge nose. She *needed* to smile.

God, he longed for the authority he had in the navy. There was little or no class structure in the clan. These people were kin. Clansmen, especially the women, didn't hesitate to make their opinions known and argue with every single action he took.

"He's only forgotten three times," Nila answered, spreading her arms to protect her son, who was twice as tall as she was. "But it *isn't* his fault."

"And whose fault is it, Nila?" Heath demanded.

"*Yours.* You ask too much of him. You ask too much of all of us."

Heath swore under his breath. "I'm asking you to help feed yourselves. We need those pigs so that we have bacon and hams for next winter. Or do you want another winter like this one where you are hungry all the time?"

"You are the laird. It is your responsibility to take care of *us.*" Nila spoke to Heath as if he was as simple as her son and did not understand his duties. "You talk of feeding us but then you cut the widows' pensions. You promised we would see the rest of our money, but we haven't yet."

"Don't use that tone on me, Nila. My father and my brother sold everything of value to keep this clan going but the world beyond us has changed. The old ways can't work any longer. Each of us has to learn to carry his or her own weight. And you haven't gone hungry yet. I've seen to that."

Heath knew he wasn't speaking just to Nila and her son. The others listened as well.

The immediate clan was made up of some thirty families numbering close to two hundred individuals tucked away here in the valley along Loch Awe. Once their numbers had been greater, but like Heath, many had been restless and had wanted to see what lay beyond Macnachtan lands. They had gone in search of opportunity, leaving behind the feeble, the lazy and the fools.

This morning, Heath felt very much as if he belonged in the last category. Was it any wonder that the estate was in the hands of his creditors? Brodie had borrowed deeply to save this lot, a debt now on Heath's shoulders.

That meant he must preach independence, even when drink-bitten.

And of course, he was too stubborn to walk away from it all. Nila's opinions aside, he did feel a responsibility. As had his brother and his father.

Owen Campbell's offer to buy his land rested heavy in his mind. Money would solve all his problems.

But he couldn't sell. He wouldn't. This was his legacy. His ancestors had nurtured, protected and led these people for centuries. He'd not be the one to fail them, although Nila was right about his cutting the widows' pensions. There were twelve widows on the rolls, a school and a kirk to maintain, and a host of other obligations on top of the debts.

He needed a miracle to find his way through this — and then God, in his holy humor, had sent the richest heiress in the kingdom to his door.

But she was a Chattan and he a Macnachtan.

Chattan. Stories behind that name were shared in the evenings when people wanted the entertainment of a good morality tale or to warn children of the evils in the world.

There had been a time when Heath, much younger, of course, had believed those who claimed all Macnachtan woes stemmed from Chattan deceit.

Now he understood the Chattans had nothing to do with the challenge of bringing this stubborn band of Highlanders into the modern world.

"You *will* receive your money, Nila, but *not* if I must keep spending more to buy pigs to replace the ones your son let loose."

Hearing his tone, a wise man would have stepped back. Not Nila. She stood her ground, glaring up at him in defiance.

"Well, Laird, you have your opinion, and I have mine," she announced, her hands on her hips. "Don't go believing that you can do as you please. There are the old ways, the right of tanistry."

"Tanistry?" Why was he arguing with this

81

woman? He would rather return to his bed and perhaps have another nip of the bottle to cure the ache in his head.

"Aye, tanistry," she said. "The title of chief is voted upon by us and rotated between those with the blood to have the honor," she said. "There is more than just you with the right blood. We haven't changed things yet, but we might."

"Who told you this nonsense?" Heath demanded. "Swepston? Is the man calling up the law of the Druids now? Does he believe himself some priest prince?" Heath could almost laugh at the thought except he was so bleeding angry. He wanted to shake the silliness out of Nila.

He raised his voice so that all could hear him. "Swepston whispers mutiny against me and my family. Well, hear me well, I am descended from Robert the Bruce and one of my line has been your laird from that time onward. Have Swepston come forward and place his claim. I shall settle it for him."

He'd knock him down with one blow.

Nila's response was a sniff. "Come, Irwin, I have chores for you at home." She turned and walked off with all the bearing of a queen.

Heath struggled with a strong, childish urge to run after her and give her a kick on the backside. He had just wasted his breath. She'd heard nothing.

"You knew you wouldn't win that battle," Rowlly muttered. His wife nodded her agreement. Janet practically lived at the stables when her husband was there. She was a robust, handsome woman a half a head taller than Rowlly and the mother of his four sons.

"I had hopes." Heath swallowed his frustration. "Have one of the lads follow behind Irwin each night and each morning to see the gate is closed, and be certain Irwin knows that if that pen is left open again, I will take it out of his hide."

"Aye, Laird."

And that should have been the end of it. Heath expected them all to stop standing around slack-jawed and set to work. However, any move in that direction his clansmen would have made stopped as his sisters came running down the path from the house, their long cloaks flying behind them in their urgency. Anice said, "She's awake, Heath. Lady Margaret is awake."

Even Nila did an about-face and returned to the stable yard.

There were no secrets in the clan. Stories were shared with everyone. A whisper in the morning would be an outrageous tale by evening, and Heath could swear that most of the stories were about him.

He also knew he couldn't fight it.

"The Chattan is awake?" Janet Macnachtan repeated. "She is alive, is she?" She spit on the ground to let the world know her thoughts. She wasn't the only one who had spit. At the mention of the name Chattan, there was a robust round of spitting.

Heath frowned. "We all knew *Lady Margaret* was alive," he said, using Lady Margaret's title pointedly to Janet. "And she is a guest here. I expect her to be treated as such, and no spitting on the ground. I'll not have superstitious nonsense —" He saw Nila raise her brows. "I *won't,*" he repeated, especially for her, and she could go tell Swepston as much. "If you disrespect a guest under my roof, it is the same as disrespecting me — *and I shall not be pleased.*"

There was a moment of sullen silence. Glances were exchanged . . . and then they all made a pretense of returning to their chores. But it was for show. The quality of the work would not be good and would have to be redone on the morrow.

Such was the nature of subtle insubordination.

Heath turned to his sisters, who made fine

targets for his foul mood. "We could show a bit of discretion here."

"Yes, we could," Anice replied breezily, taking his arm and pulling him off to the side. Laren followed.

"Is something the matter with Lady Margaret?" He'd sent word to her brother Lord Lyon in London explaining the accident, assuring him she was safe and appeared unharmed. Heath did not want to send another letter to such a powerful man reporting a new issue after he'd assured him all was well.

"She's fine. The picture of health —" Anice answered.

"Surprisingly," Laren interjected. "*She* was even puzzled at how she went through such an accident and escaped any injury. She wanted to see her Indian servant and seemed quite upset over his injuries. It is strange she didn't suffer any."

"It is odd —" Heath agreed, but Anice overrode him.

"It doesn't matter," Anice said. "Not now. She's well and she is healthy and Laren and I believe you should court her."

Heath took a step back. "I'm sorry, I must have had my toes in my ears. I believe you suggested *I* should court Lady Margaret *Chattan,* the woman whose name can't be mentioned without a rash of spitting. Even Janet, who always wears her best to church, spit on the ground."

Anice made a face as if he was being silly. "*You* should be in church more often, and, yes, spitting is disgusting, but this moment is like a Shakespearean play."

"God help me, Anice, don't suggest it's *Macbeth*," Heath said. "I have no desire to chase witches in the forest or stab people in their beds."

"No, it is like *Romeo and Juliet.*"

Heath directed his attention to Laren. "She wants me to drink poison?"

"She wants you to wed the Chattan heiress," Laren answered.

"It might be easier to drink poison," Heath responded.

Anice made an exasperated sound. "Why are you deliberately not understanding what I'm saying?"

"Because you are not being clear, dear, and Heath is teasing you," Laren said. "Heath, here is a brilliant opportunity to solve our debts. You must court the Chattan heiress. You should marry her."

"And then the Chattans and Macnachtans will set aside our differences," Anice announced. "Just as the Montagues and Capulets ended their feud and that is what

I meant about Romeo and Juliet. I don't want anyone bit by an asp."

"Asp? That is a different play, Anice," Heath pointed out.

"It's unimportant," Anice argued, too wrapped up in her ideas to quibble. "Asp, poison, what does it matter? Not when it is as if fate wants you to claim the Chattan heiress. And she is lovely, Heath. I considered that the bits I've read about her were exaggerations, but they are not. She is a beauty."

"Although," Laren said, dropping her voice a notch, "she behaves a bit odd."

"And what do you mean by that, Laren?" Heath asked.

"She has suffered a terrible accident," Anice said, defending their guest.

"Yes, but she is, well . . ." Laren's voice drifted as if she couldn't explain, her lips pressing together.

Anice jumped in. "Poo. She's fine. And everyone in society admires her."

Heath didn't trust the worship in his sister's voice. "She isn't any better than the two of you."

"Except she's rich," the ever-practical Laren answered. "And even if she does act a bit funny, you should consider her for a wife, Heath."

The idea was tempting and ridiculous at the same time. What would his sisters say if he confessed that he'd secretly lusted for the woman? He'd not embarrass himself with that confession.

Instead, he shook his head. "Can you imagine the likes of her arguing with Nila? Or organizing the charity baskets and herding Janet and the other churchwomen into doing good works? Or seeing to the wash and the cleaning the way you girls must?"

"The cleaning wouldn't be a problem," Anice said stoutly. "If you marry her, we'd have so much money, none of us would have to do those things. Of course, we will need to clean *you* up if you are going to impress her. I don't want to be rude, Heath, and you are not a bad-looking man — well, perhaps a bit arrogant —"

"And he does have a temper," Laren agreed.

"Yes, he does," Anice answered. "But the worst of it is that right now, Heath, you smell strongly of the pigpen."

"And the marsh," Laren agreed.

"And you need a barber."

Heath held up his hands to stave them off. "*Enough.* I'm not courting Margaret Chattan. I'll grant you she is lovely, but you know nothing of the world beyond Loch

Awe. It's different than it is here. Lady Margaret Chattan could not survive in these mountains. Furthermore, what your papers don't tell you, Anice, is that she is known for being difficult and arrogant and conceited. Traits I acknowledge in myself but doubly unpleasant in a wife. And then there is the name they have for her in London. They call her the Unattainable because she is cold and distant. Is that truly what you want for me?"

Worry lines marred Anice's forehead. She looked to Laren, and Heath understood. They knew the debt he carried. And he knew that unless he did something about it, his sisters were doomed to be spinsters.

All the marriageable lads for a hundred-mile radius knew the Macnachtans were done up. No sensible ones came to pay their respects.

At one time, he'd told himself it was because they were in mourning for Brodie . . . but the year had passed and no one knocked on Marybone's doors.

Well, that wasn't true. There had been an older widower looking for a mother for his eight children, and a few buffoons who thought his sisters were desperate enough to consider them. Heath had sent them all on their way.

He placed a brotherly arm around their shoulders. "Money is tight, but we will see our way through this. Do not worry —"

A woman's sharp voice interrupted him. *"Macnachtan."*

The word rang through the stable yard. Heath turned to see Lady Margaret Chattan standing on the path leading to the house. She wore a red cape and her black hair curled around her shoulders. Her face was pale, her cheeks were rosy, and her blue eyes were lit with the fires of righteous anger.

Here was not a pampered society miss, but a medieval queen ready for battle.

Heath stepped forward, suddenly *too* aware of the beard stubble on his jaw and the muss of his hair. He could smell the pigs on him . . . just as he caught the scent of her. She smelled of the forest, of dark greenness and night air.

God, he'd lost his mind. In a second, he'd be spouting poetry. That was how strong his reaction was to her.

"I am the Macnachtan," he said.

She pulled her arms free from her cape. In her hands she held a pistol.

Heath recognized the weapon. He'd discovered it himself when they been collecting her things around the accident. He'd placed it in her traveling case along with a bag of black gunpowder. He hadn't thought it was hers or that she would have the desire to use it.

She now proved him wrong by leveling the gun on him.

Her hands shook slightly.

Rowlly and several of the other lads stepped forward as if to overpower her, but Heath held up his hand, warning them back.

This woman was frightened, even though they had done nothing to harm her. He wanted to hear what she had to say.

He also suddenly, blessedly, felt very alive. She could pull the trigger and shoot him dead. This was the edge of danger, of adventure he missed from his military days, and he reveled in the moment.

"What is it that you want?" he asked, his voice calm. "If you wish to shoot me, fire away . . . but I must warn you that your gunpowder was very wet when I found it. Your weapon could misfire."

"I want Fenella's book. I must destroy the curse," she said. "I want it over and done."

The damn curse. He did not need her jabbering superstitious nonsense. Everyone would start spitting again.

He folded his hands in front of him, keeping himself relaxed. "And how may *I* help you?"

"Tell Fenella to stop." Desperation edged her plea.

Heath frowned. Fenella was the name of an ancestress of his, but the woman had died centuries ago. He didn't know of whom Lady Margaret spoke. "Who is Fenella?"

"The witch. The one who cursed us. She's here."

A collective gasp seemed to rise from the crowd behind him, and Heath wanted to shake his head. There would be more stories around the table tonight.

"My lady," he said softly, "there is no curse and Fenella died long ago." He dared to take a step forward.

She cocked the pistol. "The curse lives, and well you know it, Macnachtan. You took my book. I want it returned."

His good humor faded. No one called him a liar. A rascal, yes, but a liar, no. "I know nothing about a book. Whatever you had that we found, we placed in your room. And, although I am surrounded by women, my lady, none are witches. Come, give me the gun."

She shook her head. "Fenella *is* alive. She never died, don't you understand."

"I understand I am beginning to doubt

your sanity." Heath raised his voice, speaking to his clansmen rather than to her. "My ancestress Fenella is dead. Long gone. You need not fear her. Now, hand the pistol to me, Lady Margaret, and we shall discuss this in private."

Her grip on the gun tightened. "I don't trust you. I don't trust any of you. Fenella *murdered* my companions. She caused the accident."

"How so?" Heath asked.

"She swept us off the road."

"The wind through there is high during a storm. The road is not good. The locals know that."

An angry muscle worked in her jaw. "That is *not* what happened. The road was good. The wind swept us off it as if we were crumbs on the table. They *all* died because of her. *I* should have died. *I did die.*"

Heath wasn't certain what she meant. "But you didn't, my lady."

"I did," was her answer, her voice shaking slightly. "I don't know how I am here now."

The woman had lost all reason.

Heath began calculating his chances of taking the gun from her. He decided the direct approach was the best.

"Hand the gun to me," he said, using the voice he used to soothe his sisters when they were unreasonable. "You are tired. You have been through a horrible ordeal. Let us return to the house so that you can rest."

"I don't have time to rest." She held her gun up higher. "I must stop this curse."

Rowlly had eased himself around her. She had not noticed yet.

"We will help you," Heath promised, "but first you must give me the gun." The poor girl, she was caught up in fear, a fear of the supernatural.

Rowlly's foot kicked a rock on the path behind her. She took a step aside to include him now in her sights. "Stay back," she warned.

"Do as she says, Rowlly," Heath ordered. He dared another step toward her. "Lady Margaret, you have nothing to fear."

How do I know that?" she demanded, the frown line between her eyes deepening.

"You must trust us," he said. He took another step.

"I can't."

"And yet you are amongst us," he said in understanding.

She shook her head. "Do not come closer."

"The gun is no good to you," he told her. "The gunpowder was wet from the rain."

For a moment, she appeared uncertain.

"Let us discuss this matter," he encouraged, moving toward her. He wanted the gun from her. He didn't believe she would fire it. He didn't think she had the fortitude.

He was wrong.

Heath was six feet away from her when she pulled the trigger.

CHAPTER FIVE

Fire and smoke burst from the pistol's muzzle.

Margaret's arm jerked with the force of the weapon's explosion. This movement wasn't unexpected to her; however, it did make her more aware of her surroundings and what she was doing.

She was shooting at *a man.*

Margaret had fired a pistol for sport many times, but this was the first she'd aimed with deadly intent — and her action shocked her into reality.

Before the firing, she seemed to have been in a dream born of desperation and fear.

Now she understood she was *not* asleep.

The gun *had* fired.

And she wasn't someplace safe, but instead was surrounded by her enemies.

The ball hit the Macnachtan's arm, tearing through the coat he wore.

To his credit, he stood his ground. Had

he believed she would not fire?

She was surprised herself.

His clansmen surged forward. In truth, she'd been so focused upon the laird that she'd barely registered the presence of a stable yard of people around her. Now rough hands grabbed her arms, reaching for the weapon and pulling her this way and that.

"Stand back, lads," Laird Macnachtan ordered.

The three men who had come for Margaret dropped their hands but did not move, holding her prisoner with their bodies. "Are you all right, Heath?" the shortest of them said.

The Macnachtan looked down at his coat where her ball had ripped through the material. "You missed my heart, my lady." His voice was deep, his accent not as pronounced as the others'.

"I hit where I aimed," she informed him.

That was not true. She *had* been aiming for the heart. This was Harry's gun. The sight would be true, but perhaps the fact that the powder had been damp may have impacted the ball's direction.

She didn't know if that was what had happened or not, but she was lucky she *hadn't* killed him. His clansmen would have seen her hanging without hesitation.

The lines of his mouth tightened and there was knowledge in his eyes that he knew she lied.

Gray. His eyes were a clear, almost silver gray. The impact of them almost knocked her from her feet. They were the sort of eyes that registered everything, cataloguing details, gauging their importance.

This man could speak with his eyes, or hide his thoughts behind them.

Those eyes now told her that he'd decided to be magnanimous. "Then I shall be thankful," he said, "that you didn't aim at my heart, my lady. Apparently your powder was *not* that wet."

He was giving her back her honor. Allowing her to keep it. "A Chattan always protects the powder," she answered, and took the arrogance out of her words by offering the gun to him.

"Very wise," he murmured approvingly, stepping forward to take the weapon from her. He was a tall man with dark brown hair in need of his barber. His beard had a day's growth, maybe more. His teeth were white and straight, and the set of his jaw told her he was not one to suffer fools gladly.

He appeared disheveled, impatient and very, very masculine.

Here was a man who could take charge and make the world turn on his terms or die trying.

He was also her enemy. She must remember that.

For the briefest of moments, they both held the pistol. A lightning bolt of energy seemed to pass between them.

She let go of the gun, startled by the sensation, and then felt embarrassed. Had he noticed her abruptness? Did he experience that awareness — ?

Suddenly, she wasn't feeling well and it had nothing to do with this confrontation with Laird Macnachtan. Her head began to ache as if gripped in a vise and her stomach churned.

He placed the gun into the deep pocket of his coat. "I'll know better than to keep that pistol and powder where you can reach it in the future."

"Is that all you are going to do? All you are going to say to her?" his sister Anice demanded. "She could have murdered you, Heath. I've lost one brother. I'm not anxious to lose another."

"She's right," Laren agreed. "I truly thought she'd killed you, Heath." She threw her arms around his shoulders. Anice did as well.

For a second, Laird Macnachtan appeared startled, as if he didn't know what to do with his arms full of sisters. "I'm fine —" he started, but Laren cut him off with an exclamation of horror.

"*You are bleeding.* Her shot *did* hit you," she accused. She pulled back her hand from his arm to show the smear of blood on it.

"Oh, Heath, how can you just stand there bleeding?" Anice said.

"It's a flesh wound. A mere scratch. The ball went through. One of you lads fetch a clean cloth from the tack room so I may apply a bandage."

A boy of about ten ran as if wings were on his feet to do his laird's bidding.

"A bandage from the *tack* room?" Laren repeated as if not believing her ears. "Do you want a fever? Or worse?"

"*Worse?*" he echoed, mimicking her, widening his eyes. "What could be worse, Laren?"

"You could lose your arm," Anice answered, her brother's disregard for his own safety obviously unsettling her.

"Then I wish the bullet had gone in my head," Laird Macnachtan said, "because I wouldn't mind losing it right now."

"That is your own fault for drinking so much last night," Laren replied.

That announcement was met by a boister-
ous round of comments from all within
hearing and some suggestions of what their
laird could do with his head.

Margaret watched all this, confused, the
pounding in her head growing stronger.
This was not how servants acted at her
brother's estate. This easy camaraderie was
not a part of her experience.

Nor did his sisters take offense. They accepted that all had a voice, from the oldest
to the youngest.

This was a different world from the one
she lived in. This was foreign, strange even.

"Anice, Laren, easy now," he said. "I'm in
no danger. I've been shot worse before."

His announcement did not calm his sisters. Their brows came together in alarm,
their mouths opening to ask a million questions, and he held up a hand to beg for
quarter. "I was in a war. Remember? Do
you think in boarding a ship, men throw
thistles at each other?"

"The world might be a better place if they
did," Anice announced, and the men around
her laughed.

"You may have been shot at by the
French," Laren said, "but we didn't expect
you to be shot right here before our eyes.
You could have been mortally wounded."

"But she was not aiming for my heart," he reminded them. His voice was light. He seemed to be enjoying himself.

A new voice spoke up, one as grating as a crow's caw, and it belonged to a small, grubby-looking woman. She appeared to have only two teeth in her head and her nose was impossibly big. But it was her tiny, shrewd eyes that put Margaret on guard. "I believe you should rid yourself of the Chattan," she announced, and then spit on the ground. "No good will come of having her here."

"The woman is our guest, Nila. Remember that," Laird Macnachtan bit out. "And quit spitting."

Nila did not take well to the order. Her eyebrows almost disappeared in her hairline. For a second, Margaret anticipated her spitting again, but grumbling several opinions to herself, the crone had the good sense to withdraw.

Meanwhile, the stable lad returned with a roll of clean wraps used for horse legs. Laren took the cloth from the boy and began wrapping the wound to stop the bleeding without bothering to remove the laird's coat.

Margaret had to speak up. "You should remove his clothing if you wish to stop the bleeding."

"Well, aren't you something, *my lady.*" Anice spoke with scorn. "First you shoot him and then we are not tending him well enough for your tastes. I fear everything they say about *you* is true."

"Everything they say about me?" Margaret repeated, mystified and, yes, feeling very guilty.

But Anice and her sister were not up to answering. They, Nila and the few other women in the stable yard gathered around the laird.

Nila informed them she'd heard of a remedy for healing that called for putting chicken droppings on the wound. Anice shouted, "Someone, fetch a chicken."

The women might have been serious in the order, but the men in the stable yard hooted with laughter.

That was enough for the Macnachtan. "If any of you brings a chicken, I'll wring its neck, *and yours,*" he warned as he pushed his way out from the midst of the women. Laren followed him, her hands holding the bandage she'd wrapped around his arm.

"And here we thought it would be making you smell better than the pig stink you are wearing, Heath," one of the men said, and the others laughed.

A dull red crept up the Macnachtan's neck.

He'd taken their earlier comments in stride, but this one had touched a nerve.

"I haven't finished tying the bandage, Heath," Laren complained.

"It is good enough," he barked out. "And don't the rest of you have tasks to be doing? Or are you going to stand around grinning like great apes all day?"

The men quickly went about their business, a sign that they did respect him when he used a tone of voice that warned heads would roll.

Laird Macnachtan turned his attention to Margaret.

The drumming in her head was louder now. She was suddenly very, very tired and she could not afford to be so. She needed her wits about her to find Fenella's book.

She meant to say as much to him, but when she opened her mouth, no words came out.

She swayed. Laird Macnachtan put out his hand as if to steady her.

It was the wrong thing to do.

To her horror, Margaret bent over and was frightfully ill.

All over his boots.

She looked up, scandalized. This was

beyond a lapse in manners. She'd never disgraced herself in such a way before. "I'm so sorry," she whispered, and then swooned.

Heath caught Lady Margaret before she hit the ground.

For a second, he held the woman, stunned by what had transpired.

He wasn't the only one. Everyone who had witnessed Her Ladyship's disgrace also appeared dumbfounded.

It was Anice who broke the silence. "I'm not certain Lady Margaret likes you, Heath."

He shot his sister a look that could have straightened the curls from her hair. He lifted Lady Margaret up in his arms and began walking toward the house. His body now smelled in so many wretched ways that he couldn't bear consideration, and his boots were in need of a cleaning from marsh water, pig offal and — well, he didn't want to think on it.

For once his clansmen kept their raucous opinions to themselves, although he did overhear Nila mumble something about "Chattans" and spit on the ground.

He didn't chastise her this time.

At the house, Heath kicked off his boots by

the door. It wasn't easy since he still held the unconscious Lady Margaret. He'd always heard that the cream-at-the-top ladies of society prided themselves on nibbling like birds. Lady Margaret obviously didn't share that habit. She'd grown heavier with every step he'd taken along the path to the house.

"Good heavens, Heath," Dara said, catching sight of him standing at the back door struggling with balance and boots. "What has happened to you? And how did you come by Lady Margaret?"

"What *hasn't* happened to me since last we saw each other over breakfast, Dara?" he said. She was his brother's widow but he considered her like a sister. "Let's see, I've been chasing pigs, arguing with Nila —"

"Again?" She heaved a world-weary sigh.

"I seem to never learn," he agreed. "Then I was shot —"

That caught her attention. "With a gun?"

"Is there another sort of shooting? And then Her Ladyship added insult to injury by — How shall I say this delicately?"

"You don't need to do so." She sniffed the air and then pulled a face. "I believe I understand."

Heath grunted his response as he finally kicked off his last boot. "I shall take her upstairs."

"I shall move your boots to the back step," Dara said, using a corner of the apron she wore to protect her fingers from touching them.

"I need to have a wound bandaged," he called after her as she walked away.

"I shall meet you in your room. I'll also see water is prepared for a bath."

"Thank you, Dara."

"Don't thank me. I'm doing this for the rest of us, Heath," she said, disappearing down the hall.

In stocking feet, Heath carried Lady Margaret up to her bedroom. He laid her on the bed. For a moment, he considered removing her cloak, and decided things were best if he left it alone. He did untie the strings at her neck.

When she'd first swooned, she appeared very ill, but now the color was returning to her face.

He was tempted to feel her forehead to see if she ran a fever, but he knew that would be just an excuse to touch her. He moved to the foot of the bed. She was so lovely . . . but there was something else about her that drew him. And it wasn't any idiocy like the curse.

It was a yearning that seemed born from

the deepest part of his soul.

And speaking to her, having that strange and violent interaction in the stable yard, had not dissuaded him. In fact, she had courage, a quality he respected.

He looked forward to their next exchange. "Hopefully, my lady, it shall not be as fierce."

Her answer was the silence of sleep.

Heath left the room. He was no poet. No woman had ever claimed his heart. Then again, the day he'd caught sight of Lady Margaret on that London street, every other woman he'd met had paled in comparison.

He went to his room. Theirs was a humble household. He served as his own valet, just as his sisters were their own maids. He wondered what Lady Margaret would make of such circumstances.

The cook's husband, Tully, served as a jack-of-all-trades. He had already delivered the tub to Heath's room and appeared with two pails of steaming water while Heath was undressing. He poured them in and fetched a pail of cold.

"Good enough for you, Laird?" Tully asked. He was silver-haired and stoop-shouldered and he'd known Heath since the day he was born.

"Yes, Tully, thank you."

"Lady Macnachtan will want to be seeing to that wound," Tully said.

Heath had removed his shirt, and although he'd been correct and the ball had gone through, there was a bit of pain in the muscle. "She'd best bring some compresses."

"Nila says putting chicken droppings on a wound like that will heal it without a scar." At Heath's glare, the older man held up his hands. "I was just saying, Laird. Offering to help."

"If you want to help, keep Nila and the chickens away from me."

Tully chuckled. "Aye, I'll try to do that, Laird, although the chickens and Nila have a will of their own." He left the room.

Heath wasted no time finishing undressing. He crossed to the set of drawers and opened one. He pulled out a cloth bag. Inside were some of the items from his naval career. He rarely looked at them now.

One was a bar of finely milled, sandalwood-scented soap. He held the bar up to his nose. The scent reminded him of the day in Amsterdam when he'd purchased it. That day hadn't been long after he'd seen Lady Margaret in London.

The officers he'd been with had teased him. The soap had been an extravagance.

Heath had always sent the majority of his pay home, then he saved a portion, and spent what was left on necessities.

The soap had not been a necessity, not with cakes of lye soap selling for a half penny, but today, he was glad he'd purchased it.

His arm was beginning to hurt.

He climbed in the tub and gave himself a good scrub. It felt good. It had been a long time since he'd done this. *Too long, perhaps?*

And he was ashamed.

He knew that he'd started drinking more than he should in the evenings. Part was the burden and nature of his responsibilities. He felt like Sisyphus of Greek myth who'd been forever doomed in Hades to roll a rock up a hill, only to see it roll back down again. Every day it seemed he had to do the same things over and over and say the same things repeatedly. He was ground down by the boredom.

But the other reason he numbed himself with spirits was fear.

He'd never imagined that he would take Brodie's place. His brother had been so full of life, of confidence, it still didn't seem possible to believe he was dead.

There was a knock at the door. It was Dara. "Heath, are you ready for me to bandage your arm?"

"One moment." He climbed out of the tub. He would toss the water out the window later. Using the shirt he had just removed, he dried himself off and then quickly dressed in fresh breeches and stockings.

"Heath?" Dara said.

"I'm dressed, save for my shirt. One moment."

The door opened. "Don't bother with your shirt," she said. She carried a roll of clean bandages that looked very much like the horse leg wraps he had used and a container of salve. "It will be easier to bandage without it and I'm an old married woman. The sight of your chest won't make me missish. Here, sit on the edge of the bed. It will be easier for me to reach your arm." She stopped and sniffed the air. "Heath, is that good smell you?"

"Tend my wound, Dara."

Her eyes lit with laughter. "Well, Her Ladyship may be silly for shooting you but at least she has done one favor for all of us."

"My arm, Dara."

"Yes, Laird," she said, and then her laughter turned to a frown as she studied the wound. Dara had been a minister's daughter

111

in Dalmally. In that role, she had done a fair amount of nursing. Even Mr. Hawson, the doctor, deferred to her. "It isn't bad but it needs to mend." She began wrapping his arm. "I can't imagine what Lady Margaret was thinking, firing a gun at you," she said as she worked.

"Pull tighter," he ordered.

She did as bid.

Heath winced. "Not that tight."

"You might need a stitch."

"I hate stitches."

"I hate unruly patients," she answered calmly, tying a knot in the bandage. "If it doesn't start mending up tonight, I'll put a stitch in it on the morrow."

Heath would see that didn't happen.

He stretched his arm. It hurt like the devil but he'd heal. He always healed.

"Speaking of patients, how is Lady Margaret?" he asked.

"Still sleeping. The woman is exhausted." She paused. "It is odd that almost everyone traveling with her died and yet she survived with a nary a scratch."

Heath shrugged and pulled on the clean shirt he had taken from his drawer. "Accidents happen that way," he said. "I've seen crews hit by cannon fire where the ball took the life of one man and the man standing next to him didn't receive so much as a scrape."

Dara shivered at the thought. He tried not to talk too much to the women in his family about war. They were gentle, happy souls. They would not understand the grittiness of being in battle or why he had thrived on it.

He must also remember that Dara would be more sensitive to such talk after losing her husband in such a grisly fashion. He ran a hand over the growth of whiskers on his jaw. He rose from the bed and crossed to the washbasin. He began sharpening his razor.

Dara leaned against the post of his bed. "You are shaving, as well, Heath?"

He caught her mocking glance in his mirror. He had been too busy the day before to apply a blade to them.

He'd also been too busy the day before that as well.

"I've gone to seed here," he said.

"You have had your hands full," Dara said sympathetically. "Perhaps it is good Lady Margaret is here. Perhaps her presence will help you think about what you want to do."

Heath poured fresh water into the basin. "What do you mean?" He began lathering soap to shave. He should have cut his hair weeks ago. He had grown as shaggy one of the Jack-Tars aboard the *Boyne.*

"I'm talking about the offer from Owen Campbell that you discussed with me. I haven't said anything to anyone, although sometimes this house has ears."

"I haven't really given it much consideration," he lied, shifting his gaze to his shaving.

"You need to," she said. "Your sisters need dowries. You don't want them branded spinsters."

Heath frowned. "Rowlly said the same to me several days ago. Have Laren and Anice complained?"

"Oh no," Dara hastened to say. "They wouldn't do that. It is just that I know what it is like to be a girl without a decent dowry. Until Brodie, I had no other callers, and no future."

He rinsed the razor in the washbasin and faced her. "It's been a year since Brodie's death, how are you feeling, Dara? We never talk about it."

She straightened. "For good reason. I miss him, Heath. I wish we'd had children. *Sons,*" she elaborated. "Then you could be off sailing the world and fighting the French."

"All our lives changed with Brodie's

death." He dried his hands on a towel thoughtfully and then said, "I will find the man who killed him, Dara. I promise you I will."

A sad look crossed her face. "It no longer matters to me. He's gone. Nothing will bring him back." She lowered her head and then said quietly, "I wish I knew who murdered him as well . . . but life must go on, as hard as it is to think in such a manner. I need to start considering what I should do."

"There is a place for you here. You are family."

"Thank you, Heath. That is good to know. When things begin changing, it is hard to know one's place." She paused a moment and then said, "I must warn you of trying to change things at Marybone. Brodie tried to make changes. The crofters and the like resisted him and he was often as frustrated as you have been. I know you have grand plans —"

"Actually, some are Brodie's plans. The improvements I'm suggesting are the ones he'd started or left notes indicating what he wanted done."

"Brodie had high hopes for us all," Dara said. "He always saw our best and ignored our flaws. I fear that is one of the reasons we are in such debt. He truly believed that he could breed horses and could save us." There was a bit of silence. She sighed, the sound heavy, lost.

"Don't worry about the debts, Dara. I shall see to those. What is important is that you make wise choices for your life."

"I know." She picked up the salve from the bed. "And you should think of the choices you have to make as well, Heath. I know you feel a responsibility to all the people here. But if you decide to sell to Owen Campbell, I'll support you. I'd like to think as Brodie's wife, my approval might mean something."

"Thank you, Dara. It does to me."

"So, have you given his offer any thought?"

Heath walked over to his wardrobe and pulled out his brown woolen jacket. This time he admitted the truth. "It's all I can think of."

"Then you will sell?"

He looked to his sister-in-law. Brodie's death had been hard on her. "I don't know yet, Dara. This is my birthright."

"But you have not been here in years."

"Aye, and it is harder to keep this lot in line than seven frigates of sailors . . . but it is the legacy of my ancestors."

"And it is not my decision," she said as if

to remind herself. "I know you will do what is best for yourself and your sisters. As for the rest, I'm certain Owen Campbell will treat them well."

"Or turn them out."

"Do you truly believe he would?" She sounded surprised.

Heath shrugged. He honestly didn't know what Campbell would do, and there were days even he wanted to walk away from all of this. "I can't leave. Not yet. Not until I know who murdered my brother. I owe him that much."

"Brodie wasn't the sort who would have held you accountable."

"He wasn't," Heath agreed. He opened a drawer and pulled out a neck cloth. He quickly tied it around his neck as he admitted, "It's myself who needs answers."

She'd walked up to him, waved his hands away and retied the knot he had sloppily managed. Lifting her eyes to meet his, she said, "You'll know soon enough what it is you should be doing." She stepped back. "Dinner will be within the hour. I'll see you then."

"I'm going downstairs as it is," he answered, and opened his door for her. He followed her out into the hall and down the stairs. He had an hour to waste. It was an incredible luxury. He should do paperwork, but then he rejected the idea. Lady Margaret's arrival had disrupted the normal order of things at Marybone. She'd reminded him of the taste of the world he'd had and might not have again.

Heath decided to walk to the stables and see how the pregnant mare was faring. The animal had been anxious all day. It was too soon for her to foal but Heath had learned a long time ago that God and nature had a way of playing tricks.

Stretching out his bandaged arm, knowing that moving it would save the muscles from stiffening, he walked toward the back hall when he heard his sister Laren shout, *"Help me."* A crash punctuated her words.

The call came from the library that also served as his study. Heath ran in that direction, reaching the library door a step before Dara and Anice.

He was shocked at the sight of Laren and Lady Margaret struggling against each other. Her Ladyship held a book in her arms and Laren fought gallantly to take it from her. Lady Margaret battled just as earnestly to keep it, shoving his sister back against his desk with her shoulder in a move Heath had used himself just a few days ago in his brawl at the Goldeneye.

Laren lost her hold and Lady Margaret turned to dash out the door with her prize. Instead, she ran right into Heath.

Chapter Six

The moment Margaret's nose ran into Laird Macnachtan's hard chest, she knew she had made a grave error in judgment.

His hands came down upon her shoulders. Manacles could not have been stronger than his grip. Incongruously, the scent of sandalwood surrounded them, tickling her nose and making her blink. He smelled much different, and far better, than when last they'd met.

"Lady Margaret, why are you raiding my library?"

She tightened her hold on the precious book, *Fenella's book,* clutching it close to her body. She wished she had managed to sneak in and out of the library without being discovered.

Margaret had come to her senses earlier to find herself returned to her bed. She'd been embarrassed that she had swooned in front of the Macnachtan. That wasn't something she did. She didn't even own a bottle of smelling salts.

And yet, when she'd woken, the distressing headache she had suffered before fainting was gone. She'd felt fine, and she needed to find Fenella's book. Time was of the essence.

She knew it wasn't in her room and decided to start her search on the first floor. When she'd come down earlier, she'd noticed the library.

Sure enough, upon entering the small, masculinely furnished room, she'd spied a leather-bound book tucked into one corner of the shelves that lined the walls. She had just opened it and discovered handwritten entries when Laren Macnachtan had come upon her and demanded she turn over the book.

Margaret was not about to give up Fenella's book now that she'd found it. The book belonged to her.

Every person in the household, including the laird's female relatives and a bosomy woman who smelled of flour and the kitchen fire, seemed to be here now. They crowded around the door, their heads craning to see around Laird Macnachtan.

Margaret met his hard gaze. Earlier, when she'd shot him, those eyes had held a touch of humor. He was not amused now, and he was intimidating.

He was too male, too strong, too *everything.*

It was hard to even speak when she was around him.

His sister Laren had no such difficulty. "I caught her stealing a book, Heath. I asked her what she was doing and instead of answering, she tried to push past me. She shoved me out of the way. You saw her."

Heat rushed to Margaret's cheeks. Listening to Laren's description of her behavior, she realized how erratic she must appear. It was in keeping with how erratic she felt.

None of this made sense — from the accident to her being here, whole and healthy.

For the first time she considered that perhaps *they* didn't know any more than she did.

Margaret took a step back. "This is my book. I brought it here."

"This is the book you accused me of having stolen before you shot me?" Laird Macnachtan surmised.

"*Yes,* the *one* you said you *didn't* have." The words exploded out of her, propelled by righteous indignation. She drew a deep, exasperated breath, trying to calm herself. "I *need* this book."

"Apparently." His gray eyes upon her were unreadable, the set of his mouth stern.

He turned to the others. "I wish a moment alone with Lady Margaret."

"I don't believe that is wise," Laren protested. "She is very strong. Look at this red mark on my arm."

Margaret looked with the others. Laren had pulled up her sleeve to show a red welt. She must have hit her arm hard on the desk when Margaret pushed her.

"Is it broken?" Laird Macnachtan asked.

"It hurts," Laren answered, her expression tense.

"Move your fingers," her brother ordered. She could move them.

"You will be fine," he said. He stepped aside so that she could pass. "And so will I, Laren, but if you truly fear for me, stay out in the hallway where you can come running if I need help." There was a hint of humor in this last suggestion as if he didn't believe it would be necessary. His sisters weren't so certain.

"We *will* be out here," Anice declared, her threat directed more to Margaret than her brother. Laren nodded her head in agreement, holding her arm gingerly now, something she hadn't been doing only moments before.

"I will feel safer," he assured them with the forbearance of an overly tolerant older brother, and signaled with his hand that he wanted them to leave.

Laren still hesitated. *Out,* he mouthed.

She left with the others.

Margaret had started studying the grain in the hardwood floor at her feet. She would not give up Fenella's book. She wouldn't.

"Would you have a chair, my lady?" he asked.

Margaret didn't answer. If she could, she would *will* him away.

"Well, I shall have a chair. This has been what one would call a challenging day."

She listened as he moved the wooden chair behind the desk and sat in it.

Margaret braced herself for his questions. She moved her stare from the floorboards to a point in the far corner of the room.

He didn't speak. Instead, he waited.

She knew what he was doing. Her brother Lyon used this trick all the time. If he waited long enough, people usually told him what he wished to know. Of course, she'd proven herself more stubborn than her oldest brother on many an occasion. She could also outwait the Macnachtan.

Cold and darkness seeped into the corners of the room. There was no fire in the grate.

He didn't seem inclined to light a candle and was at ease as the late afternoon shadows took over the room.

Slowly, a bit of tension inside her started to unwind.

She dared to look at him. He sat at his desk, calm, relaxed, self-assured; everything she wasn't. It almost hurt to look at him.

And so, she *had* to break the silence. "I'm not stealing the book. This is mine. *You* took it from me."

"If that is what you believe —"

"*It is what I know.* This is *my* book."

"Then you may have it."

She frowned, not trusting him.

The laird leaned forward, placing one arm on his desk. "My lady, the book has been on that shelf since this house was built. For all that time, no one has looked at it. You are welcome to the book."

The Macnachtan sounded too calm, too reasonable to be lying. Or perhaps he was the best sort of liar. Margaret had learned men had the gift of telling a woman exactly what she wanted to hear, true or not, without a pang of conscience.

"However, may I look at the book?" he asked. "Just so I know which one you are taking?"

Her guard went up. She shook her head.

He leaned back in the chair. "What is so special about this book?"

"You know. You took it from me."

"Did I?"

There was challenge in his voice.

"Someone did," she answered.

"Are you certain that is *your* book?"

He was cleverly planting seeds of doubt. She knew it, and yet she couldn't help but look down at the book she held. The cover was similar to Fenella's book — or was it?

Suddenly, Margaret feared she was the one being unreasonable and a bit mad.

She didn't understand herself any longer. One moment she felt confident, and in the next seemed a shambles. She weighed the book in one hand, placing the palm of her other hand on the cover.

"I shouldn't have shot you," she confessed, staring at the cracked leather of the book.

"You were afraid."

There was no accusation in his voice but a simple statement of fact.

She nodded. She was afraid. She was *very* afraid.

"Your trip has been hard on you," he said. "You lost many people in your party."

Tears burned in her eyes. Her throat tightened. She held the tears back. It never did any good to cry.

126

"It's hard to lose people we are close to," he continued, his deep, melodic voice soothing. "Or to be close to death ourselves."

Faces came to her mind — of Balfour her coachman, and Thomas her driver, and Smith. And then there were her brothers. They, too, could die. They were in the process even as she stood here.

He rose from his chair and came around the desk. He turned the chair situated in front of the desk toward her. The seat was upholstered so that it would be comfortable. "Please, sit, my lady. Let us discuss this."

Still, she did not move. It was as if she was powerless.

He held out his hand to her. She startled, on guard — and then realized he was offering a kerchief. In spite of her best efforts, she was crying. Tears streamed down her face, dripping off her chin.

Some women were more lovely when they cried. Margaret was not one of them. Her face grew splotchy and her eyes red. She was losing both pride and looks in front of him. It was too much.

"My brother Neal never carries kerchiefs around," she whispered. "Neither does my brother Harry."

"I have more sisters than they. If they were

in my shoes, they'd have one in every pocket."

His mention of her brothers broke down the last barrier. She took the kerchief. Worse, she, who was said to epitomize grace and good manners, blew her nose in it, making a decidedly ungraceful sound.

"Please, sit, my lady."

Margaret sat.

She expected him to attempt to snatch the book from her, but he made no move toward it.

Instead, he watched her with an air of patience.

"I don't know what to make of you," she confessed. "Did you not know we are enemies?"

"I don't participate in feuds or grudges beyond one year's endurance. I also don't believe every tale whispered in my ear. Did my sisters tell you we buried your companions?"

His change of subject disarmed her. The tightness started to build again. She nodded. "I would like to pay my respects," she whispered.

"I will personally escort you to their graves on the morrow if you are feeling able," he offered.

"Thank you," she managed. She crumpled

the kerchief in her hand. He would not want it back. Her fingers were trembling, her hands resting on Fenella's book.

"So, how do you know that is your book?" he asked.

"Because on the inside cover is a list of names," she said, opening the book to show him — and then stopped.

There were no names there. Margaret frowned at the blank page as if she could will the names to appear. She started leafing through the pages.

He watched her, the only sound between them the turning of old, brittle pages.

Nor were there the spells or wives' tales or sound advice that she'd read numerous times on her trip to Loch Awe. She realized now that this book had more to do with the managing of the estate and much had been written in a man's hand.

"This isn't the same book," she replied, her voice hoarse with dismay.

"What book are you searching for?" he asked.

Margaret looked up at him. "You didn't find any book in my things?" she demanded, uncertain whether she could trust him . . . and then realizing she had no choice.

She crushed the kerchief in her hand. She'd never felt so alone.

■ ■ ■ ■

Heath was concerned.

He'd witnessed men behave the way Lady Margaret did, men who had seen too much of battle, men who believed all was lost.

Lady Margaret's actions might not make sense to him or anyone else at Marybone, but they did to her.

Heath was also worried about her health. She had deep circles under her eyes and her hands shook.

She was dressed simply and without the artifice of a wealthy woman. She'd pulled her hair back at the nape of her neck and it curled down around her shoulders. She looked young and scared and very vulnerable . . . and vulnerable women were a weakness of his.

"I sent word to your brother Lord Lyon that you are safe," he offered.

She raised a hand to her forehead as if his kindness burdened her all the more. "It may already be too late," she replied, not looking at him. "Lyon might be dead and Harry could not be long after him."

He knelt so he was on eye level with her. "Let's examine this logically. Speak to me of the accident," he said, wanting to make

130

sense of her strange belief in a curse. She was a modern woman. Certainly she understood that spells and curses did not exist? "You claim a strong wind forced your coach off the road?"

A small frown line appeared between her brows as she said, "I told you everything. I don't remember much."

"Then tell me what you do remember. Start at the beginning. You were coming here because of the curse my ancestress Fenella placed upon your family."

She raised guileless blue eyes to meet his. A man could lose himself in her gaze when she appeared so defenseless. This was also *not* the proud woman who had caught his attention in London all those years ago.

"The curse states when a Chattan falls in love, he will die," she said, her voice low. "Both Lyon and Harry are in love and both are deathly ill. The curse killed my father and my grandfather. Over the generations, many have come to Scotland to search for a way to end the curse."

"They have come knocking on our door more than once."

"And you wouldn't help them."

"We couldn't, my lady," he said. "A curse is words. Nothing more."

Her shoulders stiffened. She did not

agree. She continued her story. "We are desperate to save Lyon. In spite of what has been done in the past, Harry hoped to try a new tact and was the first to come to Scotland. We didn't know of Fenella until by chance he found Fenella's book. It was in Glenfinnan, which was once the seat of the Chattans."

"Why was it there?"

"I don't know the book's history and I don't believe his wife does, either. She said she discovered the book in her attic. It just appeared —"

Her voice broke off. She frowned as if a new thought had occurred to her.

"What is it?" he prodded.

"My sister-in-law discovered the book at the same time she found a small white cat. It's a strange cat. Her ears are folded over and she has huge eyes that seem to communicate her thoughts. I called her Owl because she reminded me of one."

Heath didn't like cats, and he didn't know why Lady Margaret was talking about one, until she said, "No one could see the cat, except for Harry, his wife, and myself. Rowan, Harry's Indian servant, the one upstairs, told me he believes Owl is a reincarnation of either Fenella or her daughter Rose, the one who took her own life and caused the curse. Do you understand what a reincarnation is?"

"I've heard of it," Heath admitted, hesitant. Her story had taken a decidedly odd turn.

She appeared not to notice his skepticism. "When Rowan told me he thought Owl was part of the curse, I left the cat on the side of the road. I hated doing it but my servants had all convinced me I was the only one who saw her."

"Perhaps they were playing a joke? And they *could* see the cat?"

Lady Margaret frowned at him. "Why would they do that?"

"I'm not certain."

She leaned forward, placing her hand on his arm. "You believe I sound strange, as if I am imagining things."

He couldn't deny her charge.

"I fear I am as well," she said, sitting back in her chair. "And yet you asked me to start from the beginning."

"I did."

"Then understand, I am telling what I know. Or what I *think* I know. And I warn you, my story is going to sound more unrealistic."

"I shall brace myself."

A flicker of annoyance went through her

eyes. His dry understatement was not lost on her and she did not appreciate his humor. She lifted her chin and continued, "Shortly after we left the cat, the storm came up. We were less than an hour from Loch Awe, certainly on the last miles of the journey."

"There has not been a large storm over the past week, my lady. Rain and mist is always present, but the weather has not been violent."

"I can only tell you what I experienced, Laird Macnachtan. The storm arrived suddenly, surprising us. It was powerful enough to sweep us off the road as if we were crumbs on a table. I could hear the men swearing at the horses. And then the horses started screaming. It was horrifying. The coach went off the road and began rolling down the mountain. Smith — she was my maid — and I were inside . . . and I could feel my bones break. I *experienced* the pain. I lost consciousness and when I woke, I saw Smith not far from me. I could tell she was dead. I knew I would be dead soon as well. I could feel myself failing."

Heath stood, frowning. "When we found the accident, you were not located close to the maid where you could have a line of sight of her. In fact, it would be impossible for you to have seen the maid from where you were."

"I was within feet of her," Lady Margaret insisted. "I was staring into her face."

"You must have moved because I discovered you away from the wreckage. You were on a bed of pine needles. There was copse of pines and you appeared as if you were sleeping there, your hands folded at your waist."

"I was on my back?" She shook her head. "That could not be. I remember that I was on my stomach. And I could not move. I saw Fenella's book. That's how I knew it was in the wreckage. It had been in the coach with me and was within my view when I first regained consciousness. I tried to reach for it, but my arms wouldn't move. They were broken."

"They are not broken now —"

"*I know,*" she said, rising to her feet and dropping the book into her chair. "I don't understand it. I don't understand *any of this.*"

Heath leaned back against the desk. "I don't believe in myths and legends. There is always a rational, logical explanation."

Perhaps Lady Margaret was part of some ruse . . . and yet he could not imagine any reason that the Chattans would orchestrate the deaths of their own people for a pretense.

"You are thinking I am mad," she said.

"I don't know," he conceded. "Perhaps you are merely confused."

"I can understand how you might not believe me." She straightened her shoulders and then said, "So, in the interest of you concluding that I am *truly* and completely deranged, let me finish my story. After I couldn't reach for Fenella's book and discovered I could not move in any way, I knew I was going to die. I expected it. A person *knows* when death is upon them."

Heath had heard that before.

"That's when Owl came to me," she said. "The cat curled up next to me. I don't know how she found me, but in that moment I was so thankful to not be alone."

"You said you left the cat on the road behind you."

"Yes, miles behind us, but there she was." Lady Margaret drew in a deep breath and crossed her arms. "I try to make sense of it all. I can only conclude that Fenella was trying to stop me from reaching here, and Owl saved my life. She revived me . . . from death."

Heath didn't know what to think. "Why was coming here so important?"

"This is where it all began. Don't you understand — ?" She stopped, pushing a stray strand of her hair behind her ear. "Of course, you don't. I'm not explaining myself well. You see, I am the first female born to our line since the days before Charles Chattan, the man who betrayed Rose Macnachtan. Harry believes that if anyone has the chance of breaking the curse, I do. And Owl," she said thoughtfully, as if just beginning to understand, "protected me. Owl wasn't evil like I feared. That is why I left her behind on the road. I feared her. And yet, now, I know she needed to be with me. She healed me when I was about to die."

Heath made up his mind about her — she was as mad as a hatter. She was telling him a story that only an idiot would believe. And yet his attraction to her was strong.

She was the standard by which he'd compared all women. He hadn't been so bold as to think that a woman of her class, of her bearing and wealth, would have any interest in a Highland ruffian like him, but he didn't want his image of her tarnished, either.

He also didn't want to encourage her wild-eyed beliefs by telling her something he knew — Marybone was nowhere close to the tower from which Rose Macnachtan was said to have jumped. She'd traveled to the wrong place.

"You think I'm balmy, don't you?" she said.

The air changed between them. He felt her withdraw. The vulnerability left her and a mask seemed to cross her face. Right before his eyes, she became Lady Margaret Chattan, the Unattainable.

"I need your help," she said, the words stiff, as if she had to force them. He was certain she was not accustomed to asking for assistance.

"What may I do for you, my lady?"

"Fenella's book may still be where you found the wreckage. Will you take me there? I shall pay you for the service."

"That is unnecessary —" Heath started to say, only for her to interrupt him.

"Of course, it is. You are a Macnachtan and I am a Chattan. I'm beginning to realize that my talk of a curse sounds fantastic to you, but it is very real for me. Is a hundred pounds enough for the trip?"

"A hundred?" Heath repeated, stunned by the amount.

"Very well, two hundred," she said, taking charge and putting him in his place.

Heath's pride bristled, but his common sense and the dire need to pay off the estate's debts stepped in before he could refuse the money.

Still, a man shouldn't humble himself.

"*Three* hundred pounds," he answered.

She blinked surprise and he felt a score of satisfaction. Her expressive eyes took on scorn. He met her gaze with a hard one of his own.

"If I'm going to be bought, my lady, I will not go cheap."

There was a moment as she digested this and then she said, "Very well. When can we leave?"

"Tomorrow, depending on your strength."

"Excellent."

"Then tomorrow it is. First light."

She nodded and took a step toward the door. "I shall be ready." She studied him again and he saw her adjust her opinion of him. She had thought him safe.

He wasn't.

"I would like to spend this evening at Rowan's bedside," she said.

"You may."

She took several more steps and then stopped. "I don't want you to think me ungrateful. I do appreciate all that you and your sisters have done. Is it possible on the morrow that I may pay respects to my servants?"

"Of course. They are buried in the kirk yard. It is on the way."

"If there were any expenses —" she started, but Heath didn't want to make the air more strained between them.

"There were none, my lady."

"But the doctor for Rowan and myself?" she suggested.

"You are my guests. I only charge for outlandish requests."

She frowned. "You believe we won't find anything?"

"I'm certain of it. We were thorough in our search, Lady Margaret. We collected everything we found around the accident. The book you are looking for was not there."

She placed her hand on the door handle. "I have a sense that you are wrong, my lord. My tale is unbelievable, and yet, you would be wise to believe." With those words, she opened the door and almost walked right into Laren and Anice.

His sisters attempted to pretend that they were not eavesdropping, but they were not good actresses.

Even Dara was lingering in the hall.

"Excuse me," Lady Margaret murmured, and gracefully walked away.

The women watched her go down the hall a moment before charging into the library.

"You did tell us we could wait in the hall," Anice said in defense to his unspoken accusation.

"Yes, but not with your ears to the door," Heath countered.

"Did you believe what she was telling you?" Laren asked.

"If I could write this for the papers in London, I would," Anice said. "People would be very interested in the reasons for her trip here."

"Yes, brought on by the Macnachtan witch," Heath gently reminded them. "We'd all be scandal broth, and you will do nothing of the sort, Anice. She's a guest and she has been through a traumatic experience."

"Where she died and a cat that only she can see saved her," Laren said, revealing how effective their eavesdropping had been. "What nonsense. That tale is pure superstition. And if you think we'll let you ride with her to the wreckage alone tomorrow, you are wrong."

"Wrong?" Heath questioned.

"Yes," Anice said. "We are not so much worried about witches as we are about Lady Margaret bewitching you."

Heath started to laugh at his sister's tart comment. "She's *paying* me to take her," he said in his defense, now believing the payment a good idea. "Don't let your suspicions run wild."

But his sisters were unconvinced by his protest. He could see their doubts in the lift of their stubborn chins and tightness of their shoulders.

They'd also be right.

Lady Margaret fascinated him. She was a glimpse of the world beyond, the world responsibilities had made him give up.

That evening, Lady Margaret did not join them for dinner. Laren sent up a tray but Cora reported Her Ladyship was not in her room. Instead, she was sitting with her servant as she had said she would.

When he went up for bed, Heath paused in front of Lady Margaret's door. He considered knocking, but backed away.

Instead, he found himself going up the stairs to the Indian's room. Here was the one person who could corroborate Lady Margaret's wild story.

The door to the room was slightly ajar and Heath caught a glimpse of her presence before he barged in. He stopped outside the doorway out of respect for her privacy.

Lady Margaret was on her knees by the bedside, her hands folded, her head bowed in deep prayer.

The woman he'd seen in London, the

Unattainable, was not one whom he had imagined praying, especially on her knees. That woman had been — what?

Beautiful? Yes. Celebrated? Certainly. Scores of men had followed her and the crowd on a busy London street had been aware of her presence. She was wealthy, young, a jewel of London society.

And then his memory caught on something else, something he had not noticed at the time but he realized now — she'd been unhappy. Whether he had recognized it or not, he had sensed it.

She'd been surrounded by hordes of admirers, and alone.

And here she was keeping vigil by a servant's bedside.

He had few regrets in life. He was a man of action, not studious contemplation, but he recognized in her the weight of remorse . . . and he did not understand why.

Heath backed away from the door, giving her privacy. Nor could he shake the image of her humbled from his mind. He went to bed, but did not sleep until he heard the sound of her bedroom door closing, a sign that she had finally gone to her room.

The next morning when he came downstairs prepared to travel, not only was Lady Margaret dressed and waiting for him, but

Laren and Anice were there and ready to ride as well.

CHAPTER SEVEN

Heath hesitated on the last step of the staircase. He'd hoped his sisters had forgotten their threat to ride with him today, and well they knew it.

Laren had the audacity to look smug. "It's such a lovely day for an adventure, Anice and I couldn't be convinced to stay behind."

The day was not that lovely. The weather was overcast and cold.

And while Laren had an excellent seat, it was well-known that Anice was a skittish rider and would prefer being anywhere save the back of a horse.

Heath looked from one sister to the other and wondered if they knew how foolish they were being.

But he'd not tell them that.

"Fine. We shall have an outing of it," he said, turning his attention to Lady Margaret.

She truly looked stunning. Her riding

habit was made of a blue material so fine and a cut so excellent it fitted her figure perfectly. The collar was black velvet and the buttons silver. She carried a whip topped with a silver and white ribbon tassel and wore a hat with a wide brim and low crown. Both items had some damage from the coach accident. The hat had lost some of its stylish shape and there was dirt on the ribbon tassel that would never be removed.

Still, in contrast, his sisters' riding clothes appeared shabby and ill made. The material was stiff and the style obviously dated.

"Well, let us break our fast then," Laren was saying, and led the way to the dining room. As she walked, she held the extra length of her skirt up in one hand in a gesture that was not common for Laren. He remembered their mother chastising her to stop dragging her hem on the floor. Just last week, when she'd gone riding, Heath had noticed that she still let her hem drag — but not today.

He disliked the fact he noticed.

Her Ladyship herself was very quiet. Tension seemed to radiate from her.

"You cut your hair," Anice whispered, and brushed her fingers against the back of his collar. Heath was wearing a brown hunting jacket and black breeches. Not only were his heels worn, his boots also needed a good polish. He'd meant to do the task last night but had been called away over a dispute involving two of his crofters, both of them highly inebriated, the bloody fools.

"What did you say, Anice?" Laren asked in her lady-of-the-manor voice. "Please sit here, Lady Margaret, next to me at the table."

"Heath cut his hair," Anice repeated.

Laren snapped her head around to look. It was as if she had not truly noticed him when he first came down. Now she frowned in disapproval. He glared back at her.

Yes, he'd cut his hair a bit. It was still too long. There was no barber, save his sisters, and he hadn't asked their help because he knew they would read too much into the action. They would believe he'd done it for Lady Margaret, and he had.

Yesterday afternoon, they had been encouraging him to snatch her up for a wife.

Now they behaved as if she was a leper.

They needn't worry. Lady Margaret would have to be blind or a fool to take a fancy to someone like him. He had far more problems than solutions.

But he was male, and she was beautiful, and if his sisters wanted to scowl with disapproval, so be it —

He stopped his musings and frowned at the dining room table.

It was different.

Usually, they either went down to the kitchen or little Cora would help Cook by bringing their breakfasts to them. They kept their life simple.

However, today the table was set with the best linens and dishes. Heath couldn't remember the last time he had seen these linens.

Now it was his turn to frown at Laren. So she mocked him for trying to impress Lady Margaret while she was doing the same?

Sisters!

He pulled out his chair at the head of the table. "What shall be next this morning, Laren?" he murmured. "Will Cora come out dressed in Macnachtan livery?"

He received his sister's coolest stare for his effrontery as she and Anice took their chairs.

Lady Margaret noticed none of it. She'd taken her seat, still very quiet, a small frown on her forehead.

Heath shook out his napkin. "I'm surprised there isn't a little bell for me to ring for the servants."

"She knows we are here," Laren said stiffly.

Cora proved her correct by coming into the room with a tray. The girl was a wee thing and the tray held several bowls of morning porridge and slices of fresh bread and butter. Heath rose from the table to help her. He couldn't keep from whispering in Laren's ear as he set her porridge in front of her, "I'm surprised we are not having beefsteak."

"We thought about it," Anice said as he served her, and Heath started to laugh. "Behave," Anice ordered quietly. "Laren truly wants to let Lady High-and-Mighty know that we are every bit as good as she is."

But they couldn't. His sisters knew nothing of the world beyond Marybone, but Heath had experienced the wonders and luxuries of London, things that Lady Margaret would accept as a matter of course, as her due. He doubted she noticed their extra efforts.

"Thank you, Cora," he said as he took his chair and lifted his spoon. Porridge. It was the best they had to offer. At night it was fish, and noonday it was usually cheese and bread. "I assure you, Lady Margaret, you have never had porridge like this before."

Her response was to look up with a distracted air as if she hadn't even realized she had food in front of her. She turned her attention to her bowl. "Oh, yes, thank you," she said, and picked up her spoon, only to set it down.

"I must say something," she said, "and I'm going to apologize before I say it because I am certain I shall do a very poor job of it." Lady Margaret turned to Laren. "Miss Macnachtan, I owe you an apology for behaving the way I did yesterday. It was poor form. I . . ." She paused as if reconsidering her words and then bravely pushed on. "I don't say I'm sorry very often. I usually keep a firm distance from people. I've found it safer. This is new to me. I don't know if Laird Macnachtan told you but I made the wrong assumption yesterday about the book in your library." She looked around the table to Anice and Heath. "I may have assumed the worst of all of you. And in doing so, I've created a bad impression of myself. Please, I'm sorry. I know to an outsider my behavior seems bizarre. I no longer see you as enemies — and I know that sounds odd since you probably never even knew I existed until you found me on your land. But I am deeply appreciative and *humbled* by all that you've done for my staff and myself."

Her words seemed to hang in the air.

He understood the courage it took to apologize. Now *he* was the one humbled.

Anice was the first to recover from her surprise. "You have nothing to feel ill at ease about," she said to this woman she'd admired only through *on dits* in the papers and the like, a woman who'd had no substance to her until this moment. "We are honored to help you."

"Yes," Laren agreed. "You have been through a terrible experience. I seem to have forgotten that. Perhaps I should apologize myself."

"Oh, please, there is no need," Lady Margaret said.

"Oh, but there is," Laren returned, her earlier coldness giving way to her usual generous spirit.

Heath was bemused by the ability of women to forgive so easily. All it took was a word, a gesture for them to band together.

"The porridge smells delicious," Lady Margaret commented, picking up her spoon.

"It's not the sort of dish you are used to," Anice demurred.

"I like porridge for breakfast," Lady Margaret said graciously, and Heath didn't know if she was lying or not, but it didn't matter. The tension in his sisters had eased, and they wouldn't be teasing him about cutting his hair.

He'd just finished his bowl when a footstep at the door claimed his attention. He was surprised to see Dara there, dressed for riding.

"I'm pleased you haven't left," she said, entering the room. She reached for a slice of fresh bread. "I've decided I'm going with you."

Heath stood. "Dara, do you truly want to come? You know where the accident was?"

She squared her shoulders, pausing long enough for him to see the struggle inside her. She swallowed the mouthful of bread. "I know, and, yes, I wish to accompany you."

He released his breath in surprise. She had never gone to the place Brodie had died. For a second, he debated arguing with her, and then decided not to. It helped him to visit that oak tree. Perhaps it would help Dara in her mourning as well.

"We'd best start out then," he said. "I told the lads I wanted the horses ready for half past eight and you know they shall be. There are not many hours of light on a winter's day so we'd best be on with it."

They left the table and headed out.

■ ■ ■ ■

"Why did your brother hesitate when Lady Macnachtan asked to accompany us?" Margaret asked Laren and Anice.

Her apology had torn down the wall between them. She now rode an even-tempered, well-bred mare with Laren on one side and Anice on the other. The sisters were truly kind and giving. They didn't seem to harbor petty jealousies like so many women she had known. Then again, London society was very competitive.

Laird Macnachtan and Lady Macnachtan rode on the road ahead, their heads together in deep conversation. A pang of jealousy annoyed Margaret. She usually didn't experience such an emotion, but Heath Macnachtan had captured her interest, as perhaps should be expected considering the role his family played in her life.

Except it was the man himself who attracted her.

In spite of his devil-may-care manner, as exemplified by the haphazard knot in his neck cloth this morning, and his almost raw masculine energy, there was a more complex side to him. He'd been kind to her yesterday and patient with her agitated confusion.

Anyone else would have locked her up.

She'd caught enough of the conversation he was having with his sister-in-law to know he discussed their tenants. It was a perfectly reasonable discussion for them to have, although Margaret was unreasonably aware of how lovely Lady Macnachtan was. She had a fragile air and Margaret couldn't help but wonder about her story. Dara Macnachtan was too young to be a widow for long.

When Anice and Laren exchanged glances without answering her question immediately, Margaret worried that perhaps she'd overstepped her bounds.

Then, Anice said, "Our oldest brother was murdered. He was attacked on his way home from visiting one of our crofters. Someone shot him with a crossbow. Our trip will take us right to the place where he was killed. Dara has never been there since his death. Heath is right to be concerned."

"I'm so sorry," Margaret whispered, stunned by this information.

"We are as well," Laren said solemnly. "I think the loss wouldn't be so deep if we'd found who killed him and could ask why someone would take such a good man's life."

"There was no justice?" Margaret said.

"None," Anice said, "and that hurts. Brodie didn't have any enemies —"

"He had one," Laren pointed out.

"Well, none that we knew. He was such a good brother and kind husband. It has been well over a year since his death, but we'll never stop missing Brodie."

"Especially as long as his killer is free," Laren agreed. "I can't even imagine how Dara feels. Brodie was her protector. He'd rescued her."

"What do you mean?" Margaret asked.

"Her father was the minister in Dalmally. He died unexpectedly and she had no relatives to take her in. Brodie had always been sweet on her. Even though they were both very young, he asked for her hand."

"How old were they?" Margaret wondered.

"Just barely sixteen," Anice answered. "Brodie had to talk to convince our father to agree to the marriage. They were together a long time."

"And no children?" Margaret asked.

"None," Laren said sadly. "Brodie would have been a wonderful father. Then again, there was still hope they would have a bairn or two. An heir."

"This is very sad," Margaret said. "You *do* understand what it means to lose a brother and why I am anxious to save mine."

"We know all too well," Laren said.

"The only good that came of Brodie's death was that Heath finally returned home," Anice said.

"Where had he been?" Margaret asked, her every instinct alert for news of him.

"He was in the navy," Anice answered. "He had a commission and was gone for years at a time. He seemed to thrive on sea battles and adventurous places." She gave a shiver as if such danger was distasteful. "He had to come home after Brodie died to take the title."

"Is it an old title?" Margaret asked.

"Aye, very old, if you are Scottish," Laren said. "It means something here, although I doubt if the rest of the world cares. We've always been too poor to advance our political fortunes."

"But at one time, we were important," Anice insisted. "And I believe Heath will see us through this crisis."

"Do you mean the death of your brother?" Margaret asked.

"And the settling to the estate's accounts," Laren said. "What we lack in money, we make up for in pride."

Margaret didn't know how to respond. Of course, she had noticed that the Macnachtan were not wealthy, but she didn't think them poor. What they had, they took care of. An example would be the horses they were riding. Someone had a good eye for horseflesh.

And yes, the sister's riding habits weren't as fine as Margaret's, but they either knew someone who was clever with a needle, or they were themselves, because their outfits were well constructed and showed a bit of personality.

Margaret's fashion taste was the product of dressmakers with critical eyes. She lacked the talent for individual flair and appreciated it in others.

But she was saved from further conversation by their brother, who circled his horse around to join them. "We are at the kirk," he said, and directed them down a well-worn path to where a small stone church sat in an inviting dell surrounded by evergreens. A graveyard was off to one side.

Margaret was riveted by the sight of freshly dug graves. Seven in a row.

She rode up to them and dismounted without waiting for help from Laird Macnachtan.

For a moment, she feared she would be overwhelmed with loss and guilt. She walked around each grave, offering a prayer. She couldn't believe the hearty Balfour or the steady Thomas were gone.

Laird Macnachtan joined her, while the others, still mounted, kept a respectful distance.

"You even gave them markers," she said. "How did you know their names?"

"Most had some sort of identification. Balfour also had a list in his pocket."

"Balfour. He was always thorough," she said, her jaw hardening.

A Chattan didn't show emotion in public. It was not seemly. She could almost hear her mother's voice chastising her. Then again, her mother had never demonstrated the tenderest of feeling to anyone, not even her children. These servants had been closer to Margaret than either of her parents.

"I should have written Harry," Margaret said. "It's all so confusing. Everything is happening so fast."

"I did send word to London to your brother Lord Lyon," he reminded her. "I'm sure he will tell their families."

"Thank you."

She sounded so civilized but in truth a rage was building inside her. How dare that witch claim them all? The servants were not a part of this. How dare she take their lives as if they were nothing?

158

Margaret faced the laird. "I'm going to beat her," she vowed. "I shall not let that witch win."

He nodded, yet there was a wariness in his eye and not of Fenella, but of her. He thought she spoke nonsense. No one believed save her, and Margaret realized she must protect them all.

She was *here,* where Fenella had once lived. Harry had been right. The battle would take place here and Margaret was not going to shy away from the reckoning. But she must be wary or more lives could be lost.

"Take me to the site of the accident," she ordered, purpose filling her words. "I must find that book."

"Of course, my lady," he said, his doubts in his voice. Well, let him think she was a lunatic. She no longer cared what anyone thought of her. Her sole purpose was to defeat the curse.

She started to let him help her mount her horse, when a new concern struck her. "You said you sent a messenger to my brother. When did you do this?"

He shrugged. "When we discovered the accident."

"Should you not have heard something from London by now? Can a man travel to

London and back in that span of time?" A heavy weight settled upon her. "Perhaps my brother is already dead."

He shook his head. "You are leaping to conclusions, my lady. Perhaps you would be wiser to focus on facts. On what is real and true. My man has not been gone four days and I have no reason to believe he will travel faster home than he did on the way to London. Have patience."

Margaret looked around the churchyard, suddenly feeling as if the trees could listen to their conversation. "Fenella could have stopped your messenger. She would if it suited her purpose."

His brows came together. "Or there might be some reasonable delay such as the weather."

"You still don't believe," Margaret said. "I understand. I would have my doubts as well. But you are a fool to not heed my warning —"

"Is something the matter?" Lady Macnachtan asked, riding up to them, with Laren and Anice alongside. They had all been on the other side of the clearing.

Laird Macnachtan made an impatient sound and faced them. "Nothing is wrong. Lady Margaret and I were discussing the messenger I sent to her brother." He started

160

walking to his horse. "Come, we need to be on our way."

The distance to the site of the accident was a good five miles' ride.

Laird Macnachtan turned off the road, riding through a forest of pine, their breathing coming out in puffs of cold air. The ground was wet, marshy even. The mare picked her own way and Margaret had the good sense to let her have her head.

They reached higher land. The woods changed here. Gone were the mighty pines. In their place were bare-limbed trees, dry shrubbery and layers of damp leaves padding the ground.

Margaret's pulse picked up a beat.

She recognized this place.

She'd dreamed of it shortly before the accident. Here were the gnarled limbs of ancient trees looming over a forest path.

And there was the bend in the road, straight ahead of her.

She reined in her horse.

"Is something the matter?" Laird Macnachtan asked.

"Where are we?" she demanded.

"In the shadow of Ben Cruachan."

"This is where you found the accident?" Alarm gave her voice a strident tone.

"Around the bend and a bit of a ways, my

lady." There was a pause. "Are you all right?"

She shook her head, not answering, but she moved her mare closer to his horse. She felt safe when she was with him.

The dream was very clear in her memory.

However, there had been a green glow hovering just around the bend in the road, and there was nothing now except for the hazy light of winter. Nor did the trees seem as threatening as in her dream.

They rode on. Margaret braced herself, uncertain of what to expect, and was rather disappointed to ride around the bend and discover only more trees, more brown brush.

But there was one tree among all the others that commanded attention. It was massive oak whose branches seemed to spread over the forest —

"It was *here,* wasn't it?" Lady Macnachtan said, reining in her horse.

Margaret had been so involved with her own turbulent emotions, she had almost forgotten what significance this route held for the laird's sister-in-law.

"Yes," he answered. Laren and Anice flanked Lady Macnachtan with their horses. They all waited, Margaret included, for what Lady Macnachtan wished to do.

"Is that *his* blood on the tree?" she asked.

There was a dark stain on the oak above the mistletoe. It could have been the oddity of nature, or something else more sinister.

"It is," he confirmed. "One would think it would be worn or washed away, and yet I see it still."

Lady Macnachtan's frown deepened. She raised a gloved hand to her eyes. "He died alone," she whispered. "All alone."

Anice leaned forward with a comforting arm but Lady Macnachtan shook her off, her gaze fastened on the tree. She sat quiet for a long moment, and then said in a small, hoarse voice, "I wish to leave now."

"If you would like to return to Marybone, I shall go with you," Anice said.

The answer was a shake of the head. "Let us go forward."

Laird Macnachtan sat a moment in silence as if reasoning something out in his own mind, and then said, "I was visiting this place where Brodie died, when a stag came through the forest and stopped right here almost in front of me. He was a magnificent beast and for a moment we took each other's measure, but he was frightened away by a piece of clothing the wind blew through the air. It seemed to fall out of the sky but then I noticed more clothing and debris from the accident. I followed a trail of clothing up the slope."

As he spoke, he kicked his horse forward. There was no path here. Margaret's mare pushed her way past the branches of shrubs and small trees that tried to catch up on them as if to hold them back.

They were in the shadow of the mountain and Margaret saw broken trees where her coach had come tumbling down the mountain.

Shattered, splintered pieces of wood and harness tracings still littered the ground.

Margaret dismounted, her heart pounding in her ears. Fenella's book *must* be here.

The laird and his sisters also dismounted.

"Where did you find me?" Margaret asked, swiping at the brush with her crop.

"This way," he said, and led her up the slope to a small clearing protected by stately firs. Their evergreen branches shut out the light and deadened sound, giving this place a sense of being another world. "You were in here."

Margaret frowned. "This is not what I remember. I was on hard, cold ground without any layer of pine needles."

"Are you certain?" he asked. "Sometimes our mind plays tricks upon us."

"Where was my maid's body?" Margaret asked.

"Over here," he said, and walked down the hill a bit to a level spot against a beech tree.

This was the place she remembered. "Someone moved me." She looked to the laird. "Is that possible?"

"It might be. You were on your back, your hands folded at your waist as if someone had posed you in that manner. Everyone else looked as if they had been tossed to the ground like rag dolls, but you appeared to be merely sleeping."

Anice had wandered away from their little group. She now stood as if listening.

Margaret tried to listen as well. There was no sound save for the wind in the trees — and then she heard it. Someone was coming toward them through the woods and there was the smell of burning tar in the air.

Laird Macnachtan heard as well. He stepped over to his horse and removed a pistol from his saddlebag. He placed himself in front of the women.

Within seconds, a party of five men came marching through the woods. They apparently had not expected anyone to be there and their steps slowed when they saw Laird Macnachtan.

Two of the men held torches. The group was led by a tall, thin man who wore a black

tunic cloak that reached below his knees
and no hat on his balding head. Tufts of
gray hair grew around his ears, and his
beard was separated and braided into two
long plaits that almost reached his chest.
Tucked under his arm was a book.

Fenella's book.

Margaret started forward.

Laird Macnachtan anticipated her movement and held out an arm to block her.
"Stay behind me."

"He has Fenella's book," she said.

"All the more reason to stay *behind* me,"
the laird repeated in a voice that brooked
no disobedience.

"Who are these men?" Margaret asked.

Laren answered. "Swepston and his kin."
She reached for Margaret's hand as if wishing to protect her. "Heath has had problems
with this lot. They are set against his improvements."

"Improvements?"

"With the land and the way I've chosen to
do things. Brodie had problems with them
as well."

"He believes he should be laird," Anice
confided.

"What?" Margaret said in surprise. The
man appeared more jester than noble.

"Swepston claims his ancestors were

166

cheated out of the chieftain by ours," Laren said. "It is a silly claim. Some believe Swepston may have been behind Brodie's murder. We believe he has been behind some mischief against us because of it."

"Mischief?" Margaret asked.

"Small thievery and the like. He truly disapproves of Heath. Even Brodie would listen to him, but Heath has no patience for the man and his followers."

It appeared they were about to discover who was stronger.

Swepston stopped ten feet from Laird Macnachtan. Margaret noticed that his men weren't the only ones with him. In the forest shadows was a silent host of others including women and children. She wondered if the laird was aware he had an audience.

Swepston's group was a motley lot, dressed in homespun shirts and well-worn boots. Some, like their leader, sported braided beards.

"Good day, Laird," Swepston said. He had a booming voice, one that commanded authority.

"What brings you to this remote place, Swepston?"

Swepston gave Margaret the full force of his icy gaze. His mouth had the set of the uncompromising. He obviously disliked what he saw. "Send back the Chattan, Laird. We don't want her here."

"Lady Margaret Chattan is my guest, and I'll be determining if she stays or if she leaves."

"She leaves."

"And what makes you say so, Swepston?" It was a match of two strong wills.

"Because that is the way it *must* be" was the cryptic answer. "We know you don't believe in the old ways —"

"Not believe?" Laird Macnachtan challenged. "Have I not sweated and worked to see my clansmen safe? Are not the crofters still in their homes that they shared for generations and their bellies filled? I have honored the commitments made to my people over the ages."

Swepston held up Fenella's book. "You have no understanding of the *old* ways, Macnachtan," he repeated.

Although his focus seemed to be completely on Swepston, the laird could see that his audience had grown, and when he spoke, his voice was louder, as if he wanted all to hear him. "Don't challenge me, Swepston. I am of the direct line from Michael, first chieftain of this clan. The blood flowing through my veins dates all the way back to the House of Alpin." His brogue had grown stronger as he spoke to these men, a reminder that he was one of them. "I lead by the right of my clansmen." He had tucked the pistol in the waistband of his breeches, a sign he did not fear Swepston. "You are holding a book that does not belong to you. You stole if from this place. Return it to me."

"*It was stolen from us.* Lost, only to be returned as the curse is fulfilled," Swepston announced. He directed his remarks to Margaret. "The curse will never be lifted. Not until the House of Chattan has been destroyed. Macnachtan pride will not allow it."

Margaret felt her knees start to shake. Laren took one hand, Anice the other.

"Are you saying *I* have no pride?" Laird Macnachtan asked, his voice dropping to a dangerous tone.

The men behind Swepston shifted their weight as if realizing they might be crossing a line unwise to contest.

Swepston did not so much as blink as he said, "I'm saying, Laird, that you have been away from Loch Awe a long time."

"My pride in my heritage, my feelings are as strong as anyone else's, Swepston. And I'll battle the man who says nay."

"This book belongs to all of us," Swepston answered. "I am now the keeper of the curse. I am one of those whose task is to keep it alive."

Margaret could stay silent no longer. "Is the answer to the curse in that book?" she demanded, shaking off Laren's hold and coming to Laird Macnachtan's side.

Swepston sneered at her, but before he could say anything, the laird interjected, his tone almost conversational, "Thank you for that, Swepston. We've been concerned over Lady Margaret's sanity. It is a wild story, is it not? Curses and witches. The ridiculous garble of children's tales or the ranting of the feeble-minded."

"It is our history," was the ominous reply.

"Aye," the laird said, "but I find myself wondering who has actually been cursed? The Chattan? Lord Lyon is a rich man and enjoys the high regard of his peers. He is known for service to his country and dines with the king. Even his father and father before him have reputations for being formidable men."

Laird Macnachtan bypassed Swepston to address his people. "Now look at the Macnachtan," he said. "We have *not* prospered so well. Our corner of Scotland is small and growing smaller as change takes place. Our crops do not give us good yields. Our livestock do not replenish themselves, and we struggle to find the coin to purchase better. At one time, the name Macnachtan rang through the Highlands with pride. We were powerful and our counsel sought. Now we are alone and in danger of losing all." He faced Swepston. "So tell me, *who* has carried the curse? In all these years that have passed since the woman who wrote that book shouted her curse, who has prospered and who is in danger of truly dying out? Oh, and before you make more claims, remember I am of her line, the connection between Fenella and the present, the here and now. And there is one thing I know, hate *never* reaps a good reward. We have cursed ourselves, and the time has come to bring it to an *end.*"

His was a rallying cry, and it did not land on deaf ears. Heads nodded. They understood his reasoning, and Swepston was not pleased.

Laird Macnachtan turned to him. "Hand the book to me. You stole it from this woman and I shall not tolerate thievery."

Swepston's response was to grab a torch out of the hand of the man nearest him, throw the book on the ground, and set it afire.

CHAPTER EIGHT

The torch flared and the book burned with the speed of dry tinder.

Shocked, Margaret cried out. She lurched toward the fire, even as the laird began stomping on the flames. She fell to her knees, reaching forward, ready to save the book with her gloved hands.

Laird Macnachtan caught her by the wrists. "Don't be foolish."

"But I can't let it burn."

"It's gone, my lady. It's gone."

He was right. The book had been so old that it was close to ashes in a blink of the eye.

Margaret felt as if she had been ripped wide open and thrown asunder. The book was her one link to Fenella. It was all she had.

Swepston stood over them, raising his hands, and announced, *"The curse lives.* It will never end until the last of the Chattan are gone —"

Laird Macnachtan leaped for Swepston, grabbing him by the throat and cutting off his words.

Swepston raised his hands to his neck but he was no match for the laird's angry strength. The laird lifted Swepston into the air until his toes barely touched the ground.

"Did you move Lady Margaret when you came upon the accident?" Laird Macnachtan demanded. "Answer me, man. Did you know of the accident and tell no one? Did you touch her?"

Swepston appeared stunned at his laird's anger. When he didn't answer immediately, Laird Macnachtan gave him a forceful shake. *"Did you touch her?"* he repeated.

Lady Macnachtan came forward. "Heath, please, he can't speak. You are choking him to death."

The laird loosened his hold and Swepston fell to the ground. The man started dry heaving. Laird Macnachtan stood over him. He prodded Swepston with the toe of his boot. "You can answer me now."

Swepston's gaze flicked over Margaret before he managed to say, "I did not touch her. I thought her dead."

"*Where* did she lay?" the laird ground out.

"There. She was right there. Lying on her

belly." Swepston pointed to hard ground and the place where Margaret had remembered herself being.

Laird Macnachtan knelt so that he was eye level with Swepston. "And what of my brother?" he asked. "Did you put an arrow through my brother's heart? Did you murder him, Swepston?"

Now the man reacted with true fear. He held up his arms as if the laird's words were blows.

"Did you murder my brother, man?" Laird Macnachtan repeated. "Do you hate us so much you would kill?"

"I did not," Swepston said. Gone was the arrogance. In its place was fear for his life. Nor did any of his followers rush forward to help him. They drew back as if wanting to put as much distance as possible between themselves and Swepston.

"I don't know if I believe you," the laird said.

"You *must* believe me. I'd not ambush a man. Did I not confront you directly just now?"

Laird Macnachtan seemed to consider this and straightened to his full height. He was taller, stronger, and more powerful now than his nemesis. "To the devil with you, Swepston. Leave here and never return to these lands again. I *banish* you."

"You cannot do that," Swepston answered.

"I already have." Laird Macnachtan stood and lifted his voice so that all could hear him. "Angus Swepston is no kinsman of the Macnachtan. He shall receive no succor from one of us. He shall sit at no table amongst my clan or step foot upon my land. The man that aids him, that shelters him, is banished as well as is his family."

The pronouncement rang through the forest, carrying a power that was both thrilling and frightening.

"You are cursing me?" Swepston said with angry surprise.

"Aye, I am *cursing* you, Swepston, and as Fenella was *my* ancestor, know that I shall destroy you if you return to these parts."

Swepston's manner changed. He had gone from defiant to terrified.

He began crawling backward on the ground away from the laird. As soon as he was able, he scrambled to his feet and went running through the woods.

The laird looked at the others gathered round. "And what of you?" he demanded. "Are you *my* men or not? If you are not, then leave, for your fate shall be Swepston's."

They began bowing and backing away

from him. "We are your men, laird," one dared to say as they left. The others nodded and faded back into the woods, taking their families with them.

Laird Macnachtan watched them go before muttering, "Aye, and they'll turn their backs on me at the first chance."

Anice stepped forward. "Heath, you were magnificent."

"Brilliant," her sister Laren echoed. "I now feel sorry for the sailors who were under your command, brother."

"Do you believe him when he said he had nothing to do with Brodie's murder?" Lady Macnachtan asked.

"I don't know what I believe," the laird said, no satisfaction in his voice. "But if I meet him again, I'll put an end to him. His accusations and pronouncements have only served to keep us poor."

Margaret barely attended their conversation. She was distraught.

The book was gone.

She was still on her knees. A new wind swirled around her, colder than it had been before. It picked up the last charred remnants of the Fenella's book and blew it through the air to where she knew not.

One small bright ember of burning parchment whirled right by her face, its edges glowing before it turned black and disappeared.

There was nothing left.

And Swepston was right. The curse *would* last forever. Both of her brothers would die and their sons would carry this terrible burden.

She'd come to fight with everything she had, and now it was over. She had failed.

There would be no stopping Fenella.

Her shoulders lifted with the horror of her thoughts. She heard a keening and realized it came from her. She'd felt such despair, her body had to set it free —

Strong arms took her by the shoulders. She tried to push Laird Macnachtan away. He held fast.

"Hey now," he said, his voice low near her ear, "is this the lass who was brave enough to put a bullet in me?"

She shook her head and tried to free herself.

He tightened his hold. "You can't give up. Not now." When he could see that she was not going to listen, that she refused, he gripped her shoulders, bringing her to her feet and turning her so that she had no choice but to face him. *"Margaret,"* he said in a stern voice, "you must not give up."

She heard him. She knew he was wrong.

"You have Scots blood in you, woman. Scots do not give up."

"I have very little Scots blood, and I've lost the one connection we had to Fenella. It has taken years to find it. *There is nothing else,*" she said, the words like knife points in her throat. "*I* have lost."

"You lose only if you give up. And don't be thinking you are alone. I'll not let my clan be ruled by superstition. This curse has roused my temper. I'm by your side in this battle."

"He is right," Laren said, words echoed by Anice.

"And there *is* something more we can do, my lady," the laird said.

"More?" Margaret raised her head. "What more can be done?"

He took a step away from her. She frowned, suspicious. "*Is* there something?" she demanded.

Drawing a breath and releasing it as if he feared he might have regrets over what he was about to say, he said, "We can go to Macnachtan Keep," he said. "That is the ancestral home, the one in being at the time of Fenella and Rose."

"Wasn't Marybone built on the grounds of the keep?"

"No, the ruins of the keep itself are on an

island in Loch Awe."

His words were not only a bane to her spirits, but a stimulus for her anger. "Why did you not tell me this before?"

"Did it come up in conversation?" he asked rhetorically. "I believe not."

"You know I'm in search of *anything* that can help destroy this curse," she shot back.

"The tower is a pile of rock," he explained. "If anyone jumped off it now, they might sprain an ankle, no more, no less."

Margaret could barely speak. He made a perfect target for her frustration over losing the book.

"I know that look," he said. "My sisters give it to me often. You are thinking I am responsible for something I am *not* responsible for and you want to take me to task. It won't work. Be honest, if you were I would you believe your story? But then Swepston shows up with a book and supports what you've said of being injured in that accident and we find you without a scratch, and, well, I have to start to believe there is some truth in it, don't I?"

She looked into his eyes, realizing he was handing her a victory. "Yes, you do."

"Can you wait for the morrow to go?"

"Do I have a choice?" she countered.

"Not a logical one."

"First light then," she said.

He nodded.

Margaret reached for his hand and brought it up to her lips, kissing the back of his gloved fingers. "Thank you," she whispered. "Thank you so much."

Heath gasped.

Even through his gloves he could feel the warmth of her breath, and something tight and defensive inside him gave way to feelings he'd never experienced before. Ever.

He'd always sworn he'd been born to be a bachelor. He'd had no desire to put his feet up in front of any hearth. He'd chafed at the responsibilities of being laird. Hated them.

And yet, in this moment, he sensed he was exactly where he wanted to be.

There was a connection between them, something more than the simple lust a man had for a lovely woman.

Yes, he desired her. He'd wanted her from the moment he'd laid eyes on her. If he hadn't been with the other officers of his ship, he might have fallen in line with her other admirers. He might have trailed after her with a moony look on his face and a quill for writing poetry in his hand.

With a glance or a gesture, she could make

him feel ridiculously noble. He wanted to please her.

He wanted to lay a hand on her silky hair, to pull her close, to hold her, comfort her . . . love her.

Heath took a step away, startled by the direction of his thoughts. He turned to see his sisters watching him with speculation in their eyes. They were no fools and they knew him better than anyone else. Anice appeared almost gleeful while Laren's brow was furrowed in concern. Dara frowned.

He looked around this place that had seen so much death, trying to redirect his thoughts. "If Swepston did not move you to the pine grove, I wonder who did?"

"I do not know," she said.

"What are you thinking, Heath?" Laren asked.

"I'm wondering if that person might also be involved in Brodie's death," he answered.

At that moment, the wind whipped through the trees around them. A wind that knew what had happened to Brodie.

"Perhaps we'd best leave now," Laren said, a hint of apprehension in her voice. "It will be dark soon."

She didn't have to make the suggestion twice. An ominous feeling seemed to have crept around them. Even Lady Margaret was ready to go.

However, he noticed as they left the woods, she turned back for one more look at the ground where the book had burned.

CHAPTER NINE

"I'm so glad you are all here without our guest," Dara said as she entered the sitting room where Heath, Laren and Anice had gathered, waiting for supper.

They'd enjoyed a moment to refresh themselves after the ride. Anice stood in front of the fire, slightly lifting the back of her skirts to warm her legs, a habit of hers even from childhood. Heath sat in the wooden chair not far from her enjoying a nip of whisky, his favorite method of heating his blood.

Dara glanced at the hallway stair. "Is she joining us for dinner?"

"I don't know," Laren answered. She had her darning in her lap as if she wished to mend a few things before dinner, but the light was not good and Heath knew they were all tired. She set aside the sock she'd been planning to sew. "She said she was going to see to Rowan."

"Rowan?" Dara repeated.

"Her Indian servant," Anice supplied helpfully.

Dara frowned slightly. Sensing she had something on her mind, Heath asked, "Is all well, Dara?"

There was one last glance at the stairs, and then Dara said, "I believe you should send Lady Margaret on her way with all due haste."

"And why is that?" Heath asked. Dara had been quiet on the ride home. He'd noticed because he'd kept an eye on her considering the importance of her visit to the place where Brodie had died.

"Why is that?" she echoed before saying, "Is not her tale of curses enough? Or her erratic behavior? Such as shooting at you?"

"She is not the first woman who has wanted to do that," Heath admitted.

"Please, tell me she is the first woman who has actually carried through with the idea," Dara responded without any humor.

He set his glass on the side table. "Dara, what is truly bothering you?"

She came over to sit in the chair opposite his, her expression tight. For a second, she clasped and unclasped her hands before saying, "I know she is a guest, but I don't have a good feeling about her . . . especially when it comes to you, Heath."

"What do you mean?" He didn't like this conversation.

"One could easily see today that she has you wrapped around her finger. And I fear you may do something foolish."

"She's paying Heath to help her," Anice said.

"And you are obviously quite taken with Lady Margaret yourself," Dara challenged. "And that is what has me concerned. You all appear happy to give her the benefit of a doubt." She turned so that she was including Laren in the conversation. "What if this is all a hoax?"

"To what purpose?" Heath asked.

"I don't know," Dara said. "Perhaps the Chattans were bored in London and decided to play a game to amuse themselves."

"People died in the coach accident, Dara," he responded. "That would be an elaborate and criminal hoax."

"Yes, yes, I know." Dara sighed her frustration and then said, "Perhaps it is seeing that tree where they left Brodie . . ." Her voice trailed off, tears welling in her eyes.

Anice and Laren went immediately to her side. Heath stayed where he was. It was understandable that the sight of the oak would upset her.

Dara took Anice and Laren's hands and said to Heath, "I suppose I'm troubled because while we entertain Lady Margaret's wild notions, we are falling deeper in debt." She paused as if gathering herself, then continued, "I believe you should sell Marybone to Owen Campbell."

"And why is that?" Heath asked, startled by her abrupt change of subject. His sisters were equally surprised by the turn of the conversation. Laren and Anice were aware Campbell wanted Marybone and of the family's woeful financial affairs. However, he'd not yet discussed his meeting with the solicitor because of Lady Margaret's accident and his own desire to avoid the unpleasant topic.

"Because," Dara said, squeezing each hand she held, "your sisters deserve better than what they have here. They need dowries and husbands. You deserve better as well. I watched you today, Heath. I noticed you enjoyed your confrontation with Swepston. You are a man of action. You like a fight. But you are not a farmer. Brodie was . . . and that is the big difference between the two of you."

Heath sat silent a moment. She was not saying anything he hadn't already been told or thought himself.

The clock on the mantel seemed to tick off the moments of his life.

Finally, he spoke. "I'm not ready to give up yet."

"Is it giving up to follow a path you prefer? You don't have too much time left," Dara answered. "I know how severe our circumstances are. Are you thinking that the richest heiress in England will fall into your arms? Don't pretend different," she warned. "I can see your interest in the way you look at her. Marrying her would solve all your problems. But don't forget, Heath, she may depend upon you now, but the two of you are from very different classes. She would never see you as a man."

There was truth in Dara's words and he disliked them all the more because of it.

Before he could answer, she continued boldly, "Be your own person. Let us have our pride restored to us."

"By selling Marybone?"

She turned her head from him as if she could not meet his eye. "There are so many memories here," she whispered. "Sometimes *too* many."

Anice and Laren's gazes softened in empathy, but Heath sat forward. "Dara, if you are not happy here, tell me where you wish to go."

"I have no place," she replied, the set of her mouth stiff. "My fate is yours." And then as if rethinking the way her words might sound, she said, "All right. *Yes,* do what you must to force the Chattan heiress to marry you. I shall tell no one."

The comment was ridiculous. Heath started to protest — when he heard a sound in the hallway. Lady Margaret stood in the doorway.

Heath stood, wondering if she'd overheard them and then deciding she couldn't have if she'd just come down the stairs.

She appeared, in a word, lovely. Her hair was styled simply and she'd changed to a green dress that seemed to bring out the color in her eyes and the cream in her cheeks even better than her blue riding habit had.

"I hope I'm not disturbing you?" she asked. There was always that air of distance about her as if she feared letting anyone too close to her. He was beginning to understand. Her aloofness didn't rise from a sense of superiority but out of uncertainty.

"Of course not," Heath said, coming forward. "We were just going in for dinner. How is your servant?"

"Still not well. Perhaps we should send for the doctor again?" she suggested. "I shall see to the expenses."

Perhaps she *had* overheard what Dara had been saying.

"That is not a problem," Heath started, but Dara had her own thoughts.

"Thank you, my lady," she said, coming to her feet. "That is generous of you." She took charge. "Shall we go in to dinner?" She moved so that she came between Heath and Lady Margaret.

"I'm famished," Lady Margaret confessed, allowing Dara to draw her toward the dining room.

"As we all are," Dara said.

Heath let his sisters go ahead of him. As she passed him, Laren said, "Anice and I do not want you to worry about our marriages. Make the right decision, Heath. We can live with what happens."

But he didn't know if he could.

Heath had never thought of himself as particularly noble when it came to women other than his sisters. He was surprised to discover over the fish and potatoes that was their meal this evening that he had come to include Lady Margaret in the circle of women he would protect.

As he watched her sip her soup and nibble on Cook's fresh bread, he no longer saw her as the Unattainable. She had become very human to him.

He felt very human around her.

And Dara, Anice and Laren watched every move they made.

At the end of the meal, Lady Margaret did not linger but excused herself, rising from the table. "I fear I must search for my bed. This has been a hard day and I don't know what to expect tomorrow."

"Let me see you to the stairs," Heath said, already to his feet, suddenly wanting a private moment with her.

Lady Margaret hesitated. She looked to the other women. Anice and Laren seemed to encourage her. Dara's frown deepened.

Heath decided not to wait. He moved around the table to her, and together they went out the door.

"You didn't need to accompany me," Lady Margaret said. She had not met his eye. He did not like that.

"You heard us discussing you earlier," he suggested.

She shook that off. "I'm not offended. Gossip is rampant in London. I could not survive there if I listened to it all."

She was lying. He knew that.

They'd already reached the stairs. She started to go up them, tossing a quick "good night" over her shoulder.

Heath caught her hand, stopping her.

For a second, he didn't know who was more surprised by his action, Lady Margaret or him.

She looked at his hand holding hers.

He thought of apologizing for the gossip, of telling her that marrying an heiress was not an idea that he had contemplated — except what reasonable person would believe him?

"I'm not what you think of me," she said slowly. "I'm not what you want."

"How do you know what I want?" he asked.

She was silent a beat and then she amended, "I am not what you deserve."

Their voices were quiet, for their ears alone — and in that moment, he'd never wanted a woman more.

She stood two steps above him so that they were almost equals. Her smile grew sad. "You are not what I anticipated, Laird Macnachtan. You are a good man."

"You are not what I anticipated. You are a good wo—" he started to echo, but she stopped him, pressing her lips to his.

It was a quick kiss, a chaste one, and yet it sent a jolt of awareness through his being. Just that momentary contact, and he wanted more. He would have leaned in but she turned away. "I can't. I —" she started, and then broke off.

"What is it?" he asked.

"It is nothing," she whispered, her eyes cold, bleak. "Nothing at all." She pulled her hand from his and all but ran to her room.

Heath stood on the step until he heard her door shut.

He'd been listening so intently, he'd not heard Dara come up behind him. "She is beautiful, Heath, but I hope you are thinking with your large head and not your 'little' one."

Her comment jarred him. "A bit crude, isn't that, Dara?"

She shrugged. "I've been married. I know men."

There was a hint of a boast in her words.

And he realized that, in truth, he didn't know her well. He'd left for the midshipman's apprenticeship with his mother's uncle when he was twelve. Dara had been a distant presence in his life then, a lovely girl that his brother eyed. He had not been surprised when he'd received word that they had married.

One aspect he had enjoyed since returning to Loch Awe and taking Brodie's place was rebuilding friendships with his sisters as adults. He had also grown to appreciate

Dara. By all accounts she had made his brother a happy man.

But there was also something distant about her as well. Secretive, even.

Laren speculated Dara's aloofness came from growing up in the church. A church-man's family was never free to be themselves.

His older sister might be right, but there were times, as now, when he had an unsettling feeling about Dara. He didn't quite trust her, although that could be because there was no blood link between them.

"You needn't worry about me," he said.

Dara hummed her disbelief and went up the stairs.

Margaret shut the bedroom door and leaned against it.

Slowly, she sank down, her arms on her bent knees. She rested her head upon them, wishing she could curl herself into a ball . . . and perhaps disappear?

How many times had she wished that in her life? That she could just evaporate? Vanish? Be no more?

She was an illusion, a bit of fantasy, a shell that others seemed to value. Inside, she was empty. A purposeful nothingness.

She had kept herself that way, only allowing herself to care deeply for her brothers. The rest of the world did not matter. She refused to let it do so.

Or so she had thought.

Heath Macnachtan had found his way into the abyss she nurtured inside herself.

She wasn't certain when it had happened. Was it today when he'd grabbed her by the shoulders and held her fast against her worst fears? Or when she'd held a gun in her hand and he had fearlessly confronted her while protecting those he loved?

Loved.

She hated the word "love." It meant nothing, and yet all the world thought it should.

There had been a time when she'd opened her heart enough to love. God, she would have tossed everything aside, her family, her pride, and her heritage for love.

For love she'd humbled herself to a groomsman. Mark had been nothing more than a stable hand.

Yes, she'd been young, no more than fifteen, but the intensity of her feelings for him had been very real. She'd given him the one thing that had been truly only hers to give.

Margaret had not even known her father was aware of her shame until she'd learned that the groom was no longer in the country, let alone in their employ. She'd thought it was her secret . . . and that was when she'd learned of how completely Mark had betrayed her feelings. That he'd bragged about his conquest so loudly that her father had discovered what they'd done. Mark had not loved her. He hadn't even cared for her.

From that moment on, she hadn't trusted men.

They liked her looks, the surface, the shell, but she realized they weren't concerned about her. They wanted her money, her family connections, and the boost to their pride at having a lovely wife.

Luckily, time had passed and her past remained unknown to members of London's *ton.* There had been a time when she'd thought she could go through with what was expected of her — the debutante years, the courting and wooing — until she'd realized that she had no desire to be nothing more than an actress in her life. Men called her beautiful, but did not want to know her soul or value her intelligence.

Because she had wanted something more, they had labeled her the Unattainable, a mocking term that appealed to their competitive natures. She was a challenge, a game, a mountain to be climbed. And then, from what Margaret could observe of other women's marriages, she would be tucked into a stall like a prize mare to be trotted out or ignored depending on her husband's whims.

Her most courageous act had been to sit Harry and Neal down after their father's funeral and explain to them that they must all let the curse end now, with them. They should not fall in love or ever marry where children could be created.

What she'd really been doing was giving herself the rationale to never marry. Her decision had removed her from the marriage game.

Now, leaning against the door, Margaret realized a secret truth: She still believed in love.

She *wanted* to believe. She also knew that she was spoiled goods for any worthy man, the sort of man she could love. He would not want a wife who had foolishly tumbled with a stable lad. He would not trust her.

Margaret pushed the weight of her hair back from her face. Her life was so confusing. She could not rely on anyone other than herself . . . with, perhaps, the exception of Heath Macnachtan.

Had he betrayed her by not telling her about the island?

She thought not. He'd been protecting his

family and her story was outlandish.

But she'd also witnessed how this man would step forward for what he believed.

And she was starting to notice other things about him as well. The small things, the details women cherished.

She liked the way his eyes laughed and had noticed how well shaped his hands were. He had calluses on them. He was not afraid of work, but his hands moved with the grace of ability.

Then there was the broadness of his shoulders and the leanness of his jaw. The haphazard way he tied his neck cloth. The interest and respect he showed for his sisters.

And there was the way she was beginning to feel when she was around him. She caught herself watching him, depending on his judgment.

Trusting him.

There lay danger. This man was the sworn enemy of her family and yet he had treated her with nothing but deference.

And she no longer knew herself.

She had not meant to kiss him. It had just happened.

Margaret pressed her index finger to her lips, savoring that brief contact — and knowing she must not let the passion in her nature betray her again.

For a second, she could swear she sensed him on the other side of the door. She sat still.

The rapid beat of her heart measured off the minutes.

And then she felt him withdraw.

A moment later, she heard a bedroom door shut. *He had been there.*

She brought her hands down around her legs, uncertain, reminding herself that a witch waited. Like an actress in a play, Fenella was in the wings, biding her time.

Margaret could imagine the air in the room breathing, pulsing with the presence of that which they did not understand.

Fenella was here . . . but so was the laird. A certainty fell upon her. She was *meant* to be here, in this moment.

The witch had tried to destroy her once and had failed. Who was to say she would not fail again?

And Margaret thought of little Owl, the cat who had saved her and then disappeared.

Exhaustion fell over her. It had been a day of tumultuous emotions. She needed sleep.

Margaret rose from the floor and undressed, letting her clothes drop where she took them off, too overwhelmed to pick them up. She climbed into bed and was soon dreaming. She dreamed of pine forest and a fire, but it wasn't Fenella's book that was burning.

It was she.

CHAPTER TEN

Laren, Anice and Dara did not accompany Heath and Lady Margaret to Innis Craggah, the island with the ruins of Macnachtan Keep.

Anice informed him that venturing out on Loch Awe in winter was not their idea of an adventure. "And we doubt if she will find anything, Heath," she confessed. "The island is deserted. There is nothing but rock left of the keep from that time."

He agreed, but another part of him was curious. There was a mystery surrounding Lady Margaret and he found himself anxious to solve it.

Instead of the women, Rowlly and two of the stable lads rode with them. Cook had prepared a basket of bread and smoked fish, and they were in good spirits when they set out.

Frost covered the ground, but the sky was clear and blue — a rare day, indeed, and

Heath took it as a good omen.

Because of the cold, he wore several layers of clothes beneath his coat. Lady Margaret wore a red cape trimmed in fur over her riding habit. He couldn't take his eyes off her.

He'd had trouble sleeping because of her. She'd wandered in and out of his dreams. No woman had done that before.

Last night, after she'd given that brief peck — he wouldn't dignify it by calling it a kiss — he'd stood outside her bedroom door, a part of him wanting to knock. He imagined drawing her out, talking to her about nothing, or everything. He was keen to push the tenuous connection between them. He wanted more.

But he'd held back. He'd not knocked on her door. She was accustomed to being chased. Men threw themselves at her feet.

He, and his pride, needed to be a bit more rational. After all, why would a Venus ever value a Scottish lout like him? He could think of no reason.

She was very quiet as they traveled.

He attributed her silence to concern over where they were going. Innis Craggah was the place where it had all begun.

They rode along Loch Awe's shoreline. A fine mist covered the water, and the wind was cold.

At last, they came close to their destination. Heath reined Admiral around to ride beside Margaret. "Do you see the island closest to us in the loch? You can make out its shape in the mist. That is Innis Craggah, Island of Rock. It is about a mile long and a half a mile wide."

As he spoke, the mist decided to lift and revealed an island covered with winter brown undergrowth mingled with the deep green of firs and the gray barks of trees.

"Where is the tower?" she asked.

"You can't see what is left of it from here. When we go ashore, there is a path that leads right to where the keep once was."

"How will we reach the island?" she asked.

"We have friends," Heath answered, and kicked his horse forward. To his pleasure, she did the same.

They rode along the road at a fast clip, their mounts breathing heavy in the chilled air, until they came upon John Gibson's cottage. The fisherman was bundled against the cold while he went about his tasks among his boats lined up and turned over on the shore.

"Laird Macnachtan," he hailed Heath as they rode up, "imagine seeing one such as yourself out here today. And you look hale and well. My clansman Augie swore his knuckles had sent you to a bed for a week."

"*Och,* man, are you believing Augie?" Heath said, letting his brogue deepen as he jumped down from his horse and approached the fisherman. He held out his hand.

"Not for a moment," Gibson answered, a smile splitting his face. He was a burly man with a mass of red hair on his head and chin and smelled of fresh air and dead fish. "You look a sight better than Augie does. Of course, as long as you keep popping him in the head, no harm will be done." He laughed at his own joke and then greeted Rowlly, mentioning something about his role in the fight at the Goldeneye. His eyes strayed to Lady Margaret.

Of course, as would any man, he had been aware of her since the moment they had ridden up.

He bowed, recognizing Quality when he met one.

"John, this is Lady Margaret Chattan," Heath said.

The man's reaction was almost humorous. "Chattan?" For a second, Heath feared the man would spit. Instead, he swallowed and said, "There is one of them here? With you?" He added in almost a whisper, "A

203

female one?"

"Aye, and she is with me. We want to pay a visit to the ruins of the keep. Will you take us across?"

For a second, John eyed Heath as if he had just suggested he wanted to cut out his tongue.

"Will you or won't you?" Heath prodded.

"I will," John answered, as if still uncertain Heath jested. However, he recovered enough to negotiate the cost of rowing them over.

That done, the stable lads and Rowlly helped John right two of his skiffs into the water. The boats had sails but John said the water was calm and the distance not far. "We could row in less time than it takes to mount the masts."

Heath helped Lady Margaret dismount. One of the lads would stay with the horses.

Mrs. Gibson, John's wife, came out of the house, her arms crossed. "You are going out, John?" she asked.

"Yes, Mary. Send out Donald. We need young arms to help row." She went inside and a moment later John's oldest son, a scruffy lad of about twelve, came out. He'd bundled himself warmly. Gibson placed a step by the boat for Lady Margaret and the rest of them to use to climb aboard.

In short order, they were on the water.

The current was with them.

If his sisters had been here, they would have been huddled in the boat against the weather. In contrast, Lady Margaret sat at the prow of the boat. She'd thrown the hood of her cloak back and appeared as if she relished being on the water. The wind caught her hair, loosening a few strands from the pins.

Heath manned the oars closest to her. John was also in their boat, while Rowlly, the stable lad and Donald were in the other.

One end of Innis Craggah was a rocky beach. The other end had a blunt shape formed by a rock cliff as if a portion of the island had been parsed away by the hand of God. Lady Margaret pointed at it and said, "Could that be the cliff that Fenella jumped from when she threw herself on her daughter's funeral pyre?"

"I don't know," he told her. "They say there once was more shoreline beneath that cliff. The water there is very shallow. My brother and I would row out here when we were lads. I have swum the perimeter of this island at least a dozen times. The water below the cliff is not as deep as my knees."

Lady Margaret nodded. The small worry line had reappeared between her brows. Heath hated seeing it, especially since he believed she would be disappointed in what she would find on the island. There was very little left of the old keep.

They were approaching the shore. John used his oar to guide the boat as close to land as possible. Heath jumped ashore and pulled the prow of the boat in. He reached for Lady Margaret, who was already standing. She offered her hand but he knew she could not jump the distance and would find her shoes wet for the effort. He placed his hands on her waist, swinging her up into the air to settle her on the rocky shore. Her weight felt good in his arms.

He tried not to think of it. Instead, he focused on helping John secure the boat.

Rowlly's boat reached the shore. Heath helped drag it up on land. "We want to look at the ruins," Heath informed the others. "It should not take us long."

"There isn't much to see," John agreed. "We'll be here."

"What do you want us to do while we wait, Laird?" Rowlly asked. He'd thought to bring Cook's basket with them.

"Whatever you wish. We should be ready to leave within the hour," he answered.

He turned to Lady Margaret but she had already discovered the path overgrown with spiny brown heather and hawthorn's sharp-needled branches and was pushing her way through it.

He hurried to catch up with her.

Margaret had expected to feel something upon setting foot on the island.

If there had been clouds with thunderbolts around it, she would have felt better than seeing it as an ordinary piece of land like so many other small islands in Loch Awe's waters.

When her feet had touched shore, she'd not felt a tingle, not even a twinge.

Noticing the faint trace of a path from the shore into what was a surprisingly dense, overgrown forest, Margaret knew she should wait for Laird Macnachtan and yet now she was here, she wasn't just impatient, she felt compelled to go forward. So many had sacrificed so much for her to reach this place. She didn't want to delay in beginning her search.

She heard Laird Macnachtan as he came up behind her. He leaned around her and pushed branches blocking her path away. It was a gallant gesture for which she was grateful, just as she'd appreciated his helping her from the boat. It was good to not be alone in this venture and she valued his many strengths.

"How far are the ruins?" she asked. The air was not so cold in the forest.

"We are almost upon them. At least half of this island was once Macnachtan Keep. They built it here to protect themselves from raiders. The Campbells had a bigger fortress up the loch. There are also ruins on a few of the other islands. This forest wasn't here back in the day. It's grown up over the years since we've been gone."

"Why did your family abandon the keep?"

"Our family's interests were on the shore. We no longer needed to protect ourselves from raiders. I find it interesting that they didn't even build on the shore across from the Innis Craggah. My father said that was because of our alliance with the Campbells. With that clan, you'd best secure your borders and watch everything you own or it will be gone in a blink."

"Even now?" she asked.

"No, generations ago. They *buy* property now. Owen Campbell has made a bid for mine." He now walked ahead of her, clearing the way.

She gathered her cape around her. The thing was cumbersome in the woods. "Would you sell?"

He ducked under a low-hanging limb. "I'll not lie, I've thought about it. We need the money and there have been times when I'd rather do anything other than chasing pigs and worrying about petty squabbles and empty bellies."

"I imagine after the scene with Swepston yesterday, there will be much less arguing," she said.

He shrugged. They had been hiking uphill. He wasn't winded but she was feeling the exertion of the climb. She unfastened her cloak and took it off, folding it over her arm. She could use a walking stick.

As if reading her mind, he held out his hand. "Here."

For a second, she debated refusing. He already claimed too much of her mind.

Then again, they both wore gloves . . . and she appreciated his assistance so she accepted his offer, and just in time. They had to climb a small ledge of rock. In her heavy, long riding skirt, she would have been clumsy and undignified without his help.

This point of the island was higher and steeper than she had anticipated, and provided a good vantage point for surveying all activity on shore and up and down the loch.

They took a moment to catch their breath.

"Would you go back to the sea if you sold Marybone?" she asked.

"I miss the sea," he admitted. "However, this is my birthright. My home. Then again, I think about my sisters. Dara has pointed out they should be finding husbands and they would if everyone didn't know the Macnachtans were so bloody poor."

"Your sisters are lovely girls. Is a dowry that important? Even here?"

"It is not important to old men with motherless children, or the equally poor," he answered. "Granted, we've just emerged from mourning. Perhaps Laren and Anice would each find someone worthy of them. Dara has her doubts, and it is true our debts weigh against my sisters. They should have marriages that add to their prestige, not detract from it."

She could not argue. He was right.

"Where do you believe your fortunes would be if Charles Chattan had not left Rose?" she asked.

He frowned. "What do you mean?"

"You said it yesterday. When you confronted Swepston, you claimed that the Macnachtans were the ones who were truly cursed. That Fenella's actions weighed upon you as well."

"It's true when one considers the matter. The Chattan have fared far better than we have."

"The curse has caused us death," she pointed out.

"And you believe there is nothing worse than death?"

Startled, she said, "Is there?"

He held up a placating hand. "I'm not belittling the costs to your family. I do not mean to mock those deaths you say the curse has claimed —"

"I don't 'say.' *It has,*" she said, bristling under his continued doubt.

"Yes, as it is," he returned in concession, but continued, "However, superstition has kept us isolated. When I was growing up, we lived and farmed the way my father's father did and his before him. Even the stones of Marybone came from the keep although they say it was a time-consuming, ridiculous endeavor to ferry them across. Even building Marybone was one of the foolishnesses that broke us. We didn't have the money then. And one of our problems now is that the young and the able leave and those left behind listen to the likes of Swepston or those who expect me to answer all of their problems. *Me.* The one who can't solve his own brother's death."

"Perhaps there was no reason for his murder," she suggested with sympathy. "A random act such as robbery."

"His money was still in his pocket, although he didn't have that much."

"Was there a vendetta?"

"I thought of Swepston, but you saw him yesterday. I believe he was genuinely shocked when I accused him of the murder."

"Could he be a good actor?"

The laird considered her words a moment and then shook his head. "No. He has strong opinions and eccentric habits, but at heart the man is simple. I can't see him in the role of murderer."

"Whom do you see then?" she asked.

He looked up to the cloudless sky that was the deep blue that was only seen in winter. "I believe his attacker was someone he trusted. Someone who could lead him to that place. But I don't know how it was done and there has been no sign or clue of why." He shook his head, his manner changing. "Enough of that. This day is about you and your welcome to Macnachtan Keep." He bowed as he said the last, a mocking gesture, and indicated with a wave of his hand the top of the knoll where she now stood.

Startled to think she had reached this place without realizing it, she turned and faced nettles and brown grasses that hid a low rock foundation of what had once been a good-sized structure generations ago.

Margaret could not hide her disappointment.

"I warned you it wasn't much," he said. "Right here would have been the location of the tower. You can see a corner of it there. And the front gate was to the left."

He walked over to show her where the entrance had been, but she didn't follow.

Instead, she stepped forward so that she stood in what might have been the center of the tower.

According to the legend, in this place Rose Macnachtan had contemplated jumping to her death. Several feet away would have been the inner yard. The ground was still hard there, as if it had been pounded down to a shelf of rock. Dry grass, nettles and thistles had forced their way even here, but among them she saw the imprint of a horse's hoof.

"They had livestock here?" she asked.

"Of course. I assume we ferried animals and people back and forth to the mainland." He'd not moved with her into the courtyard, but stood beside the tower foundation.

"I am disappointed the tower isn't here," she murmured. "That there isn't more." Margaret held out her arms and turned in a circle.

"What are you doing? Chanting?"

"I'm trying to imagine how Rose was feeling. She would have been looking in this direction, toward the road leading to the far shore."

"What makes you believe that?"

"Because they say she died on Charles Chattan's wedding day. She was waiting for him. She believed he wouldn't marry the Englishwoman. She thought he would return to her."

The far shore could not be seen over the brown brush and trees that blocked the view, but from the height of the tower, Rose would have been able to watch the road from the south.

Margaret moved to the outside perimeter of the tower. "Did she fall here? Or would she have jumped to the inside?"

"The inside would have been stone pavers. They are now the walkways at Marybone and the stable yard."

"So I've been walking on the stones where Rose may have fallen?"

"If she jumped to the inside of the keep."

"That is what I would have chosen to do," Margaret said. "If I was in such despair I could only cure it by taking my own life, I would want to be certain I did not survive."

She drew in a deep breath, holding it in,

recognizing the disappointment. She released it. "You were right."

"About what?"

"There isn't anything here," she admitted. "I believed I would sense or feel something. But it's normal. All is as it should be." She unfolded the cloak she held over her arm and put it around her shoulders. "A cold winter day." Indeed, it felt colder here than on the shore and should have been windier —

Margaret paused, struck by a realization. "Except that it is quiet here. *Too* quiet. The wind doesn't even rustle the grass."

"I take great comfort in that," the laird answered. "If there are ghosts here, I wouldn't want a lot of noise to rouse them."

"There *must* be something," she said more to herself than to him. "The coach accident was to *stop* me from coming *here.*" She pointed to the ground. "But *why*?"

"Why couldn't the accident be just what it was? A mishap on the road?"

She frowned at him, giving him her back. He believed in what he could see and what he could touch.

But she *knew* differently.

She began walking the line of the foundation. In some places the wall was taller than in others. In one far corner, the wall was almost ten feet high and in better shape than anywhere else. She walked toward it, realizing that the reason the wall still stood was that it had been a fireplace, a huge one. There were ashes in the pit, and a stack of wood and brush had been collected for future fires.

The laird joined her. "This is where the kitchen for the keep was." He kicked at the ashes. They were cold. "When Brodie and I had a chance, we'd spend the day swimming and then build a fire and sleep overnight. The wall radiates heat."

"Whom do you imagine built this fire?" Margaret asked.

"Anyone. There are people on and off these islands all the time."

Margaret frowned. She wasn't finding the answers she sought. "Let us go to the cliff. Is there a way to reach it from here?"

"This way." He began walking into the forest. Margaret hurried after him.

The path he followed was worse than the last. He seemed to know where he was going even though she could find no logic for the direction he took. Sweat trickled down her back although her cheeks and hands were cold.

Just as she was preparing to remove her heavy cloak again, he stepped back. "Here is your cliff."

The brush and trees went almost to the edge of the cliff's rocks. She moved forward, and there was the breadth of Loch Awe before her.

"I imagine in Fenella's time that the forest wasn't this close to the edge," he said.

"The view is magnificent," she murmured. Something stirred in her soul at the sight of the lake's bluish gray waters nestled in the protection of Highland mountains and a sky marred now by only a few large clouds. "This place has power. It is where I would cast a spell."

She looked down. The water was so clear, she could see the bottom even from this height. She edged forward.

His hand grabbed her arm. "Careful," he warned. "I don't trust the rocks here."

Margaret ignored his warning, or perhaps she trusted his strength to protect her. It didn't matter which. She was caught up in the moment. "Fenella would have built the funeral pyre to the left."

"How do imagine that?" he asked.

"The left hand is connected to the heart," Margaret said. "I read that in her book. Several of the recipes, or spells, were very precise on which hand should be used before incantations." She frowned, picturing the size of the fire that would have been built, imagining Rose's body burning.

She could see it in her mind. Fenella would have stood exactly at this point so that when she leaped, she would not miss landing on the fire.

Margaret had to take another step forward. Her weight freed several rocks to bounce down the cliff's side into the water.

"It is higher than I pictured in my mind," she said. "Anyone jumping from here would not expect to survive unharmed."

"Which is a good reason to step back from the edge," the laird pointed out, pulling on her arm.

She obeyed his tug and moved back.

There *must* be something here that she was meant to discover. She began searching, pushing back shrubs, bushes and bracken that could hide clues.

"Do you even know what you are looking for?" he asked.

"No."

He made an impatient sound. "My lady, there isn't anything more to be discovered. Do you understand? You have seen it all. It's rubble and forest, little else. We'd best be on our way so we can return to Marybone before dark."

"Just a minute more." She walked in a

circle, relooked where she had looked before.

"You have seen all there is, my lady. There's naught much else."

Margaret moved once again to the cliff. Her frustration knew no bounds. She stared out onto the loch. *Why would she have been brought so far for nothing?*

"Come," he said, his voice sympathetic. "We shall return to Marybone and regroup."

"How can 'we' regroup if you don't believe the story?" she asked, bitterness in her words. "I came here not expecting to fail. Perhaps my confidence came from Harry. He'd been right about Glenfinnan and finding Fenella's book. He believed *I* could be the key to end the curse."

"If that is true, then another way will be made known to you," he answered. "Perhaps the magic is in the rocks we used to line our garden," he suggested. "You can spend tomorrow going around sensing them."

She didn't like the gentle disbelief in his voice. "If I had a rock in my hand, I would throw it at you right now."

"Ah, but that would be the one you needed, my lady, so I'd advise you not to waste it." There was humor in his voice, but his gaze held concern for her. He held out his hand. "Come, we need to return to the boats."

He was right. The hour was growing late. Reluctantly, she placed her hand in his. He led her down a new path, this one easier to follow since it trailed the shoreline.

"Is Innis Craggah always this silent? It's eerie," she said. "There hasn't even been a bird flying over our heads."

"It's not quiet," he answered, not breaking stride. "I hear plenty of sound."

"Such as?"

"The sound of our steps on the path." He kicked a loose stone ahead of him for emphasis. "Or the wind through the trees."

"*I* don't hear the wind through the trees," she countered — and she didn't.

"You aren't listening, my lady," he said. "There is sound. I can hear the water against the shore, the rocks beneath our feet, your breathing, mine —"

At that moment, the men waiting at the boats hailed out to them.

"Do you hear them?" he asked.

"Of course, I do," Margaret answered, feeling surly.

Laird Macnachtan stopped. "My lady, don't make any more of this curse than what it is."

"And what is it? You have never believed

there is a curse."

He drew a breath as if praying for patience. "I've been helping you, my lady. If that isn't putting faith into something, I don't know what is." He started to take a step away but then returned to say, "And instead of blaming a curse for the course of events, perhaps you should consider other factors that could be causing the deaths in your family. Your kin may have weak hearts or another malady. Blaming death on ghosties and ghoulies serves no purpose."

He didn't wait for her answer but began walking toward his men.

And Margaret felt like the most churlish of women. If she wasn't careful, she would lose his support, and she discovered she did not want to do that. She needed his help . . . she wanted it. She liked counting on his strength and intelligence. She'd begun expecting it. *She,* the woman who prided herself on not expecting anything from anyone, actually enjoyed being with this Scottish chieftain with his generous nature and adventurous spirit. She relied on him, and Margaret wasn't certain that was wise.

He didn't understand, and if she truly cared for him, she'd keep a distance. His doubts aside, she knew her line was tainted.

She walked toward the boats, head bowed.

Laird Macnachtan said something to her but she ignored him. He'd believe her in sour spirits over his directness. She wasn't. She was just beginning to realize she had more to fear from her feelings toward him than she did from the curse.

Was this what had happened to her brothers?

Had they been like her, determined to not fall in love, and then found themselves being drawn to *one* person?

One very special person? The sort that didn't hesitate to speak his mind or treat her as an equal?

She'd never met a man like Heath Macnachtan before. She doubted if she ever would again.

And the realization created a hollowness in her belly and a tightness in her heart.

He was not safe.

She would have climbed into the boat by herself if possible. It was not. So she had to endure the thrill of Laird Macnachtan picking her up in his arms. For a second, the presence of him enveloped her.

And was it her imagination, or did he act as if he felt something for her as well?

She could usually detect when a man was attracted to her, but she wasn't certain this time . . . perhaps because she would not be averse to him?

Within minutes she was settled in the rear of the boat. Beneath the warmth of her cloak, she crossed her arms. The boat rocked in the shallow water as the laird and Gibson climbed aboard.

From their boat, Rowlly, Gibson's son, and the stable lad waved. "A race to the other side with a bit of a wager?" Rowlly asked.

"Name it," the laird said.

"Two pints apiece at the Goldeneye," Rowlly answered. "Who knows? We may see Augie again."

All the men laughed, including the stable lad. Gibson made a comment that he wouldn't mind being present for another meeting of the laird and Augie.

Margaret didn't understand what they were talking about. She kept her eyes on the shoreline.

There was a splash as oars hit water. The men would waste no time reaching the other shore —

A flash of white at the edge of the trees close to the path leading to the keep caught Margaret's eye. It was a cat. A small one.

It was Owl. There was no mistaking the odd shape of her head.

Margaret turned toward the laird.

"There's my cat. I see Owl." They were now ten feet from the shore. "You must take me back," she ordered.

Gibson, sitting in front of her, frowned in the direction she pointed. "Where is there a cat?" he said. "I don't see one."

"Right there on the shore," Margaret insisted. How could he not see Owl, who had padded down to the waterline and meowed as if begging her to return? The cat placed a paw on the water as if to come after her and then quickly backed away. "Please, take me back. I must catch my cat."

Laird Macnachtan was mid-stroke when he Lifted his oar. He frowned. "My lady, I see no cat."

"She's right *there*," Margaret said, frustration making her angry. Why couldn't anyone see Owl save her? What madness was at work?

Owl meowed one more time. Margaret could hear her plainly. Owl turned and began trotting toward the woods. She would disappear into the underbrush in a minute.

"Take me back," Margaret begged. She knew she couldn't leave Owl.

The men had not moved. They stared at her in concern. Rowlly's boat kept going, racing away and unaware of the discussion.

Margaret had asked for a sign, and Owl

was what she'd been searching for. She realized that now.

The cat sat on her haunches at the edge of the forest as if waiting for Margaret to return.

"You *don't* see the cat," she stated, wanting them to confirm one more time they were blind to what she saw.

"There is no cat," the laird said, even as Gibson demanded, "Will you row? We will be paying for pints if we don't put our backs in it."

Margaret stood up in the boat. The wind had picked up. They were now close to twenty feet from shore.

She knew how to swim. She also gambled that the water would still be shallow here. She threw off her cape and jumped into the water.

"What the devil — ?" Gibson shouted.

Her habit weighed her down but her determination was strong. The bitter coldness of the water went straight to her bones. But her determination was stronger than fear.

Thankfully, her booted feet touched bottom.

Owl disappeared into the trees as if knowing Margaret would follow.

Behind her, Laird Macnachtan was shouting.

She didn't answer. She couldn't. The waves around her had suddenly become stronger and were trying to push her away from the shore.

She stumbled, caught herself, and surged forward, refusing to give up. The effort to reach the shore required everything of her, but she succeeded.

On the shore, she took a moment to catch her breath. She struggled to her feet and looked to the boat. The men were trying to row back to her and yet the current now carried them farther away. And the sky had changed. It now roiled with heavy, dark, thunderous clouds that seemed to have appeared out of nowhere.

But the danger of a storm didn't matter. Margaret was where she knew she must be.

She threw the hem of her water-heavy skirts over one arm and rushed to the point in the forest where she'd seen Owl disappear.

CHAPTER ELEVEN

Heath couldn't believe Margaret had jumped out of the boat. He swore furiously. The water was freezing. She would not survive. He shouted for her, but she ignored him, *of course.*

Why should she behave any differently when her life was in jeopardy than she had from the moment they'd met?

"Bring the boat around," he shouted to Gibson. "I'm trying, Laird. The current is too heavy. I've never seen the like."

Indeed, white-capped waves now pressed against the boat. In less time than it took to say one's name, thick clouds had begun churning over their heads and the wind had picked up speed.

"It's as if the world has gone mad," Gibson declared.

And he was right.

Heath saw Margaret reach shore. She was soaked to the skin, but at least she'd made it. Her wet hair clung to her shoulders and she was shivering.

She started to her feet but tripped over wet skirts. Again, she tried.

"Margaret, stay right there."

Either the rising wind whisked his words away from her hearing or she chose to ignore him, because she lurched to her feet, gathered her skirts and, with a hobbling gait, ran into the forest.

"Row," he ordered Gibson, digging deep into the water with his oars. "Take me back there."

"We aren't going anywhere," Gibson answered. "I've never seen the loch like this." He was pulling back against the water as he spoke and there was the sound of a crack. His oar broke. The wood snapped as if it had been a twig. The boat was adrift and began spinning.

Highland storms could be sudden and cruel, but Heath had never seen one such as this before.

He didn't understand what has happening, but a fear for Margaret gripped him. They were being carried farther away from Innis Craggah. The boat was thirty feet from shore and moving rapidly. He could not waste time. He pulled off his boots.

"What are you doing —" Gibson shouted

just as Heath climbed on the bench and dived into the water.

The cold bite of it robbed him of breath. For a second he floundered. Great waves rolled over his head. He fought panic.

He'd heard sailors tell of being in the Northern Sea, of how quickly the water could freeze a man to death. He knew to keep blowing bubbles. The sailors had said that would stop his lungs from freezing.

Heath had been swimming in these waters all his life, but he'd never felt such a strong, threatening current. It was as if there was something trying to pull him under and away from the shore all at once.

And yet, he had to reach Margaret.

His feet touched bottom. Hope surged within him. At some point, he'd lost a stocking but it didn't matter. He had no feeling in his feet as it was. He charged forward, pushing his way through the current until he fell facedown upon the rocky shore. Nothing had ever felt so good to him.

For a long moment, he couldn't move.

And then the hail started.

Hail the size of man's fist rained down from the heavens. He covered his head with his arms. It seemed to come down harder.

Struggling to his feet required herculean strength. Heath didn't try calling for Margaret. The storm was stronger than his voice.

Instead, he stumbled toward the haven of the trees, and just as he reached shelter, the hail stopped.

This was not normal weather, not even for the Highlands.

He leaned against a tree trunk, bending over to catch his breath, his gaze wandering back toward the water — and he was shocked by what he saw.

Loch Awe was a mass of white-capped tossing waves beneath a foggy mist. Any view of land or the boats was blocked. He prayed Rowlly and the others had reached shore and then pushed away from the tree and began his search for Margaret.

He was freezing in his clothes. He removed his remaining stocking and continued barefoot. His feet seemed to have turned into blocks of ice.

If he was this cold, she had to be as well.

It was snowing now, large flakes, and he was reminded of what she'd said about the coach accident, about weather they'd experienced that had not touched Marybone only miles away.

He'd assumed she would go to the ruins. However, when he reached the knoll, she was not there. His next thought was the cliff. He noted the kitchen's hearth was protected from the storm and the kindling was dry. He would bring her here as soon as found her and start a fire.

He called her name now.

There was no answer.

Heath was halfway to the cliff when he sensed he was not alone.

He stopped in the path. He saw no one, and yet his gut warned him to caution — and then he heard her voice.

"Lady Margaret?"

The voice stopped. She'd sounded as if she'd been speaking to someone.

"Lady Margaret," he tried again.

"I am here," she said, her voice closer than he had anticipated. He followed the sound and within minutes found himself in a sheltered clearing. Tall, stately firs kept the wind at bay. Here was a place of peace, away from the madness of the weather.

And in the center of the clearing, Margaret was on her knees, her back to him. Her dress was soaked. She trembled with the cold but she was leaning over, brushing wet leaves to the side.

"What are you doing?" he asked, coming up beside her.

She raised wide eyes to him. "Look."

Heath didn't want to look. He was bloody frozen to death and she was as well. "Come, we need to find shelter."

She resisted. "Look at what I've found."

He glanced down with undisguised impatience and realized there were two weather-worn, rectangular stones on the ground in front of her.

"They are graves," she said. "Unmarked ones without the benefit of holy ground. Do you know who this must be?" she asked. "Owl brought me here."

"Owl?" he said.

"The cat."

The damn cat — and he was reminded of why he was here, why his teeth were chattering in his head. "Jumping out of that boat was beyond foolishness. You could have drowned."

"But I didn't," she said. Her lips were blue and he knew his were as well. "*I saw* the cat," she said, "even if you could not see her. She was on the shore and I knew she wanted me to return. I couldn't ignore her."

He knelt to her level. "You could have just asked for us to turn the boat around. Then you would have saved us both a swim."

She looked at him as if only then realizing he was as wet as she. She took his face in her hands. "I did ask you to return. You refused. But why didn't you stay in the boat and row it back?"

232

Heath could feel his scowl deepen and there was nothing to do but admit, "There is something odd going on. This storm, it shouldn't be here. And the water became wild. It was as if it didn't want us to return for you."

"So you jumped in as well?" Her smile warmed him. "Thank you," she whispered. "That was the most gallant thing anyone has ever done for me."

When she looked at him like that, even though he was cold to his core, a part of him became very heated.

He reached for her arm. "We need to return to the ruins. I can start a fire there."

"Wait," she said. "These must be the graves of Rose and Fenella. They could not be buried in hallowed ground, could they?"

The stones were rough and aged by the weather. Lines appeared to have been engraved on one of them, lines that had been worn away by time.

"Did you know they were here?" she asked.

"I've not seen them before." And he didn't care about them now. "Come, they will be here once this storm is passed." This time when he pulled on her arm, she didn't resist but rose to her feet along with him.

He took her hand and retraced his steps

to the path. They were both shaking vio-
lently in their wet clothes. Heath reached
over and pulled her next to him. They
needed to share what little body heat they
had between them.

She fit neatly under his arm. Together, the
snow falling around them, they hurried as
quickly as possible back to the ruins and
the haven of the kitchen hearth.

While Margaret huddled in a corner,
Heath found two hard, sharp rocks that had
been left by someone who had been here
before. He began working to strike a spark
over a bit of kindling. It was not easy with
the wind.

He felt Margaret beside him, her body
convulsing with cold. "Let me help," she
managed to chatter out. "Together we make
a good wall to block the wind." She leaned
against him.

"You might want to take off some of your
clothes," he advised. "Any petticoats or
anything that is wet against your skin."

"It is *all* wet against my skin," she assured
him.

He knew how she felt.

"Please start the fire. *Please,*" she whispered.

It was almost dark. Heath tried over and
over to strike a spark. His hands didn't want

to cooperate with him. He had a strong desire to lie down and close his eyes and knew that was the cold winning over his spirit.

"Please, God," he whispered, only to fail again, but his temper flared.

He drew a deep breath, hit the rocks hard, and a spark from them landed in the dry kindling. Heath leaned over and coaxed it to life with his breath.

The wood that was dry was old and caught fire quickly. In short order it was burning warmly in the protected confines of the fireplace.

"Come closer. Lie in front of the fire," Heath ordered. He added fuel to the fire and then threw his arms around her, spooning his body against hers. His back was to the elements; however, she was neatly tucked in between him and the fire.

"Thank you," she whispered. "Thank you, thank you, thank you."

Heath could only grunt. They would make it. There had been a moment that he hadn't been certain but now with shelter and the fire going, they had a fighting chance.

"She couldn't stop us," Margaret said. They were both still shaking. The ground was bloody hard. "She tried, but she failed."

"She?" he asked. He wished he could rid

himself of his clothes. They were wet and uncomfortable. Hers had to be the same.

"Fenella. She started this storm."

Heath was too tired to be annoyed with her reasoning. He closed his eyes.

Margaret turned to him, the movement waking him. Her hair was startling to dry and there wisps of curls at her cheek. He might be tired but she appeared invigorated.

"Do you truly believe that storm was an act of nature?" she whispered. "It wasn't. *That* was the same storm that came upon us before the accident."

"It's the Highlands —" he started, until she cut him off by placing her fingers over his lips. Her fingertips were cold, or perhaps his lips were.

She snuggled closer to him. "For one moment, let yourself believe. Believe that I do see a cat that led me to those graves. Owl came with me on the road from Glenfinnan. Owl has been trying to bring me here."

"And the graves?"

"I'm certain those belong to Rose and Fenella. Mother and daughter, both buried beyond the embrace of the church."

As she spoke, the wind seemed to pick up its pace, howling even through the rocks of the wall, but the fire burned steady.

"You don't know that," Heath said. "They

were small stones. They could be the graves of babes, born without baptism and denied holy ground. Or they might have been some beloved pets."

"I *do* know," she answered, her voice low and no longer shivering with her body. "I *know.*"

And then, to his surprise, she placed her hand on the side of his face, her palms warm, and kissed him.

Her lips were soft and warm. They melded against his — and Heath forgot the cold.

She didn't pull away, either, but took her time with the kiss as if exploring and discovering how it felt to taste him.

He placed his hand on the indentation of her waist and she scooted to fit her body against his.

No kiss, no woman had ever tasted this good. Or had the power to draw him in this deeply.

She broke the kiss and pushed herself up so that she looked down into his face, bracing her weight with one hand on the ground beside him, her arm on his chest. Her bent leg rested between his. Her aggressiveness surprised him, but a new, more demanding need was building inside him.

He started to lift himself up, knowing if he didn't stop matters now, he wouldn't want to stop later. "Why don't we sit — ?" he started to suggest.

She cut him off with another kiss, a hungry, demanding one.

From the moment he'd seen her on that London street, he'd wanted her.

When he'd first laid eyes on her on that bed of pine needles after the accident, he'd wanted her.

And now here she was, offering herself to him, and her kisses were more potent than he could imagine.

He was warm now. Hot even, and he no longer heard the sound of the storm. It had been replaced by the demanding drum of desire pounding in his own veins.

They needed to stop this while he still could, but not just yet.

Heath allowed himself to kiss her back.

He teased her with his tongue.

She stiffened and he held still, not wanting to chase her away. Oh no, he did not want to do that at all.

And then she traced his lower lip with the tip of *her* tongue, and he was lost.

God help him. Margaret Chattan was more than just a beautiful woman. They say a man falls in love with his eyes, but Heath was feeling something more. He liked the way she smelled and the weight of her in his arms. Those times when he'd helped her from the horse or the boat, he couldn't help but notice how soft and perfectly formed she was.

He opened his lips, breathing her in. She responded with a soft, shuddering sigh, as if this was what she wanted, what she needed. Her breasts flattened against his chest. Her nipples were taut and firm. He could feel them even through layers of her clothes, and Heath was undone.

Margaret Chattan was made for loving. She had the sort of body most men could only dream of and she was here in his arms — warm, willing, desirable.

How long had it been since he had enjoyed a woman?

He couldn't remember. He didn't care. She was all he wanted.

She gripped his shirt with one hand as if to hold him in place. She kissed him like a woman possessed. He was surprised at her passion, but eminently grateful as well.

"Trust me," she whispered. "Please trust me."

"I do," Heath murmured as she kissed the line of his jaw. Her hand strayed down his chest to the waist of his breeches. She began twisting the buttons, first one, then another. His erection against the stiff material begged her for freedom.

Still, he was a gentleman —

Heath brought his hand down over hers. "Wait, Margaret, you may want to think on this."

Her response was to trace his ear with her tongue.

"I was mistaken," he murmured. "Don't think on it." He helped her finish the unbuttoning.

She wanted what she wanted and whom was he to argue? She rubbed his thigh with the inside of her knee. He had not expected her to be so aggressive, wanton even. Her skirt was almost up to her waist and she reminded him of a dockside whore, coaxing a man to dick her —

This was not Margaret Chattan.

The thought startled Heath. He grabbed her wrists and sat up, holding her away from him.

She lunged at him as if wanting to wrap her arms around him, to claim him. The fire beside them seemed to have come alive with a will of its own. The flames rose higher, burning brighter, their light spreading until he could see her face was no longer her own.

The evil of a thousand devils lit her eyes.

And her tongue had turned to that of a

*serpent. It reached out to lick at him, even as
her fingers curled into claws intent on attacking him.*

*"Come here," she ordered, her voice soft,
coaxing. "Come to me."*

Margaret had dozed off. She was cold in
spite of the fire but bone weary and comforted by the laird's presence.

And then she felt herself being shaken
awake.

She opened her eyes to find Heath over
her. He held her by the wrists and the
expression on his face was one of horror,
except he wasn't really seeing her. He was
dreaming — and he was afraid of her.

"Laird Macnachtan, wake up. *Wake up.
Heath.*"

For a second, she feared he would not
hear her. His hold on her wrists tightened.
He twisted her around, pressing her into
the ground.

Panic gripped her, until she reminded
herself this man was good. He was the best
she'd ever met. He'd always been everything
that a gentleman should be and more. He
would not harm her.

His face came down to hers, his teeth
clenched as if in a battle and Margaret knew
she had to do something to wake him.

Something drastic.

So she kissed him.

Her lips were numb from the cold. The contact warmed them.

He frowned, started to pull back. She reached up and kissed him again, pressing her lips to his, and she felt him relax.

His grip on her wrists loosened.

She pulled her hands from his hold and threw them around his shoulders, holding him, feeling the racing beat of his heart against her chest. His growth of beard was scratchy on her skin. She kissed him all the harder.

His manner changed. He brought his hand to her waist, pulling her to him. His kiss became more intent, more purposeful.

Margaret believed she'd known what a kiss was.

She now realized she hadn't.

Heath Macnachtan's kiss robbed her of all reason.

His lips opened and instinctively she followed his lead, finding she liked the taste and feel of him. She liked it very much.

There had been a time when she'd stolen kisses. A time when she had indulged in passion. She'd paid a terrible price for her foolishness and had vowed she would be chaste, and had been. She'd become to believe herself immune to the luxuries of the flesh.

But now she couldn't keep from kissing him. It felt good to be this close to him. It felt safe.

He broke the kiss with a huge, gasping cry as if just coming to his senses. His breathing was shallow, his face flushed.

His hands had returned to her wrists but he didn't take hold.

Instead, he stared glassy-eyed. "Margaret?" he whispered. He seemed uncertain, and she realized he'd been dreaming.

"Yes, it is me," she said. "It *is* me."

"I was dreaming."

She nodded. "You were."

"It seemed real."

"They can be that way."

His brows came together, and then his response was to kiss her again.

Chapter Twelve

Heath had rarely credited kissing as anything other than a prelude to what he really wanted. Men kissed because women liked being all sloppy. What men truly wanted was much lower on the body.

However, now Margaret taught him that a kiss was a desire in and of itself. It was communication and communion.

Had the poets, whom he'd so often mocked, claimed kisses were better than wine? He'd not thought so . . . until this moment.

Memories of the dream evaporated. Responsibilities, doubts and worries disappeared.

There was nothing of more importance in this world than this woman in his arms.

She opened so sweetly to him that he knew theirs was not one-sided desire.

Of course, the kiss grew more heated. He wanted her in a way he'd never yearned for a woman before.

He began undressing her, tentatively at first, and, when she didn't object, with more purpose. The storm raged around them, but here in front of the fire, protected by the crumbling walls of Macnachtan Keep, they were safe.

Had his buttons been hard to unfasten in his dream? They were doubly difficult now. His fingers were clumsy in his excitement and he would not let his lips leave hers. She was so soft and yielding. He'd rather struggle with wet clothing than part from her.

Her hand came down to help him. He reached for her waist, searching for the lacing of her skirt. That same skirt served as their covering. His jacket and breeches became their mattress.

Undoing her jacket was a challenge. The silver buttons were slippery.

She laughed at his inept attempts, breaking the kiss. She sat up and saw to the task herself.

Heath used the moment to throw more wood on the fire. He was naked and not ashamed of the hard desire he showed for her.

Margaret blushed, but then she rose up on her knees and opened her jacket. Thin, white lawn material covered her breasts, and he was reminded of that day by the great oak when her petticoat had drifted through the air.

Her black-as-a-raven's-wing hair curled around her shoulders. He reached for the white lawn and pulled, bringing her toward him, even as the material ripped. The back of his fingers touched her skin as he kissed her.

This kiss was demanding. He wanted her and he wanted her now. Her breasts were full and tight, the nipples hard. She wanted him as well.

Her arms came around his shoulders as he leaned her back onto their makeshift bed. He pulled her skirt over them, forming a haven just for the two of them.

Their kiss deepened. He could feel her heat.

The scent of her was sweeter to his senses than any perfume. He tasted her flesh, kissing his way to her breast.

She gasped in surprise at the tricks his mouth could play, a gasp that quickly turned into small encouragements of delight.

As he moved to tease her other breast, he settled himself between her legs. She opened and arched to accommodate him. Her thighs were silky smooth against his hips.

There is a point when a man cannot turn back. Heath had reached that point.

His mind was insane with wanting her. She filled his senses. He raised himself to hungrily kiss her again —

She held her hand up to his lips. Her eyes were dark with desire. He kissed her fingers, and she sighed and took her hand away, giving him full access to her mouth.

Their tongues met, caressed, stroked — and he thrust himself deeply inside her, all the way to the hilt.

Margaret stiffened. She was blessedly tight. Too late he thought of her innocence. He called himself every worst sort of bastard, and then he could think no more as he gave himself over to the bliss of being inside her.

No woman had ever felt as good as Margaret Chattan did in his arms.

After her initial shock at accepting him, she became a full and eager participant in their lovemaking. Her movements matched his and heightened his pleasure while letting him know what she needed.

Heath was delighted. He liked a partner who didn't stint in her own desires.

Too soon he felt his concentration weakening. She overpowered him.

And then her breath quickened. She moved faster. He wrapped his arms around her and gathered her up. Deep muscles tightened and he was lost.

Heath couldn't think. He couldn't breathe.

No release had ever been this forceful. She drained the life of him and yet at the same time, he was more alive, more aware than he'd ever been before.

She cried his name and held fast to him. The strength of her completion radiated through him.

This was no ordinary coupling.

She was no ordinary woman.

In that moment, their bodies sharing the perfect summit of completion, Heath fell in love.

It startled him.

Yes, he was attracted to her. Margaret Chattan was a lovely, intelligent woman. There had been moments when he'd questioned her sanity, but he had no questions now.

The dissatisfaction that had nagged at him from the time he'd heard of his brother's death, to the daily struggle to see to the estate's debts, evaporated. The niggling doubt that life held anything of importance to him vanished.

In their place was a sense of wonder.

Margaret released her pleasure in a sigh of contentment. The ringing of church bells or the music of birdsong could not have been more pleasing to his ear.

He held her, studying her face as if with new eyes. He now saw beyond her looks. He knew her soul.

And he realized that all the events that had taken place in his life had happened to bring him to this one moment.

This one woman.

A dreamy look crossed her face. She raised her lashes and smiled, satisfied.

Only then did he realize he'd been holding her, bracing her in his arms. Gently he let her rest upon their makeshift mattress. She raised a hand to rest against his jaw. He knew his whiskers were rough but she smiled as if their prickly growth pleased her.

"I did not know it could be like that," she whispered.

He hadn't, either.

Heath brushed her curls away from her face. He adored looking at her. He knew he would feel the same even when her beauty faded with age — no, her beauty would never change for him . . . because it was her spirit he loved.

He loved. Heath Graham Davis Macnachtan had fallen in love, and it was the most precious, exciting, thrilling emotion of his life.

And then a coldness stole through him. She was easy to love; he not so much. She was the Unattainable, the glorious toast of London, and he was a penniless Scottish chieftain. Margaret Chattan had more sense than to love a man like him.

She drew a shaky breath and he realized he was on top of her. He edged over so they lay side by side.

"Why are you looking at me that way?" she said, but didn't seem to need an answer because she smiled and brought her palm down to press upon her belly. "I'm still tingling," she admitted. "I never want this feeling to leave."

It wouldn't, he wanted to say, *if she loved him.* He'd make her feel this way every night.

But his usual smooth manner had disappeared. The confidence he'd always had with other women was gone. And he knew that was because he wanted her so much. They had done more than just make love. She had changed him forever.

She pressed a kiss to the underside of his chin. "It's good to be here with you. I'm not afraid. For so long, I've been afraid."

He found his voice. "You need never fear anything while I am here to protect you."

Margaret shook her head as if denying his words. He captured her face in his hands. She was so finely made. So delicate and soft, while he was hard and rough.

"This was *meant* to happen," he said almost fiercely, wanting to impress the fact on her. He had her now, and he was never going to let her go.

Margaret rested in the haven of his arms, her body still humming the joy of their coupling, and she wanted to believe him.

But she knew better.

"Tomorrow it may all be different."

"Tomorrow will be no different than this moment," he vowed. "Margaret, I mean what I say. I'll not let harm come to you."

She adored the sound of her name on his lips. She liked the way his accent drew out the first syllable, the way he lingered on the last.

He then sealed his pledge with a kiss, a kiss that again quickly became heated, and she was surprised that he was already hard for her.

Years ago, out of love, she'd given herself to a man she had wanted to believe was worthy of her. He had not been. But he had

revealed her passionate nature to her. She'd
tried to deny this aspect of her character.
She'd kept her desires carefully under
control. She'd allowed no man near her.

Was it the storm that had broken down
her defenses?

No, she knew better than that.

Heath was cut of the same cloth as her
brothers. He was an honorable man, a good
one, and nothing like Mark, who taken
advantage of her youth and innocent need
to be loved.

Heath didn't speak idle words. He would
defend her with his life if need be.

She pressed her naked breasts against his
chest, basking in the feel of the hard,
unyielding planes of his body. She could
relax her guard with him.

And Margaret wanted to make love to him
again.

She leaned against his shoulder, pushing
him onto his back. She surprised him when
she rolled on top of him. He laughed, the
sound deep and masculine.

His lips brushed her hair and she searched
them out, letting her kiss say to him what
she dared not speak aloud.

Of course, the kiss became heated.

Margaret straddled him, pushing up and
breaking the kiss. He tried to follow as if he

could not bear to release the contact of their kiss. She appeased him by settling herself upon him.

He leaned back to the ground now that he knew her intent. He thrust up, reaching the very core of her, inciting new, stronger yearnings within her.

She threw the skirt that served as their blanket off her so that she could sit upon him boldly. There was no more storm, or at least she couldn't register its existence. She was too taken with the tempest of her own emotions.

Her lover was a handsome man. His hands cupped her breasts. She held him inside, feeling wildly pagan.

And then she could take it no more. A sharp pinpoint of sensation grew inside her. She had to find release. She moved with greater purpose, reveling in the intensity that built with each thrust.

He was smiling, the glint in his eyes one of wicked enjoyment. She was doing this to him. He was as overpowered by her as she was by him.

She could feel the tension building in his loins. His hands came to her waist and he urged her to move faster, deeper. She didn't believe she could. The heat between them was hotter than the fire.

Heath's hold tightened. He pushed her hard against him, once, twice, and in the third, she felt the tension break.

For one sweet moment, she seemed to hover between earth and sky, life and death.

Once again, he had shown her that what she'd thought she'd known of what happened between a man and a woman was only a meager portion of the whole.

She experienced it all now. She could feel the force of his very being melding with her. She would never let him go. She held him as long as she could . . . and then slowly, she released her hold and fell down upon him.

His strong arms came around her.

He held her tightly. "You are a jewel," he praised her, bring the heavy skirt of her riding habit around them. "A gift from the gods."

Margaret knew differently. However, she did not correct him. Instead, she fell asleep, her cheek against his chest, the beat of his heart in her ears.

She knew these moments would not last.

They could not.

Heath had never slept so well in his life. He wasn't certain what woke him, but it was morning when he opened his eyes. He stretched his body as he came awake, and then remembered he was not alone.

Margaret, his Maggie, was curled up beside him, her back to his chest. She appeared completely at peace, without any of her former anxiousness. He liked seeing her this way.

Her hair was a tangled mess. He stroked it lightly and felt himself harden. It was only an hour after dawn. They had been up most of the night. If he was kind, he would let her sleep.

Then again, her passion was as demanding as his own. He was certain she would want him to wake her —

A movement of white at the edge of his vision caught his attention. Something sat on the edge of the low wall not far from the fire. He frowned and came up on one arm, the better to see what the white was . . . and found himself staring into the large, wise eyes of a small cat. Her ears were folded over, giving her face the unusual impression of —

"Owl?"

The cat's response was a low-throated purr before she jumped off the other side of the wall, disappearing from his view.

Here was Margaret's cat, the one she had been willing to drown for.

The one he had not been able to see.

Heath climbed out from beneath the skirt that served as a blanket and came to his feet.

Now he felt the aches of sleeping on hard ground. He walked over to the wall, uncertain if he truly saw the cat or if his mind was playing tricks. Perhaps he wasn't awake. Perhaps he was dreaming.

The cold air of a winter morning assured him he wasn't. And when he walked to the wall and looked over it, the cat was still there, sitting on her haunches close to the woods.

For a long moment, they held each other's attention, and then Owl came to her feet and with a swish of her tail went into the forest.

Heath reached for his breeches and began dressing. His clothes were dry. He thought little of that considering the heat from the fire he'd built. Even now the embers still burned.

Seeing that Margaret was snuggled under the covers, he added more wood to keep the fire going until he returned. He was going to catch that cat. He had a plan to bring her to Margaret and show her that the animal was not some ghostie that could disappear, but real and very earthly.

Then, perhaps, she would accept that her family was not caught in the grips of some witch, but that there had to be, *must be,* very real, concrete reasons for the deaths of the males in her family.

If there was anything of the magical happening around here, it was the way they made love. That had been astounding, and he firmly planned to see that they did it again. Often.

But first, he was determined to banish the shadows in her life.

He had nothing for his feet but that did not bother him. He'd been colder and in worse circumstances on board a ship a time or two. The secret was to keep moving.

Climbing over the wall, he headed in the direction where Owl had disappeared. Standing on the edge of the woods, he listened. As if teasing him, he heard a faint meow and caught a glimpse of white.

The chase was on. Owl teased him by always staying ahead of him. He followed her into the densest part of the forest. A time or two, Owl almost let him catch her. His fingers just brushed the long, fine fur of her coat before she would leap out of his reach and playfully run in a new direction.

Heath was growing winded. The cat was leading him across small streams and over fallen trees. He knew they traveled in circles.

Slowly, his opinion changed. This was no ordinary cat. She understood what she was doing . . . and he realized she was leading him somewhere.

The moment he stepped into the small clearing surrounded by firs, he recognized the place. This was where he'd found Margaret the day before.

Owl waited for him. She sat between the two headstones, her expression sphinxlike.

Heath stopped. "Clever cat," he said. "We could have arrived here sooner."

Her response was an expression he could only interpret as a smile.

He didn't move closer but knelt, wanting to see what the cat would do.

The intelligence behind her large eyes, the *knowing* gave him a chill. She understood he challenged her and, in the manner of all women he'd known in his life, resented him for it.

They eyed each other, combatants at patience, and then Heath stood. "All right, I concede." His purpose wasn't to have a staring match with this cat but to capture it.

He started walking toward Owl. She waited with the air of a queen.

A step away from her, Heath decided to

make his move; he lunged for the cat, his arms going around her . . . his arms going right *through* her.

And he parted them to look at her in surprise, except she was gone. She'd vanished.

Everything he believed he knew was suddenly suspect.

Heath studied the space of ground where his own eyes had told him the cat had been. Now there was only brown grass and damp leaves and pine needles.

He searched the forest around him. There was no flash of white.

Or perhaps the cat was here and he couldn't see her, just as Margaret had claimed.

"What game do you play?" he asked the clearing.

As is too often the case when a man asks a question of the universe, the response was silence . . . the same eerie silence devoid of birds or the rustling of leaves that Margaret had commented on the day before and he'd so easily fobbed off.

And then he heard a sound. A man was calling his name. It was Rowlly. "Laird Macnachtan? Heath? Can you hear me? Tell me you made it safe, man. We've been worrying all night." He didn't sound as if he was that far away.

Heath's immediate thought was of Margaret. He had to return to her, to protect her from Rowlly and whoever was with him before they discovered her in less discreet circumstances.

Heath took off as if the hounds of hell were giving chase. He stumbled over rocks and continued on, ignoring the pain in his feet. He pushed aside branches and thorns that reached to hold him back.

Within minutes, he reached the ruins and was relieved to see that Rowlly and his party were not there, only then did he take a moment to catch his breath before charging down the edge of the knoll to the fireplace where he'd left Margaret sleeping — and came to an abrupt halt.

The fire still burned in the old hearth but there was no sign of Margaret Chattan.

At that moment, he heard Rowlly behind him, "Here you are. Could you not hear me hollering my lungs out?"

Heath was suddenly uncertain, the disappearing cat making him wonder about everything, including Margaret and what had happened between them. He turned to find Rowlly standing on the knoll with John Gibson. "I thought I'd meet you here," he murmured.

"And *I* thought you'd be freezing cold and anxious to leave this place," Rowlly answered. "I'd forgotten about the old hearth. Smart of you to use it. A pity Lady Margaret didn't find you."

"Aye," Gibson echoed, "she's lucky to be alive. So are you. I didn't believe you could swim that current."

"You found Lady Margaret?" Heath asked.

"She found us," Rowlly answered. "She came running down to the shore, looking just as disheveled. I can't believe the two of you were on the same island and couldn't find each other."

Had Margaret told them that?

"Yes, well, the storm forced each of us to seek shelter where we could," Heath answered. Something hard was building inside of him. He told himself that, of course, Margaret would want to make it seem as if they had spent the night apart instead of rogering each other for everything they were worth. "Did she say where she was?"

"She said she found a clearing surrounded by firs that kept the storm at bay." Rowlly shook his head. "She tried to describe where it was, but I don't remember such a place. Do you?"

Heath shook his head. "Is she at the boat now?"

"Aye, waiting for us," Rowlly said. "Ah, yes, and your sisters are here. We made them wait at Gibson's house. Worried ill they are. Even Dara came."

"Then let's go. My feet are cold," Heath said, speaking the truth, but his words made Rowlly and Gibson laugh. Rowlly clapped an arm around Heath's shoulder and told him about how they had tried to return to the island last night, but the storm kept blowing them back.

"I've never seen the loch like that before," Gibson said.

"Would you call it highly unusual?" Heath asked, wanting to know if the fisherman thought otherwise.

"*Och,* well, who is to say? Mother Nature and God always hold surprises."

"I hope not to experience that surprise again," Heath answered, and they again laughed. He pretended to laugh as well but his mind was on Margaret.

"Did she say what caused her to jump out of the boat?" Heath asked, curious as to what information Margaret might have shared.

"Didn't ask," Rowlly answered. "All I know is she thought she saw a cat and then dived in. Who understands the gentry? Especially the English ones. They say they are all half mad."

They came out of the woods to where Gibson's boat was docked on the shore. "We came over in the large one in case another storm brewed sudden-like," the fisherman explained.

Heath only half attended. His attention was on Margaret. She sat at the aft of the boat, her red cloak around her. She appeared to be huddled against the cold, but he knew better. She was ignoring him and didn't even bother to look up as he approached.

She wasn't alone. Rowlly had brought a few of the stable lads, and he hailed them now.

Margaret didn't look up. There was no smile for him, no acknowledgment of what had transpired between them.

Heath wanted to believe that perhaps she was being wise, that it was prudent to not offer anyone a clue to what they'd spent the night doing.

But he knew differently.

She had shut him out, and he wanted to know why.

CHAPTER THIRTEEN

Margaret focused on keeping herself warm and on examining the way the boards of the boat were fitted together. She'd not considered boat construction before. With Heath Macnachtan climbing into the boat and pretending not to glare at her, now was a good time to focus absolutely on anything but him.

Once again, her passionate nature had brought her trouble.

She'd believed that after Mark's betrayal she would have had a better head on her shoulders. And she had. *For years* she had.

Then last night, she'd tossed all common sense aside. She'd compromised herself, her own vows that she'd made, her own determined will. He had only to touch her for her to tumble into his arms like a randy milkmaid.

And she'd liked it. Dear sweet Lord, she had liked it very much.

With Mark, there had been an excitement about having a secret love . . . but at the time, she'd been desperate to have someone, *anyone* love her.

The first time he'd kissed her, she'd been shocked, but she'd wanted more. In truth, when he had taken her virginity, it had surprised her. It was all over almost before it had begun, and all she'd remembered was that it had been messy and rather silly. She'd never felt with him what she did in Heath Macnachtan's arms.

She'd given herself completely to Heath and he had used her well.

Perhaps the difference was one of age? Mark had been only a few years older than her fifteen-year-old self.

Or perhaps the difference was that her feelings for the laird of the Macnachtan were stronger and far more compelling. She seemed aware of his every movement, his every gesture. She had a sense of being able to understand what he thought and felt.

Margaret also admired him. She'd not met another man, other than her brother Neal, who commanded her respect. Heath also had a bit of Harry's daring in him, and certainly that intrigued her.

She knew Heath was confused by her leaving the ruins without him. She could almost hear the questions in his mind, questions that she would not answer.

What had happened last night must not be repeated. She was certain of that. It had been too overwhelming. All-consuming. Even now she wanted to climb the distance of the boat and wrap her arms around him. She must exercise more control.

It also didn't help matters that the men in the boat might pay lip service to the idea that she and Heath had spent the night apart, but they didn't believe it. She could tell in the sidelong looks sent her direction and the smug smiles they attempted to hide. They were men, and men always jumped to conclusions.

Now the boat had no trouble gliding across the calm, gray lake. It hit the shore with a bump. The lads jumped out and pulled the boat onto dry land where Laren, Anice and Lady Macnachtan waited.

Heath stood with his back to Margaret, but she knew he was planning to help her out of the boat. He nodded for Rowlly and Gibson to go ahead of him. His sisters were already asking him questions.

Margaret barely heard what they were saying. Instead, she braced herself, not yet ready to be close to him.

He held out a hand. "My lady." There was

266

a distance in his voice. He was angry with her silence. Good. She wanted him angry.

She stood. She could ignore the hand he offered, but then that would raise more questions and she wanted matters between them as simple as possible. They'd already complicated them enough last night. She could let him help her. All she had to do was detach her thoughts from her actions. Margaret had a lifetime of practice at that.

She placed her bare hand in his. His fingers, long, competent, callused, closed over hers, and she wanted to melt into his arms. She wanted to tear off his clothes and press herself against his warm skin.

But she didn't show it. She knew how to set her expression just the right way so that she appeared pleasant and disinterested.

"We are so relieved you are safe," Laren's voice said in greeting, words echoed by the others. They had thought to pack warm clothes. Mrs. Gibson let Margaret and then Heath use the cottage to change.

And then they were on their way back to Marybone.

Laren and Anice seemed determined to maintain a good-natured chatter but Margaret knew they sensed the tension between her and Heath.

They had other questions as well. While

she was changing, she'd overheard someone mention her claim of seeing a cat before she'd jumped into the water. She was certain everyone doubted her sanity.

She noticed that Heath didn't have much to say. Nor did he speak of finding the graves. She kept the information to herself as well. In fact, she didn't know what she could do with the knowledge of the two gravestones. She didn't understand why Owl had led her to them.

Lady Macnachtan brought her horse up beside Margaret's. "Are you all right?" she asked in a low voice full of concern.

"I'm fine," Margaret answered, trying to put some emotion in her tone to sound convincing.

"That was quite an ordeal."

"Yes, it was," Margaret could agree.

"What I fear is that you were taken advantage of?" She made her suggestion sound like a question.

Heat rushed to Margaret's cheeks. She dared not speak, afraid of what she would reveal to this kind woman.

"You needn't worry about gossip or rumors. We protect our own and our friends," Lady Macnachtan assured her.

"Thank you," Margaret said with meaning. It was good to have an ally.

Lady Macnachtan lowered her voice even more. "In truth, I'm embarrassed. I fear you have been manipulated into this position."

Margaret frowned. "What do you mean?"

Lady Macnachtan looked to the others. Anice and Rowlly were arguing with Laren as their referee. Heath rode ahead of everyone, his back ramrod straight.

She leaned toward Margaret. "Of course, you know their purpose is for you to marry Heath. That's all the girls can talk about. The family is in deep debt. They saw your arrival here as a sign of Providence. Now that you have been alone overnight with Heath, Anice and Laren have been planning your wedding."

Margaret hadn't noticed such scheming from the Macnachtan sisters. Instead, her instincts warned her that if there was any scheming happening, it was from Heath's sister-in-marriage, and she didn't understand why. She could imagine no motive other than jealousy. "Laird Macnachtan did not arrange to have me alone on the island overnight with him. It was a complete accident of fate. I can assure you of that."

"Then it was very lucky happenstance," Lady Macnachtan said. "And, please, you must call me Dara if we are to be sisters by marriage. No formalities around family."

"No one has spoken of marriage," Margaret returned.

"Not yet. They will. Although," Dara continued, her tone changing thoughtfully, "I wouldn't hold you to blame if you resisted these mercenary plans of theirs. It must be uncomfortable to have everyone consider marrying you only for your money. It would make me feel like a piece of property to be bought and sold in such a manner."

This woman owed everything she was to the Macnachtans. Perhaps *she* wanted Heath and considered Margaret a threat?

"It's my lot in life," Margaret commented. "I'm accustomed to marriage schemes."

"Ah, yes, as an heiress." Dara considered the matter a moment and then said, "But know I can be your ally. Turn to me if you find yourself in trouble with their plans, I shall help you."

"And why would you do that?"

"Perhaps I understand, one woman to another, how it feels to be powerless over our fates. It isn't right. There should be more justice."

Margaret now saw Dara in a new light. The woman had experienced few choices in her life, and, of course, she would assume that it would be the same for Margaret.

"Thank you, Dara. That is considerate of

you." Margaret wasn't certain she meant those words.

"I'm not being considerate. According to Rowlly, you are most fortunate to be alive," she answered. "We have some responsibility for that. If you do decide to return to London, I shall help you make your escape. Your brother is quite ill, is he not? I would think you would want to be with him."

She did. Dara knew what argument to use.

"And I would hate to see you forced to do anything against your will," Dara said. "We, women, are honest in our emotions. Men can be expedient."

Dara's suppositions found their mark.

For all her poise, deep inside Margaret was a place that was very vulnerable. Perhaps it came from an excess of pride, as many had suggested.

Or perhaps it was because she was *already* in love with the laird of the Macnachtan.

In love. Margaret immediately rejected the notion. She had always sworn she didn't understand what the words meant. Her parents *hadn't* been in love. Neal and Harry *were* both "in love" and she thought they were fools. Love would cost them their lives.

And yet, Heath Macnachtan was not like any other man of her acquaintance.

But what if, like most men who had

wooed and courted her, he did see her only as a commodity? What if he had made love — *there was that word again!* — to her for no other reason than what Dara suggested, that he wanted to trap an heiress in marriage?

What if, like Mark, he was not the man she thought he was?

If that was true, her first instinct *should* be to run, to take Dara up on her offer of helping her return to London. But there was more at stake now than just her pride. She'd come to Loch Awe to save her brothers. She couldn't leave until it had all played out. Owl's presence was a sign there was more to come.

Besides, she had too much sense to fall in love with anyone, let alone the Laird of the Macnachtan.

"I appreciate your offer, but I should wait for Rowan to improve," Margaret said.

"Such loyalty to a servant is to be commended," Dara answered. "Although you needn't worry. We'd see to his welfare until you can make arrangements. You could leave on the morrow."

"Are you planning on leaving, Lady Margaret?" Anice's voice said. She'd caught the tail end of the conversation and now circled her horse around to join them.

Dara gave her a smile that didn't reach her eyes. "She plans on leaving eventually. I was explaining that she didn't have to make her plans in advance. We are happy to help."

"Yes," Anice agreed, readily accepting Dara's explanation. "Of course, we would help."

Heath heard what they were saying. Anice's voice always carried. His back stiffened but he didn't turn around. He seemed to have decided that since she was determined to ignore him, he would ignore her.

Margaret didn't know how she felt about that.

However, he did set his horse off at a trot, and all the others started trotting with him. It was an effective way to end all discussion and to keep her mind on her riding.

Within the half hour, they reached Marybone.

Heath reined in his horse in front of the house. "Rowlly, see to Admiral."

"Aye, Heath."

Heath jumped down, threw the reins toward Rowlly, and started to help the women dismount, beginning with Dara.

Margaret didn't wait for him but dismounted herself. Her intent was to seek the solace of her room. She needed to think clearly and she realized she couldn't do so with Heath around.

As she started up the front step, he called out. "Lady Margaret," he said, "I need a word with you."

"Perhaps later," she replied, already moving into the house.

"No, *now,*" he answered in a tone that brooked no disobedience. "Laren, Lady Margaret and I would appreciate baths. It was a long night. Will you see that Cook heats water, and have the stable lads carry Lady Margaret's bathwater upstairs for her?"

"Of course," Laren answered.

Margaret had not obeyed his command to stop. She moved toward the stairs. If she didn't look back, if she ignored him, he would be forced to leave her alone.

She was wrong.

Just as she climbed the third step, strong hands took hold of her waist. Before she knew what she was about, she found herself physically deposited over Heath's shoulder.

She didn't know who was more surprised, she or Laren, Anice, Dara and anyone else a witness to this indignity.

Margaret grabbed hold of his jacket, thinking to pull herself off his shoulder. He hefted the shoulder, repositioning her, and marched down the hall. Before she could think to do anything, he walked into the library, kicked the door shut and set her on her feet.

In the time it took her to regain her balance, his arms came around her and he kissed her.

This kiss was an order, a demand, an insistence. She kissed back, her lips hard to let him know her resistance, her own independence . . . and then softening in her desire.

Yes, even though she was furious at him, she still enjoyed kissing him.

Their kiss came to an end when they were both mellow enough to think.

"One moment," he whispered, and turned back to the door. He opened it to reveal Laren and Anice eavesdropping. They appeared scandalized to be caught and quickly hurried off. He shut the door. "Sisters," he said with a shake of his head before leaning back against the door and considering her.

Margaret raised a hand to her kiss-swollen lips. She liked the feeling of them.

"Why didn't you wait for me back in Innis Craggah before you joined the others?" he asked.

She shifted her weight. "I thought you were gone."

"No you didn't," he said, reading her correctly. "Why didn't you want to wait for me, Maggie?"

She moved toward the desk, placing it between them.

"Why did you leave?" he pressed.

"Because I didn't want you to think you owed me anything." She held her head high. It took some effort.

"You know we must talk about last night," he said.

"No, we don't. There is nothing to discuss." She spoke firmly, but perhaps too quickly. Here was what Dara had predicted and she didn't want to think that he did not have strong feelings for her beyond lust. "I know what you are going to say. You are going to offer marriage. You are an honorable man. You feel duty-bound to make an honorable offer. You may do so. Know that I will reject it."

"What?" he said, as if he hadn't heard her correctly.

"I will reject it," she assured him. "I know what you must do and you should know I don't consider you accountable for what happened between us last night."

"You have churned everything over in that mind of yours, haven't you?" he said.

"I just know what is coming and I don't want you to say the words. I don't want to embarrass you by refusing you."

He sat on the end of the desk, his expression one of confused disbelief. "Maggie, what are you talking about?"

"You," she said. "I'm explaining to *you* that you don't need to offer to marry me. I will not accept your proposal."

"Well, that is comforting," he replied. "Are you also going to share with me *why* you will refuse this offer I have not made yet?"

She had expected him to be angry. Instead, he sounded more bemused.

And then she realized she really had no reason to withhold the truth. Heath would not betray her trust as others would. If anything, he probably knew her secret.

"I can't accept your offer," she said, a tightness forming in her chest. She kept her chin up. "Because you have not compromised me in any form. I am *not* a virgin."

There it was. The truth.

She discovered it a bit freeing to confess aloud her shame and she braced herself for his censure.

Instead, he answered, "I'm not, either."

Margaret frowned. Perhaps he didn't understand?

"No one expects you to be pure," she said. "You are male."

"Oh," he said as if with sudden understanding. "You were saying that to make me jealous —"

"*I was not.* Why would saying something like that make you jealous?"

"Well, because I like you," he replied, as if it should be obvious. "But if you didn't say it to make me jealous, perhaps then you were saying it so that I didn't feel alone. I appreciate that," he announced, coming to his feet as if she'd done something clever. "I was feeling as if I was surrounded by virgins. It is difficult being the only one who is not one. Then again, Dara is not a virgin," he continued, as if weighing the merits of the matter, "that is, if my brother did his duty. And I certainly hope my sisters are because that is what brothers *should* think, no?"

His cavalier attitude was not what she had expected. "Are you mocking me?"

"Yes, I am," he said.

"I don't like that."

"I didn't believe you would," he answered. His manner grew serious. "However, perhaps it is about time someone took you off your high horse. You aren't the only one involved in what happened between us last night."

But Margaret's temper, the one she tried carefully to control, took off. "I'll have you know, sir, that I feared this day when I

278

would feel the need to admit my terrible secret. In my mind, the receiver of such news would castigate me before shunning my presence. I didn't imagine he would think this a *jest.*"

"Jest? Yes!" he said with a touch of his own displeasure. "I didn't have you pegged as someone who would walk off as if *I* meant nothing."

Her anger evaporated. "I didn't walk off."

"Yes, you did," he said. "When I returned for you, you were gone and your leaving didn't have anything to do with the boat arriving, did it? This was all some grand scheme in your mind where you were the tragic heroine and I was what? The actor in a small part who is of no importance? Or is this the way you react whenever anyone grows too close to you? We were very close last night, Maggie. And it *was* important. It *was* meaningful."

For second, Margaret was tempted to storm out of the room — but she didn't . . . because he was right.

What happened between them had been important, but couldn't he understand what she was trying to explain? And why it should be important to him, the most amazing man she'd ever met?

"You don't recognize what I am saying to

you," she said. "In London, there are those who, if they ever found out what I'd done, would ruin me. Society has long memories and unforgiving natures. I've trusted you with information I've not told another soul. But also," she continued, "*you* need to know that I'm not special. I'm not important. You must not see me as someone I'm not."

Heath moved toward her until they stood almost toe to toe. "What I see is a woman who loves her brothers and her family honor enough to battle demons for them," he said. "I don't know the story of your deflowering, and I don't want to," he hurried to add. "I'm no saint, Maggie. I can be jealous, but I'm also not the king of France. Purity is not my first consideration for a wife. You see what my sons stand to inherit. Marybone is a sad thing right now but it certainly doesn't call for the sacrifice of a virgin. What I don't want is for you to act ashamed of what happened between us last night, because I'm not. I have no regrets."

He took a step closer to her. "Don't run from me, Maggie. Don't ever run from me."

Margaret had spent years carefully constructing walls around her heart. They started to crumble in the face of his honesty.

"I didn't run. I was helping you. Heath, you don't understand the burden of the curse. I'm the first female of my line. We don't know what will happen with me, with my children. They could carry the curse. Of course, you don't believe in the curse."

"I might surprise you," he said soberly. "This morning I woke to find a wee cat with folded-over ears staring at us."

"*You saw Owl?* Why didn't you tell me?"

"You weren't there when I returned, remember? And I did more than 'see' the cat. I touched her. I felt her fur. She wanted me to chase her."

"So that is where you went. Where did she take you?"

"Back to the graves. My intention was to capture her and bring her back to you so that you could see she was real and not a ghost. But when I reached to pick her up, my hands went right through her."

"That's not happened before," Margaret said. "I've always been able to hold her."

"Perhaps she doesn't like men?" Heath suggested.

"Or perhaps she isn't going to be with us much longer." Margaret walked a few steps past him, thinking furiously. "If she is the reincarnated soul of Rose Macnachtan, then it may be she must return to where she belongs."

"Why would you believe her to be Rose?"

he asked. "Could she not be Fenella?"

Margaret considered the matter a moment and then shook her head. "Fenella would not help us. You heard that man Swepston. Those who believe in the curse think the Chattans should remain afflicted until the end of time. But what if Rose is trying to help us?"

"Then you don't want her to disappear."

"Exactly."

He held up his hands and took a step away. "I can't believe I'm having this conversation."

"I can't believe you saw the cat," she said. "No one else has seen her save for Harry and . . ." She paused. "His wife first saw the cat. Before Harry did." She frowned at Heath. "Why do you think Owl has revealed herself to you?"

Before he could answer, there was knock on the door. "We are not to be disturbed," he barked.

Dara's voice said, "I must disturb you, Heath. Owen Campbell is here. He said it is urgent he speaks to you."

Heath's whole manner changed. Tension straightened his shoulders. His brows came together. "What the devil is he doing here?"

"Who is *he*?" Margaret asked.

"Someone I don't want to talk to," Heath

answered.

"And yet you must?"

"And yet I must," he agreed, his expression grim. He opened the door where Dara waited for him. "Where is he?"

"In the sitting room. Is something the matter, Heath?"

He didn't answer Dara but turned to Margaret. "We will finish this conversation. And by the by, you may be the first female in your line, but I'm the last male. Perhaps that means something." He took off with a purposeful step down the hall.

Dara peeked into the library. "What was that about?"

Margaret ignored Dara's question, asking instead, "Who is this Owen Campbell?"

"He's a relative of the Duke of Argyll," Dara said. "I know he's interested in purchasing Marybone."

Margaret looked around the cozy library. She liked this house. Yes, parts of the building and most of the furnishings were shabby, but it had good bones and a comfortable air. "Will Heath sell?"

"He may have no choice," Dara answered with a distracted air. "Excuse me, I must go and find out what I can." She left.

Margaret stood a moment, and then decided she might want to know more about why Owen Campbell was calling as well.

She waited a few beats, and then followed Dara down the hall. She found Dara with Laren and Anice huddled on the staircase, out of the line of sight of the sitting room but close enough to hear everything.

Margaret joined them.

CHAPTER FOURTEEN

Owen Campbell fancied himself of the Corinthian set. He was a handsome, lean man ten years Heath's elder. He wore his graying hair in the windswept style, a silly affectation where the hair was combed forward over the brow and ears as if a great wind blew it from behind. The style also hid Campbell's growing baldness.

Heath didn't trust a man who spent a goodly amount of time thinking about his hair. Yes, all the young bucks in London were vain but there came an age when a man put a comb through his hair in the morning and didn't think of it the rest of the day.

Campbell's hair wasn't his only pretension. He sported a spur on one highly polished boot just for show. Heath had noticed that single spur even in church. No true horsemen would ride around with *one* spur. He'd be riding in circles.

It stood without saying that Campbell's clothes were finely tailored and definitely from London. His greatcoat had no fewer than seven capes, and it must have taken a bevy of tailors to style his breeches just right so that the padding used to fill out Campbell's manly form would not be noticed.

The man had built his fortune with the East India Company. Heath had met a number of nabobs during his naval career and there wasn't one whose greed didn't turn his stomach.

Campbell stood by the fire and as Heath walked into the room, he swept back his elegant coat, placing one gloved hand on his hip as if posing for his portrait. Heath could even imagine the title, "Corinthian Visiting Lowly Country Laird." Campbell's hat was on small table by the door and Heath was determined to put it in his hand and direct him out onto the front step as quickly as possible.

He had a conversation to finish with Margaret, and she was far more entertaining and interesting than Campbell.

Campbell smiled his greeting while giving Heath's rough appearance a critical once-over. "Good of you to see me, Laird." Campbell didn't have a title, not even a lowly one like Heath's, but he would like one.

"You said you have business of an urgent nature?"

"I do." Campbell's voice was full of confidence. He walked over to the liquor table that held the decanter of whisky and glasses. He poured himself a healthy measure. "You should be a better host. Always offer your guest something to quench the thirst from the road."

Heath frowned. This was strange behavior from Campbell. Because he coveted Marybone, his manner was usually obsequious.

This boldness, while not new to Campbell's nature, was new to their dealings together.

"What have you done?" Heath asked quietly.

Campbell raised his eyebrows in a parody of surprise. "What makes you believe I've 'done' anything?"

Heath answered him with a bitter smile.

"Very well," Campbell said. He downed his whiskey, the gamesmanship leaving his manner. Holding the empty glass, he announced, "I own your paper."

"My paper?"

"Your debts. I've bought them up. I've been in the process of it for a long time.

There was one creditor who was loyal to your brother. Brodie Macnachtan inspired that in men."

He was right.

"Do you mean Angus Trotter?" Heath said.

"I do. He refused to sell your brother's note. Said he'd promised you that he'd give you the chance to pay it off."

"He did."

"Did you know he passed away several weeks ago? He was visiting his daughter on the Isle of Skye when he took ill. He was an old man and it wasn't unexpected. The family didn't have Trotter's reluctance to sell me your debts, and at a very good price, I might add."

Heath's temper was a boiling stream in his veins. It took all his control to not grab Campbell by his windswept hair and the collar of his tailored coat and toss him out the door. He willed himself to stay still. "Marybone is my birthright."

"Yes, well, your predecessors shouldn't have mortgaged it to the hilt. I gave you a fair opportunity to sell to me and keep your respect. Your solicitor urged you to consider my offer. So, now we do this the disagreeable way." He walked to the door and picked up his hat. "You and I know you can't pay your debts. Here is my new offer — you will either pay off your debts or vacate these premises within the week. I don't like you, Macnachtan. You are an arrogant sod. I would be happy to start proceedings to send you to debtors' prison." He smiled, pleased with himself. "I can see you are upset with me. I don't blame you. You'd like to throttle me. String me up. But you can't. You don't dare. You have that much sense. If it were just you, well, then you'd do what you wish. But you have your sisters, and their fates are in your hands."

He was right, damn his soul.

Campbell started toward the door. "I expect your decision by the morrow. You know where to reach me —"

Margaret stepped into the doorway, startling both men with her sudden appearance. She had to have been listening to be this close to block Campbell's path. Her expression was one of an avenging angel.

Campbell took a step back. His gaze rolled over her, and Heath could see he was impressed. "Lady Margaret Chattan?" His whole manner changed. He became the courtly gallant as he made a bow. "I'd heard you were in the neighborhood. What a pleasure it is to meet you. Let me introduce myself, I am Owen Campbell —"

"I know who you are and I don't like you," Margaret announced. "Furthermore, you may have your answer about Marybone's debts. We shall pay them off. Immediately. Please provide a complete accounting to Sir James Smiley, Esquire of London and submit them for payment. And then don't ever show up here again with your threats. Marybone is staying in Macnachtan hands."

If she had planted a facer on Campbell he could not appear more surprised. "But I thought the Chattan and the Macnachtan are enemies."

"Not any longer," Margaret informed him. "I have accepted Laird Macnachtan's offer of marriage."

Heath was stunned by Margaret's claim, but it was also a good moment. Campbell was receiving his comeuppance.

However, having Margaret rescue Macnachtan pride was not something that set well with Heath. He had been willing to protect her honor, but he didn't expect her to protect his.

Campbell looked back at him. Heath didn't speak. He was too angry and he didn't know if he was angrier with Campbell or Margaret.

"You have your answer," she said to Campbell, dismissing him with a queenly disdain. "Now leave."

Campbell glanced one more time at Heath and then muttered something about how they hadn't heard the last of this as he slapped his expensive hat on his head. He left the house.

Margaret was immediately surrounded by Laren and Anice. Their appearance was so quick they must have been on the stairs eavesdropping. Dara entered the room with them as well.

Laren and Anice threw their arms around her. "Thank you," Laren said. "Thank you so much."

"This is the best news," Anice said. "I like you so much and now we shall be sisters through marriage. This is wonderful."

"Congratulations," Dara said, the felicitation sounding almost cold in its reserve. She'd taken a moment to see Campbell out the door.

Laren looked over at him. "Why didn't you tell us, Heath?" she asked.

"It was a sudden decision," he managed to say through tight jaws. "Will you excuse us? I need a moment with my future *wife*. And don't let me catch you listening on the stairs."

Laren and Anice exchanged a look, and for a second, he anticipated them making him truly angry by refusing his order. *Damn women. They were impossible to control. They never followed a direct order.*

Dara came to his rescue by placing a hand on each of his sister's shoulders. "Come," she said. "Lady Margaret and Heath have much to discuss."

She whisked them down the hall.

Margaret eyed Heath warily. "You are not happy with me."

"That is an understatement," he answered. He stood a moment and then picked up a glass from the liquor table and threw it into the fire, where it smashed into pieces. There had been a bit of whisky in the glass and the flames hissed.

Margaret was not accustomed to anyone's anger but her own. She straightened her back. "What have I done to make you furious?"

"I don't know," he said with a false note of mild amusement. "I believe you announced we are marrying. Tell me, was I going to have any say in this?"

For a second, Margaret's cheeks burned. This was awkward. "We had not completely finished our conversation in the library but were you not going to suggest we marry?"

"Ah, yes, the offer you refused before I

could make it."

"You make me sound bulling," she said, reaching for her pride as a shield. "I have just agreed to pay all your debts. You should be pleased."

"I pay my own debts," he said, his brogue coming out. "I don't need you or anyone else to pay them."

"Because you were doing so well on your own," she couldn't resist pointing out, and that was not the wisest thing to say. But no one, absolutely *no one* had ever questioned her actions. She was Margaret Chattan. She did as she pleased.

A fierce light came to Heath's eyes. "What you don't realize, my lady, is that the rest of us have just as much right to our pride and our choice of action as you do. Furthermore, I seem to remember you informing me that marriage was not in order. What made you change your mind? *Pity?*"

Too late, Margaret had a clarity of vision that allowed her to see how he had interpreted her actions. "No," she said, taking a step toward him. "I — I overheard —"

"You were prying," he corrected. "Let us be clear about that. My interview with Campbell was none of your business."

"*It is* if you consider that I have come to think highly of all of you," she responded in her defense. "And your sisters were on the stairs. I merely joined them," she threw out, a weak excuse for poor manners if ever there was one.

"Think highly of us?" he said. He snorted his thoughts on that. "Doing what you did, and the way you did it, tells me you don't think about any of us at all. We are a means to an end."

Margaret wanted to stamp her feet with frustration. "Owen Campbell was going to take Marybone away from you. I have the money. It's doing nothing but sitting in the funds drawing two percent."

"And now I am in debt to *you,*" he snapped.

Margaret shook her head. "No, that is not it at all. You needed help and so I offered it."

"You didn't offer it, Maggie. You rammed it down my throat." He started to walk past her but then he stopped, turned and faced her. "And the worst part is, there is nothing I can do about it. It's done."

"You don't need to marry me, if that is what concerns you."

"How little you know men," he responded. "Of course, I *must* marry you." He practically spit the words out.

"Well, you can't," she said, her pride rising. "I don't want to marry you. And I don't care about the money. I have plenty of money. I have so much money, I can't stand it." And then she walked out of the room, determined to be the first to leave. Men didn't reject her. She rejected them.

"Margaret, come back here," he ordered.

She ignored him. She climbed the stairs two at a time and raced to the haven of her room. She slammed the door behind her. Her whole body was shaking.

How dare he speak to her in that manner. She had been trying to help and he made her feel as if she had pushed her way into the conversation . . . and into his life.

"He would have lost the house," she said to her reflection in the looking glass.

And she'd meant what she'd said about letting him have the money. Money meant nothing to her, while it obviously meant *everything* to him.

The bath he had ordered had been prepared for her. The tub was an old wooden one. The servants had set it in front of the hearth although there was no fire in it. That was done *to conserve money.* She would be expected to light the peat — used instead of wood *because there was no money* — which she should have no problem doing if she hadn't started crying.

Margaret knelt in front of the cold hearth, the flint box in one hand, and let the tears fall.

She didn't understand what had come over her. She'd never in her life cried as much as she had in Scotland.

Then again, she'd never allowed herself the emotional freedom she'd discovered here.

In England, her life was controlled. No one argued with her or mistook her best intentions or accused her of overstepping boundaries. She had servants who jumped to her bidding.

No one expected *anything* of her or told her nay — until Heath Macnachtan. He had no difficulty putting her in her place. No wonder she didn't like him. He was unreasonable.

And she was still going to pay his debts — for no other reason than she *did* want him beholden to her because she *knew* how angry that would make him.

A soft knock sounded at the door. The girl Cora's excited voice said, "Lady Margaret, your servant has awakened. You said you wanted to know when that happened."

Rowan. Guilt flooded through Margaret. She'd been so enmeshed in Heath Mac-

nachtan she'd almost forgotten her brave servant.

She wiped her face with her hands. "Yes, I did." She rose from the floor and crossed the room to the door. Cora waited outside. "When did he wake?"

"Just a few moments ago. His eyes opened and he blinked." She opened her eyes wide and blinked to demonstrate.

"I'll go to him right now," Margaret said, suddenly anxious to connect with someone from her other life. Rowan would help her make sense of all this. He was her connection to her brothers, who always knew what to do. They were stronger and braver than she.

She dashed up the stairs, gave a knock at the door and entered Rowan's room without waiting for permission.

The valet looked to her. Tears filled his eyes. His dusky skin had a tinge of ash to it and deep circles underlined his eyes. His face was still swollen from bruises.

"It is all right," Margaret said, coming to his bedside and pulling the chair Cora had been sitting in closer. "There was a terrible accident, but you are going to be all right." She tried to smile encouragement. It was difficult. "You've broken many bones and so sleeping has been a blessing for you,

Rowan. No, don't try to move. If it is possible, please, keep still."

"Where are we?" Rowan asked. His voice sounded as scratchy and hoarse as hers had right after the accident.

"At Marybone, the family estate of Laird Macnachtan. Do you remember the accident?"

Rowan slowly nodded.

"We are the only two to survive." She touched the fingertips of his bandaged hands. "I don't know if we are going to win, Rowan," she confided. "There is a force here, the same one that tried to stop us on the road to Loch Awe. Do you remember?"

"The wind."

"Yes, the wind . . . but it wasn't really an act of nature, was it?"

"No."

Margaret nodded her agreement. "You are not in danger," she said, wanting to give him some reassurance. "But I don't know what is afoot, and I fear, Rowan, that any opportunity we had at defeating Fenella is past. She's too strong. I feel like a child in a dark room. I'm afraid to move. I'm afraid to do anything because I sense she is watching."

He moved his fingers, a motion for her to lean forward. When she did, he said, "Why

298

did I wake?"

The question surprised her. "What do you mean?"

"Why did I wake now? What has happened?"

"I assume your body decided it was time," she said.

He shook his head, his expression tired. "There is no such thing as chance," he murmured. "Always a reason."

This was more of his unorthodox beliefs. However, Harry always listened to him, and perhaps Margaret should as well. "If it isn't chance, then could it be that Fenella wants you awake? Owl saved my life," she whispered. "Remember the cat only I could see? I was not going to live after the accident and Owl came to me and performed some sort of protective magic. I didn't even have a scrape on my skin."

His eyes narrowed as he listened.

"Fenella's book is gone," she continued. "It was burned by this man called Swepston who came across the accident and stole it. He wants the curse to go on forever. Surprisingly, Laird Macnachtan does not agree. I had anticipated we would be enemies, but it is far different from that," she said, her mind suddenly filled with the images of the two of them making love. Of

299

their kisses. "He wishes us no ill will. Swepston did not like that fact and burned the book."

Rowan's frown deepened.

"I thought all was lost but then the laird took me to the island where Rose Macnachtan jumped to her death. There I saw Owl again, and she led me to two unmarked graves. They must be for Rose and Fenella, but, Rowan, beyond that, I know nothing else. Every direction I go has an ending without a solution. And I'm afraid time is running out. Laird Macnachtan sent a messenger to inform Lyon that I was safe. The messenger has not returned. I don't know if that means Neal is still alive or not."

"The messenger may not have reached Lord Lyon," Rowan suggested. "My lady, you are on the right trail. The cat is telling you that."

"By taking me to the graves?"

"If you see the cat, then your quest is still alive."

That made sense. "But Owl comes and goes. She does not stay with me." Margaret studied the weave of the bed sheet a moment before saying, "Laird Macnachtan saw Owl. When he woke this morning, Owl was watching him. He chased her and touched her but when he attempted to capture her, his hands went right through her body. And he says he doesn't believe in 'ghosties.' "

"What changed? What let him see the cat?"

They had made love.

It was so obvious Margaret was surprised she hadn't realized it before now.

She looked at Rowan, who waited patiently for an explanation. Harry trusted the valet, so she would as well. "We were together. For the night," she said. "On the island alone."

He nodded as if he had already concluded that. "Perhaps that was meant to be," he said.

Margaret leaned forward. "What? Am I to continue that behavior? Do you believe it seemly of me?"

"Are you afraid?"

"Of course not," she said, quickly.

Rowan drew a deep, heavy breath. "My lady, I do not know. However, there is a force here. Something beyond our understanding. In India, we have a different view about what happens between a man and a woman. If you were not titled or an heiress, would it matter so much? Follow the way you must go," he advised.

"And which way do I continue?" she asked, thinking about her recent words with Heath.

"You will know."

That was no answer, but Rowan's eyes were starting to droop with exhaustion. "Here, I have been selfish," she admitted. "You must rest." She started to plump the feather pillow around his head.

At that moment, there was a knock on the door and Laren entered with a tray of food. "How is he?" she asked Margaret.

"Healing," Margaret answered. She gave Rowan's fingers a small squeeze. "This is Miss Macnachtan, one of the laird's two sisters. They have been very kind to us." She meant those words. "Rest now. We shall talk more later."

"I hope he doesn't go to sleep immediately," Laren said. "I carried this tray up all those stairs for him. It's some of Cook's good broth. It will lift your spirits."

"Thank you," Margaret said for both of them. She started to leave, but then stopped. Rowan was right. She needed to see this through. Perhaps she had not been wise walking away from Heath. "Do you know where your brother is?"

A worried look came to Laren's eye. "He left."

"Left?" Margaret repeated in surprise.

"Yes, he left the house. I saw Rowlly a moment ago. He said Heath saddled Admiral and took off in a tear."

His leaving annoyed Margaret in a way that it shouldn't have. What should she care what Heath did or where he went? He'd made it clear he wanted everything on his own terms. Apparently if he wasn't satisfied, he rode off.

Then again, she'd stormed away from him.

But she hadn't expected him to leave the physical boundaries of the house. Indeed, Margaret realized she'd assumed that eventually they would continue their "discussion."

"Is there anything wrong?" Laren asked, concern in her voice.

There were many things wrong but Margaret didn't know if she understood exactly what they were. "Everything is fine," she murmured, and forced a smile at Rowan. "Please, rest."

He gave a weak nod and she left to return to her bedroom. It was close to the dinner hour. This had been an event-filled day.

Cold bathwater still waited for her . . . as did the cold hearth.

And Heath had gone off to who knew where without a word to her.

And Margaret felt miserable.

She told herself to stop being foolish. She forced herself to concentrate on building a fire. The flint didn't spark immediately so it was an effective distraction.

An even stronger distraction was the bath she took. It had taken great effort for Tully to bring the water to her room. She would not waste the effort. The temperature of the water was not unbearable but she made quick business of her bath. She then dressed and went down to dinner.

Heath did not join them. He had not come back from his ride.

Laren and Anice pretended that all was fine, although they had to have heard the arguing in the sitting room. Dara didn't pretend, but offered Margaret consoling looks that annoyed her greatly.

After dinner, Dara managed a private moment with Margaret by following her upstairs when she went to her room. At the top of the stairs, she stopped Margaret and said, "You seem so unhappy. Do you wish to talk about it?"

For a second, Margaret was tempted. Then again, the habit of aloneness was strong within her. She wasn't accustomed to sharing her doubts and fears. That was not what a Chattan did.

"I'm fine," Margaret said. "I just don't like arguments."

"You will have plenty with Heath," Dara

assured her, shifting the candle for the two of them she held in her hand. "He has too much of the naval officer in him. You will do as he says or he'll keelhaul you."

Margaret rolled her eyes and Dara smiled before turning serious. "He did ask you to marry him, didn't he?"

The temptation was strong to share the truth. Suddenly, Margaret didn't want to have this conversation, but she would not lie. "We haven't discussed anything about marriage," she demurred, and that was true, in a way. "I wonder where he spent this evening."

"Probably at the Goldeneye, drinking. He does that more than he should." Dara smiled sadly. "I knew he was going to pounce on you. I warned you."

"You did."

"*You* don't look happy. And the way he treated you this afternoon, that was humiliating. He acts as if he doesn't know how important you are."

Margaret stood with her hand on her door handle and decided that now might be a good moment for plain speaking. "You are working very hard at creating a division between myself and Laird Macnachtan. I'm beginning to wonder why."

Dara took a step back with a dismissive

305

gesture. "I told you earlier. I feel you are being rushed into something that I believe you will regret."

"Did you regret your marriage?" Margaret asked. She'd learned that often people accused others of their own thoughts and sins.

"Of course, I didn't. Brodie was a remarkable man. A kind man. I don't know where I would be if he had not come to my rescue."

"Everyone speaks highly of him. I wish I'd known him." Margaret meant those words.

Footsteps sounded on the stairs and they saw the glow of candlelight. Laren and Anice joined them at the top of the stairs.

"We'd wondered where you had gone off to," Anice said in her usual cheery manner.

"I'm surprised you are still awake," Laren said to Margaret. "I'd have been to bed an hour ago."

"I need to check on Rowan," Margaret said.

"Here, take a candle," Anice offered, and excused herself. Laren and Dara also murmured good nights and went to their rooms. Apparently Dara did not want to share her doubts in front of her sisters-in-law.

Rowan was asleep. His breathing was uncomplicated. He would heal. Margaret sat a long moment in the chair by his bedside, thinking about their earlier conversation and his words to her . . . and she could find no pattern or conceive of any new progress in the events of the last few days.

"I will have faith," she told him. "I will not give up." With those words, she rose from the chair and left the room.

Downstairs, all was quiet. The hall was dark save for her candle. She entered her room and shut the door. At some point in the evening, Tully had fetched her bathwater from her room. She went over to the fire and added fuel to revive the flames. She crossed to the bed and set her candle on the table beside it.

And she felt alone.

She wandered over to the window that overlooked the stables. All was dark save for the light of a full silvery moon.

Margaret started to turn away when she heard the sound of horse's hooves. She leaned close to the window, waiting, and was rewarded with the sight of Heath's silhouette on Admiral in the stable yard. He had returned.

For a second, she stood in indecision. Should she hurry into her nightclothes and ignore him the way he'd ignored her by leaving?

Or should she force a confrontation?

There were things they had to say to each other, and she didn't want them said with an audience. The women in this house were very good at ferreting out information.

Movement on the path caught her eye, the shadow of a man walking from the stable to the house. *He was coming.*

She started to undress, determined to climb into her bed and not give him another thought.

But then she sensed, rather than heard, him enter the house. He would be coming up the stairs.

After what had happened between them last night, why should she be shy about going to his room? There would be privacy there. Everyone else was asleep. They could talk. She could explain that she wanted him to have the money and he could grumble all he wanted.

Time seemed to stand still. She listened, anxious to hear a sound from him.

She heard nothing . . . but he had to be upstairs. He must be. Once he had entered the house, it would not take him too long to climb the stairs.

But what if he'd stayed downstairs? What

if he had decided to enjoy a bit of whiskey?

Then she would speak to him downstairs, she decided. That was a better plan anyway.

With firm resolution, she walked over to the door, opened it, and —

Heath stood there.

He still wore his coat although he was hatless. His hair was mussed, as if he'd combed it with his fingers. He didn't smell of whisky but of the night air and the winter wind.

Her heart filled with joy at seeing him.

His eyes were very sober. "I don't need charity."

"I know," she whispered.

"But I think," he said, sounding hesitant, "I believe I might need you."

Her response was to throw her arms around his neck.

CHAPTER FIFTEEN

Heath had been run to ground.

And he knew it.

He wasn't a man who liked being beholden to anyone. He'd hated Campbell for forcing him to be bankrupt . . . and he'd not been happy when Margaret had jumped into the fray and saved the day. Her solution had not been right in his mind. It had tweaked his pride. They would say the only way he kept Marybone was by marrying a wealthy woman.

Marriage. He'd never thought of marrying anyone before. In the navy he'd been too footloose to want to settle in one place. But now there was only Marybone.

And there was only one woman of the many he'd been with for whom he'd sacrifice all — and that was Margaret.

Headstrong, impossible to tame, infuriatingly beautiful Margaret.

After he'd left the house, he'd ridden

Admiral like a madman for a good ten miles. Then he'd gone to the Goldeneye. Augie Campbell had been there and anxious for a second go but Heath wasn't in the mood. His temper was waning and in its place was a rare moment of self-knowledge.

Yes, he hated that he couldn't pay his own bills, even though he had done nothing to create the debt. But he'd be a fool to refuse Margaret's generous offer. Furthermore, even if she hadn't had money, he wanted her. He liked having her at his side. And he'd meant what he'd said when he told her he admired her. In fact, that was an understatement: He loved her.

The truth of that feeling went all the way to his soul.

But could she love him? Could she ever respect a man who needed her money? He didn't know, but he understood that he didn't want to lose the bond that the night before had created between them.

And now she was kissing him. Welcoming him with a willingness that made him hope that she saw him as a man. A man who was an imperfect creature but who wanted to offer to her his best. A man who would do anything to keep her safe.

He backed her into the room and pushed the door silently shut with his shoulder. He tasted salt in her tears. "What is this?" he said, breaking the kiss, his arms still around her. "What are you crying for, lass?"

"I never cry," she told him, almost angrily.

"My brave Maggie. Tears have nothing to do with being strong."

She leaned her head against his chest, her arms tightening their hold around him. "I'm so glad you returned. So very glad."

"As am I," he said, and he kissed her again.

Their kiss grew more heated. He lifted her into his arms and carried her to the bed, their lips not leaving each other. He laid her on the bed, practically falling on top of her, and they both laughed, their voices low and meant only for each other.

Margaret turned on her side toward him. He would never tire of looking at her, especially when she smiled. He liked the way her eyes took on a light of their own when she was happy. With him, she seemed younger, freer, and that pleased him.

He brushed her hair back with his hand. "I'm such an ugly mutton-headed man, all rough and callused. I shouldn't even touch you."

She placed her hand on his chest. "I like your strength and your courage. I like that you aren't afraid to take hold of your life and live it on your terms. I've learned much from you, Heath Macnachtan. In some ways, I feel as if I only started living once I met you."

"*After* you tried to put a bullet in me," he corrected, and she laughed.

Dear God, he loved her laughter. He loved all of her, even the stubborn bits of her.

Margaret leaned over and kissed his neck, burrowing her nose against his skin. He adored her. Worshipped her. Began undressing her.

"I know what you want," he told her. "And you are going to receive it."

Her response was to pull him closer and begin unbuttoning his breeches.

He liked this part of her best. His Maggie wasn't some retiring wallflower. She knew what she wanted, and she had chosen him. He was both proud and humbled by her choice, because he wanted her . . . in a way he'd never experienced with a woman before.

They grew serious about their work. There was no fear of the supernatural here other than the magic they were creating. They were a man and a woman who had just discovered what they meant to each other.

And when they were both gloriously naked, Heath rested his weight upon her.

She was soft where he was hard, and completely willing.

He raised his body above hers. The words "I love you" hovered on the tip of his tongue, but he could not speak them. He was not worthy of her. She belonged to a different world, but for right now she was his.

His, he repeated in his mind as he slowly slid into her.

She gasped her pleasure as her body stretched and accommodated him. Her eyes closed, her lashes dark against her cheeks. He liked this moment best. Feeling her, knowing he pleased her.

And then he began moving and all conscious thought left his mind.

They moved together, meeting each other halfway, satisfying each other as only two people who care deeply for each other could. Heath let his body say what his pride would not allow him to speak. She was his. No matter what happened beyond this night, *she was his.*

Maggie was a quick learner. Had she been possessed the night before? He couldn't tell. She knew where to kiss him, what to whisper, how to encourage him.

There was no other woman like her and there never would be. That was what he'd discovered in the hours of running from himself.

He was no fool. He knew how complicated matters could be between a man and a woman. He had no expectations from her. He lived completely in this moment, their bodies bathed gold in the firelight as they strove together toward that moment of completion, of perfection.

She whispered his name. He answered her with his lips. He tasted her, desired her, enjoyed her —

Her legs grasped his hips. He pushed deeper, relishing the tightness of her, the quickening. Her arms embraced him as if he were a lifeline.

And then he was lost.

Margaret overtook him with her passion. She was clinging to him, the strength of her release radiating from her until he could contain himself no more.

Heath lifted himself above her, the better to thrust, once, twice, *dear God, she was a marvel,* a third time, and he was lost again.

For a long moment, joined at the hips, they held each other, truly becoming one.

And then slowly, he collapsed upon her. They were both breathing heavily. He felt himself leave her and he immediately gathered her close.

"I will not let you go," he said. "I will not."

She snuggled into his arms, without answering, her body as languorous as a cat's.

He murmured, "And I prefer making love to you on a bed than on hard Scottish soil."

"It was far more comfortable," she agreed.

Heath kissed her forehead, her hair, her eyes, her nose. In this moment, there was nothing he couldn't do. Not with his woman by his side.

Maggie smiled her pleasure.

Cool air skimmed his skin. He reached for the coverlet to throw over their nakedness.

"You are no longer angry with me?" she asked.

Under the covers, Heath ran his hand over the curve of her hip. Her breasts were against his chest. "It is hard for me to even think when I have you in my arms like this."

"Then what happened last night was not . . ." She paused as if searching for a word.

"Lust?" he suggested. "A spell or a piece of pagan magic?" He kissed her. Here was his chance to declare himself. He could tell her that his feelings were stronger than mere need.

But what would she think?

How could he even trust the strength of his own feelings? They had not known each other a week.

And yet, he trusted his heart.

What he didn't know and couldn't know was what was in hers.

Here was a woman who had been pursued by men with more power and infinitely more fortune than he. Men who were handsomer and offered opportunities he could only dream of. He couldn't expect her to settle on him.

She touched the bandage on his arm. "Does this still hurt?"

He shook his head. When she looked with such empathy, he could almost believe she cared for him as deeply as he did for her.

Then again, no one had ever claimed that he could not be a fool. Just because he had tumbled head over heels in love did not mean she had.

And he'd best remember that. Or his eagerness would chase her off.

He sat up. She made a sound of disappointment. Her nipples, those delightful bits of femininity that could make a man crazy with desire, tightened with the cool air on her skin.

Heath resisted warming them with his mouth. He pulled the covers over her. "I must let you sleep," he said.

"I'm not ready for you to leave. Heath, we

have so much to discuss."

He wasn't in the mood for conversation. If he stayed here, he'd make love to her again, and again.

"Tomorrow," he promised. Tomorrow when they could both think clearly and be in control of themselves. "Here, let me close the curtains to warm the room. I'm surprised you left them open."

"I was watching for you," she said. She pulled the covers up over those luscious breasts and he almost whimpered. He pushed aside the implications of what it could mean that she'd watched for him. He didn't want to hope. He began closing the drape, when a flash of light by the stables caught his eye.

"Why can't we talk now — ?" she started but he held up a hand, warning her to silence.

The light was out of place. The stable lads were all abed — unless something was amiss. With one hand on the drape, he waited. "Someone is at the stables."

Ever quick thinking, Margaret blew out the candle. "Would someone be down there if an animal was ill?"

"Then the person would hang the lamp on a peg the better to work. But this light moved as if a signal —"

A door opened out in the hall.

Margaret had heard it as well. They both listened as almost silent footsteps moved toward the stairs.

Heath waited, and then crossed to the door, cracking it open slightly. He caught a hint of movement. A woman's skirt . . . naturally. The only people on this floor were he, his sisters, Dara and Maggie.

He closed the door and reached for his breeches. He began dressing.

"Couldn't it be one of the stable lads?" she whispered, pushing the heavy weight of her hair back from her face.

"Possibly, but why would someone here leave her bedroom because of it?"

"It could be coincidence."

"It could," he agreed, buttoning his breeches. "I'll find out one way or the other. But it doesn't make sense that someone from the house would be leaving at this hour of the night."

"Perhaps whoever it is wishes to go downstairs? Perhaps to the kitchen? Perhaps she can't sleep?"

"All possibilities." He sat on the edge of the bed and began pulling on his boots. He noticed that Margaret had started dressing. "You will stay here," he said.

"You might need me," she answered,

ignoring him and pulling her dress over her head.

"I need you *here,*" he reiterated. "Where I know you will be safe."

"I like to be prepared for anything," she replied, pulling the lacings of her dress. "If the person is from the house, who do you believe is out there?"

"I don't know." He reached for his shirt, jacket and coat. "But *you* will stay *here,*" he ordered, rising from the bed. Before she could protest again, he opened her bedroom door and slid out into the hall.

All was silent downstairs, but there was a bit of fresh air as if someone had gone outside. Heath walked down the hall and opened the back door. He peered into the moonlit night. The shadows of the trees hid anyone making her way from the house to the stables. He started to go out the door, when he felt a presence behind him.

"Yes, I am here," Margaret whispered.

He turned, blocking her way out the door. "Go back."

It was too dark to see her face but he knew she scowled at that order. "I shall not. You might need me."

"For what?"

"I don't know."

"Maggie, I *need* to know you are safe."

"And I need," she said, "to be wherever you are in case you need help."

"I've been taking care of myself for a long time."

"Yes, and I shot you."

He made an impatient sound and was ready to argue, but she ducked under his arm and escaped out the door before he could catch her. She wore her red cloak. It was black in the moonlight.

"Come along," she whispered. "I have my brother's gun."

"Not that again," he muttered, but she had already disappeared into the shadows.

"Come," she said in a hushed tone. "Don't lollygag."

Swearing under his breath, Heath went after her. The light in the barn could be nothing suspicious, but his every sense warned him there was something afoot, and Maggie was running right toward it.

CHAPTER SIXTEEN

If Heath had thought Margaret would stay in the house waiting while he investigated the light in the barn, he was sorely mistaken. Yes, it would be better if he had Rowlly with him, but going alone was foolish and so Margaret had no choice but to protect him.

She hadn't the chance to reload Harry's gun, but the powder bag was with her and she hoped for a moment to take care of the matter.

As she followed the path to the barn, she was surprised at how much she was beginning to enjoy adventure. It gave her meaning, purpose.

Had she truly been intimidated to come to Loch Awe? The coach ride that had brought her here seemed like a lifetime ago.

And she now seemed a very different person.

For the first time, she felt as if she was truly living. A woman had more freedom here, far from London and gossipy tongues. But the change in her was more than in the proprieties. She was no longer a bystander, an ornament, a victim.

She was making the decisions.

Heath came up behind her, touched her arm to bring her back so that he could lead the charge on the barn. Margaret was perfectly willing to let him go first. If there was danger, then, between the two of them, he was the stronger fighter. She'd be happy to load Harry's pistol and shoot whomever Heath left behind.

When they reached the edge of the stable yard, he held out his arm to keep her behind him. There was no light. All seemed pitch black and quiet. The pigs snored in their pen. The horses, cow and goats were silent in their stalls.

"Do you believe the person has left?" she asked, her voice low.

"Perhaps, but let us be cautious. If someone is in the back stalls, we wouldn't see a light. I'll go first and you stay here. I mean that, Maggie. You stay right here on this spot as if your feet are rooted to the earth."

"But what if you need my help?"

"I'll shout."

"What if you can't shout? What if there is a band of thieves or Gypsies or that Swepston person? What if they have knives — ?"

He shut her up with a kiss. Right there in the night's cold darkness with who knew what sort of brigands going though his stable.

When he was done, she could barely recall her name let alone all the dangers that lurked ahead of him. His kiss was that potent.

"You are infuriating," he whispered.

"Thank you," she murmured. "I like you as well."

He chuckled, the deep, masculine sound enough to weaken her knees. "It's more than just like, Maggie. Much more."

And then he was off, moving so quickly his shadow could barely be seen in the moonlight.

It's more than just like . . .

Yes, he'd said those words.

Margaret gathered her senses enough to load the pistol, using her hands to feel for what she could not see, and then, even though he'd told her not to, she followed Heath.

The stables were Heath's second home. He took great pride in the stone and timber structure.

The moon's light did not penetrate the

walls. He could barely see his hand in front of his face, but he knew to skirt the feed stacked up by the paddock door, and to keep to his left to avoid the anvil against the wall.

He paused, listening, letting his vision adjust to this deeper darkness. He could hear the horses moving restlessly in their stalls, but they hadn't noticed his arrival. Instead, they were attuned to the very human grunting sounds that came from the far stall where there was the glow of light.

One of his stable lads was obviously enjoying himself, but who was with him from the house? He couldn't begin to imagine.

The barest sound of a footstep behind him told Heath he was no longer alone. He knew Maggie was there before she whispered, "What have you discovered?"

She reached out with her hand to find him and take hold of his jacket in the darkness while her own eyes adjusted. Then she heard the last grunt and heavy sigh of a man finishing his business.

"Oh my —" she started as the realization of what was going on hit her.

Heath placed a hand over her lips, warning her to silence. He then crouched low and moved down the aisleway, moving toward the last stall. He braced himself for what he would discover, certain he would not like what he saw, when a male voice said in satisfied tones, "I'll want to do this again. You have been putting me off too long, lass. Too long."

That was Rowlly's voice.

The shock of recognition gave Heath pause. He knelt, stunned to imagine his cousin having an affair with someone in the house. His wife, Janet, would have his hide.

"I wanted you to miss me," his companion answered . . . revealing herself to be *Dara.*

Shock gave way to relief in Heath's mind. He was glad Rowlly wasn't with one of his sisters so he'd have to hang his cousin up by his balls. But he was shocked at Dara. He would never have thought Rowlly would appeal to her.

"I missed you, I truly missed you," Rowlly said, his tone heavy with lust. "See? I'm ready again. I want more. Now."

There was feminine trill of laughter, the sort of sound women made when they knew they were in charge, followed by the smacking of lips and hungry sighs.

Heath didn't know what to do. He wasn't anxious to catch Rowlly and Dara. He'd always thought Rowlly and Janet were a couple well pleased with each other. Then again, Dara was a beautiful woman.

But always a bit closed unless she wanted to share her thoughts.

It didn't make sense that she would be wasting her attentions on the likes of Rowlly, although Heath had seen stranger pairings. He wouldn't meddle in their business. He took Margaret's hand, ready to lead her away without the two of them learning they had been discovered.

"Wait," Dara was saying. "Hold on. Not just yet —"

"Why?" That one word carried the frustration of a man who was in need.

"Because there is something you must do for me," Dara cajoled.

Rowlly groaned his frustration. "We don't have much time. I told Janet I'd return from checking the stable in an hour."

"We'll be done by then," Dara assured him, her voice laced with sweetness. "But you know there is never something for nothing."

There was a beat of silence.

Heath and Margaret had gone still, fearing that their departure would be overheard. There is a timing to these moments. Heath reasoned in another second or two, neither Dara or Rowlly would hear their leaving even if they'd rode away on a herd of elephants.

Now, they waited.

And then Rowlly's words put a chill in Heath's heart. "I'll not kill again."

"You might not have to," Dara said. "But you may not have a choice. You really must do what I ask of you."

"Or what?" The lust had left Rowlly's voice.

"Do you really want me to say it?" Dara asked. "Are you so ignorant that you don't realize what would happen if I let it be known you murdered my husband, the man everyone in the valley admired?"

Heath's world reeled with that information. Rowlly had murdered Brodie? Rowlly, his own cousin, whom Brodie had trusted almost more than he had Heath? Rowlly, whom Heath had relied upon for counsel and advice, whom he had turned to time and time again?

He started forward —

Margaret's hand caught his arm. She squeezed it tight, a warning for him to be wary.

Heath didn't want to be cautious. He wanted to attack Rowlly with his bare hands and pull the man's lying, murderous tongue from his mouth.

"You wouldn't do that," Rowlly said, his voice flat. Heath could hear the sound of clothing being rearranged, could imagine Rowlly pulling up his breeches, wanting to be done with her. "If you do, then I will tell everyone that murdering Brodie was your suggestion."

"Not mine," Dara answered, practically purring with satisfaction. "Yes, we are lovers but I didn't mean for you to do away with my husband."

"*You* put me up to it," Rowlly lashed back. "You said we could be together once you received your portion of what should be yours when Owen Campbell bought Marybone. That we would leave together. Go somewhere else. But then after I did it, there's always been something keeping us apart. You don't really want me, do you? Meeting me like this, letting me have you, it's to tease me into doing your bidding."

His voice had risen with realization at how he'd been used.

Dara's response was cool. "If you'd thought on it, you would have known. After all, why should I see anything in the likes of you?"

"You made me kill my cousin —"

"I 'made' you do no such thing. You wanted me, and to have me, you needed him out of the way. I had only to suggest how happy we would be without Brodie for you to leap at the opportunity."

"I loved him like a brother. He was a good man."

"Obviously, you didn't love him enough."

"You bitch —"

"Oh yes, call me names. But think on what you should call yourself."

"I sacrificed everything for you," he said as if the simple statement condoned murder.

"I was a married woman. I had no place promising myself to anyone. In the end, Rowlly, it will be your word against mine. Yes, I strayed as a wife. I sinned, but I didn't expect you to kill him."

"You suggested it —"

"Did I? I recall no such thing."

"I've waited for you," Rowlly said as if still not believing how neatly she'd tricked him. "You said after your mourning we could be together and I've waited. I was ready to leave Janet. To set aside my sons."

"And you've had me," she answered. "And you can have more." Her voice had turned seductive. "But there is a price."

"I'll not murder Heath for you —"

"You needn't," she hurried to assure him. "Heath can live. But I must have Lady Margaret disappear. She can't give Heath her money."

"If there is any dirty business to be done,

you'd best do it yourself." His boots moved toward the door. Heath braced himself, ready to leap at his brother's murderer.

But Dara caught him and pulled him back. "You don't have a choice, Rowlly," she said, sounding as if she commiserated on his misfortune. "If you don't help me, then I shall tell everyone what you did to Brodie and I will prove it. You gave me the crossbow to hide. I know where it is. That and my testimony will see you hang."

"You'll hang as well."

"Do you truly believe that?" she said calmly. She was cold-blooded, unremorseful. "I have a friend, Rowlly, a powerful friend who will protect you if you do what we ask."

"I can't. I won't." He was struggling with his conscience.

"You will" was Dara's reply. *"My* word against *yours."*

Heath could contain himself no longer. "And my word against the both of yours," he said, standing up and moving into the light from the stall. Dara and Rowlly turned in surprise. They had been so involved in themselves that they truly had not realized anyone was present.

"Heath," Rowlly said in alarm and then said, "You heard her. She tricked me. I

didn't want to hurt Brodie. I never would have if I'd been in my right mind. She made me crazed with wanting her. She's evil, Heath. Evil."

But Dara was not panicked. She faced Heath with an unnerving serenity.

"Why?" Heath asked. "My brother gave all that he had to you, Dara. My sisters and I kept you in our home. If you hated him so much, why would you stay?"

The lines of her face tightened and then, almost as if she could not keep her emotions at bay, she said, "I stayed because I'm in love. Because the man I truly care for asked me to help him."

"And who is that man?" Heath demanded. "It certainly isn't me."

"Of course not. It's Owen Campbell. I love him. I've *always* loved him."

Rowlly lunged for her. "Did he put you up to this?" he demanded, grabbing her by her cloak tied around her neck.

Heath reached to pull him off her. "Steady man. Don't be more of a fool than you already have been."

Rowlly released his hold. Dara fell back a step, her hands coming up to her throat. Her eyes turned to angry slits. "Of course, Owen didn't put me up to this. He's an honorable man. I had to do this *for* him.

After all, how was he going to marry me if I already had a husband? I had to rid myself of Brodie. I needed to. Just like Lady Margaret needs to leave. Owen wants her land."

"Are you lovers?" Rowlly demanded. He would have gone after her again except that Heath held his arms.

"Yes," she said to him, taunting him. "And I never need to pretend when I am in his arms the way I must to put up with you."

Rowlly roared his pain, trying to shrug Heath off. He bucked his body, kicking out. His booted foot hit the oil lantern, knocking it over.

The hay in the stall burst into flames. It was dry and the fire spread, catching the hem of Dara's cloak in the blink of an eye. The wool was ablaze in seconds. Dara started screaming. She began to run forward. Heath reached out to help her.

The flames were already going up the side of the stall. He could hear the horses neighing in alarm.

And Margaret. Where was Margaret?

A blow across his body stopped him from helping Dara. Rowlly had struck him.

"Leave her alone," Rowlly said, his voice guttural and strange. "Let her burn."

"No," Dara shrieked, while frantically trying to untie the ribbons of her cloak. Fire

lapped Heath's boots. Again, he tried to help Dara.

Rowlly doubled his fist and hit him. "I said no, Heath."

"This isn't right," Heath said. There was no time to fight, not if they wanted to survive.

"Aye, but this is the best way for it to end," Rowlly answered.

Dara tried to get by him again and he shoved her back with his elbow. She hit the wall and fell to the ground, the wind knocked out of her. Heath took a step back but Rowlly grabbed hold of his jacket, his fingers like claws, and swung Heath around. The air was filling with smoke and Heath was feeling the effects of it. The horses were panicking and kicking their stalls, trying to escape.

Rowlly's face had taken on a demonic look. "This is the best way. Let us *all* burn," he said. "And then no one will know I killed Brodie. No one will ever know —"

A shot rang out. Rowlly stiffened, and then let go of Heath. He turned to where Maggie stood in the stable door, her pistol in her hand. "She shot me," he said to Heath in disbelief.

"She does that," Heath answered, feeling absolutely no remorse.

Rowlly nodded. His face was turning pale. And then he placed his hand on his chest and dropped to the ground.

Coughing from the smoke, Heath leaped over the body to rescue Dara, managing to remove her cloak before throwing her over his shoulder, and running from the stall.

Maggie was opening the barn doors, urging the horses to rush out. They were difficult. They were afraid, but Maggie managed to coax them outside.

"I had to shoot him," she called out, coughing. "He would have murdered you."

"You did the right thing," he said.

After carrying Dara outside and lying her on the ground, Heath prepared to go back for Margaret. Flames danced across the roof of the stable.

People were coming from all areas now, drawn by the fire. Irwin and his mother were two of the first to arrive. "I didn't do this, Laird," Irwin called. "I've been doing my job. I've been doing it."

"I know you have," Heath shouted. "Free the pigs in case the fire spreads. We will chase them on the morrow." He started to charge back into the barn just as Margaret ran out. She held her arm across her face to protect her breathing.

"Thank God you're safe," he said, meaning the words. He started for the barn. Margaret caught his arm.

"What are you doing?"

"I'm going back for Rowlly."

"No, you can't," she said. "Heath, he's dead. He's gone."

"I should claim his body."

"No, Heath, it is better this way."

She was right. He took her in his arms and held her tight as he watched the stables burn. She was right.

CHAPTER SEVENTEEN

The next day was not a good one for the Macnachtans.

The fire had burned throughout the night.

At first light, Heath sent a party of men to search for frightened horses and scattered livestock. Neither he nor Margaret slept the night through, and Margaret didn't think they would sleep much for days to come.

Neighbors came to help. The animals were safe but all the equipment was lost.

The hardest moment in the day was when Rowlly's wife, Janet, and their young sons came to Heath. Irwin had just proudly announced that the pigs had all been gathered and placed in one of the many makeshift pens and paddocks hurriedly built for the livestock.

"I have not seen my husband," Janet said. "Was he here helping with the fire?"

Heath exchanged a look with Margaret and then said, "You lads stay here with Lady

Margaret." He put his arm around Janet and they walked a distance away where they could speak without being overheard.

Margaret watched as he told the woman what had happened to her husband. She collapsed against him. He spoke to her, offering her some thread of hope, Margaret prayed. They talked earnestly for a good long while.

Once Janet recovered, she called for her sons to join them. Heath and she both told them that their father was gone. The boys met the news with tears of loss.

When Heath walked over to join Margaret, she asked, "Did you tell them the truth?"

"About Dara? I told Janet. She should know. If Dara recovers and starts talking, then it is best Janet know. I did not tell her that Rowlly murdered Brodie. That will depend on what happens to Dara."

"And if Dara doesn't recover?"

"Then I believe the story of Brodie's murderer will stay between us." His gray eyes were bleak.

She touched his arm. "Can you live with that? With his death always being a mystery?"

"It's not the solving of it I wanted," he said. "I wished justice . . . and that has happened. No good will come of saddling those boys with their father's reputation as a murderer. Brodie would have wanted it this way." His expression was grim. She could tell he held back tears.

"I wish I'd known your brother," she said.

He nodded, and then, as he had so many times during that day, he touched her as if reassuring himself of her. She found his hand with her own, squeezed it, letting him know she was there for him, and a bit of the tension marring his brow eased.

"Swepston is here," he informed her in a low tone.

"The man you banished?"

Heath made a dismissive sound. "He's a clansman. A fight between us is a fight in the family. He's been helping Irwin collect the pigs and working hard. I understand why he would not want to leave. I shall not say a word to him, but as long as he is one of us, there is a place for him."

And that is when Margaret fell in love.

The realization of the fullness and completeness of love caught her by surprise. In truth, it had always been there, lingering inside her, waiting for her to open her heart as well as her mind.

She knew of few men who had the capacity to forgive. Usually their conceit demanded the world bow to them. Heath could have been such a man. Instead, he moderated his temper with compassion.

And how could she help but love him?

Love surprised her. She thought she knew the rush of emotions labeled "love." She'd been "in love" before. Her feelings had been a heady mixture of desire and longing . . . but now she learned that love was a subtle, finer emotion. It came upon her with a sense of purpose and serenity, with a security that she'd not known before. It was as if she had been standing separate and apart and now found herself as one, with him.

She valued Heath, needed him, trusted him.

She believed in him.

Heath walked away, returning to the numerous tasks that had to be attended to in the aftermath of the fire. Margaret watched him go, feeling as if she'd been changed forever. Her feelings were certain and intense.

And tomorrow, she would love him more. She had that much of it to give. Love was not finite, she realized. It was a well that never went dry. Nor did it exist for just the here and now, but was truly forever.

"Are you all right?" she heard Anice ask.

"You have the funniest expression on your face."

"How is that?"

Anice smiled. "You stood there as if you had been struck by a thunderbolt."

"I have been," Margaret admitted. "Right to the core of my being."

Anice did not mistake her meaning. "I knew there was something between you and Heath. All that nonsense yesterday about having to marry. You *want* to marry him. You love him."

"Can you tell?" Margaret asked, a bit puzzled by how quickly Anice had read her.

"You glow with love," Anice said. "I hope someday to feel that way about a man."

Anice's description was exactly how Margaret felt on the inside — glowing and more alive than she could ever have thought possible.

Margaret threw her energy back into helping clean up the fire damage. She now felt accepted by Heath's clansmen. Several times, the women came to her for suggestions. She felt productive, and it was a reward in and of itself to have purpose. It was a gift to the man she loved to work beside him.

Three hours later, Laren came down to the stable yard with the grim news that Dara had died from her burns.

Owen Campbell had not sent an inquiry about the fire, or about Dara.

That, too, Margaret thought, was justice.

And that night, in bed, she listened for Heath to go to his room. She'd sensed his disquiet. It had been building as the day and the cleanup had progressed and she worried for him.

When after two hours she didn't hear anything, she decided to check on him. Perhaps he had gone to bed and she had not noticed, but she doubted it. She was attuned to his moods, almost more so than her own. She pulled on her blue woolen day dress from her wardrobe, not bothering with stockings and shoes but walking across the hall to his room barefoot.

He wasn't in his room. She went in search of him. She found him downstairs in the library, poring over open ledgers. He had removed his jacket. His shirt was open at the neck and the hem hung loose over his breeches. His hair was mussed, as if he'd been raking his fingers through it, the way he was wont to do when challenged by a problem. Ledgers were open on the desk and he was muttering to himself.

She lingered by the door, uncertain of her welcome. She drew a breath for courage and then interrupted him. "They say that talking to oneself is a sign of madness."

He looked up. "Maggie," he said, speaking her name as if it was benediction. "You should be asleep."

Margaret walked into the room to stand beside where he sat at his desk. She glanced at the ledger in front of him. It was covered with marks and cross outs. Heath had been doing a great deal of stewing. She took the quill from his hand. The tip of his index finger was ink stained. "You should be in bed as well. You worked harder than anyone today, and we did not have any sleep last night."

"The stable was my father and Brodie's pride. Brodie had a vision that he would build a breeding program. That's why we have those good mares. Brodie told me he wanted the Macnachtan to have a reputation for something instead of just being known as the poorest around Loch Awe. Now it is all gone. Every bit of it, save the debts, and a good portion of those are in Owen Campbell's hands."

He sat back in his chair. "But the debts are not what I'm thinking on. Brodie *loved* Dara." He looked up at Margaret as he spoke. "He *trusted* her. He worked bloody hard to make her happy. And she didn't care."

"She loved someone else," Margaret said.

"Did she? She was an excellent actress. I believed she and my brother were close. Maggie, I suspected everyone of his murder but never her or Rowlly. Rowlly, Brodie, and I were constant companions when we were lads."

"She used him," Margaret said. "I'm not saying it is right, but I've witnessed men and women in society do terrible things in order to capture someone's attentions."

He nodded as if accepting her words. "I am a bit unnerved to realize how close we all were to true evil, only it isn't what I had ever imagined it to be. It was born out of lust and jealousy."

He gave himself a shake as if silently ordering himself to leave such thoughts. He looked back to his ledger.

Margaret placed her hand upon it. "Come to bed, Heath."

"I will, but first I need to add this column. It's a list of all that was destroyed in the fire and how much I still owed on it."

"And it doesn't matter," she said. "I meant what I said to Owen Campbell. I'm a wealthy woman."

"And you would give up the rest of your

life to settle my debts? Maggie, it would be like selling your soul, and you deserve better. In fact, I'm certain your brothers will have something to say about the matter."

If there had been a false nobility about him, she would have been angry. Instead, he was somber, honest . . . caring.

"I make my own decisions, Heath Macnachtan," she informed him, but what she really wanted to shout at him was *I love you.*

There it was, a truth so shining only wisdom kept her from speaking it aloud. He must say it first. She knew that. She'd witnessed women pressing men and she didn't want to be one of those. Their men never respected them, and she wanted Heath's respect. She wanted every facet of him.

He took her hand, bringing it to his lips and kissing her palm. She felt his grief as keenly as if it was her own. "Then you should make better choices," he answered. "I will not hold you to a marriage," he said. "I do have pride."

As did she.

And for a moment, she felt like every sort of fool.

He was pushing her away. She'd had every eligible bachelor in London at her feet, and the man she wanted, the man she loved, did not want her.

"I see," she said, straightening. She pulled her hand from his, for once in her life not bothering to hide her feelings. She was disappointed, devastated. Hurt. "I don't understand, but I accept."

She turned, determined to walk, no, run out of the room with as much dignity as she could muster —

He rose from his chair and grabbed her arm, making her face him.

"You don't 'see' anything," he said. "I love you, Margaret. I think I've loved you from the first moment I laid eyes on you. I was in a London street and you went by me surrounded with a gaggle of admirers. You didn't even know I was there, and I fell in love."

"That is *not* love," she threw at him. "That's infatuation. It's simple and doesn't require anything of you. With infatuation, you don't have to care for the person or consider her or involve yourself." She flung her arm up so that he had to release his hold, but instead of leaving, she stood her ground.

"Love," she said, "is admiring a person not because he has two eyes and nose and mouth fashioned in a pleasing and even form, but because he has a heart that cares about *something other than himself.*" She emphasized her words by pressing her palm against his chest over his heart. "That he isn't afraid," she continued, "to speak out when there is injustice and champions with kindness those who are weaker. Love happens when you witness this person building something that has meaning for people and striving to make the world a little bit better place for all. Love is discovering that here, at last, *finally,* is a person I can trust, someone I know will never hurt me and yet will always be honest with me. That's what is behind love. Not some 'Oh look, my eyes see a woman. She is pretty.' "

He was staring at her, his brows raised as if stunned by her response, as she was herself.

She'd put every emotion she had in her words, and she now felt as if her heart was beating outside her chest, as if she was completely exposed. She'd opened herself in a way she'd never done for anyone else in this world.

Dear God, she prayed he was worth it.

There was a long beat of silence, and then Heath said, "I'd always heard the Chattans didn't know how to love."

Her eyes burned with unshed tears. "Perhaps what we know is how to love *too* well."

Her heart lay bare in front of him.

He was quiet a moment, pensive.

"I don't come alone," he warned, as if wanting to be certain she understood. "Besides my debts, Margaret, I'm responsible for a host of the oddest characters and I'm related to most of them so there is no escape."

"I don't call them odd," she said. "I prefer the term 'endearing.' "

Her response made him smile. "Yes, they are. Even Irwin. I can't leave them. My role is to protect them as much as I can."

"I understand."

"Do you? They will come to the woman who would be my wife for every third concern in their lives. There will be times when they will wear you down."

"Do you believe I am not equal to the task?" she dared him.

"I know you are. I saw it today in the way you organized and prodded them in the cleanup and I found myself marveling that not too long ago, they spit on the ground every time they heard the name Chattan. Today, they honored you by doing as you asked." He placed his hand on the back of her neck beneath her hair to bring her closer to him. "And, yes, when I look at you, I see your beauty but it is your spirit I respect. In turn, I'm nothing more than a miserable man."

"You are not miserable —"

He shushed her protest by saying, "Maggie, I fail a hundred times a day. But with you by my side, there is nothing I cannot achieve. I love you — not the you the world sees," he hastened to add. "I love the woman who has the courage of a lioness. Who would go to the ends of the earth for her family. And who isn't afraid to battle demons, both those we can see and those we can't. I love *you, Margaret*."

"And *I love you*," she said, the words finally bursting out of her. "I believe you are the bravest, most marvelous man in the world."

He laughed and released his hold on her to take her left hand in his. "We both may be fools for this, Maggie, but now I'm doing the asking." His expression sobered as he said, "Margaret Chattan, I'm a poor man with a big heart and a houseful of relatives. Will you marry me, my love?" He paused. His brows gathered. "Will you be by my side through whatever life tosses at us? Will you always speak your mind whether I want to hear it or not? Will you bear my children, Maggie, and teach them to be as bold and headstrong as you are?"

She wanted to shout out, *Yes, of course.*

But she deserved her say as well. She squared her shoulders and said to him, "Heath Macnachtan, will you cherish me every day of your life, even when I do speak my piece — as you've asked me to do so right here and now?"

A grin split his face and she knew his answer was yes. But then she softened her voice and continued, "Will you teach me to not be afraid of my mistakes? To keep my heart open? To trust even when I'm afraid?"

"I will never let you fall, Margaret," he said.

"And I will never run from you," she answered.

"I will never betray your trust."

"And I give you my complete faith."

He leaned toward her. She met him halfway and they sealed their pledges with a kiss.

It wasn't as heated a kiss as many they'd shared. This one spoke of commitment. This one was in the knowledge that not only did they love, but they were loved in return.

And was it her imagination? Or did the very air around them sing with the joy she felt in her heart? The moment shimmered with it.

Heath broke the kiss first. They still held

each other's hands.

"Do you know what we've just done?" he asked.

"Declared ourselves?"

"More than that. This is Scotland, Maggie. We've handfasted ourselves. In the old days, it was as good as married. I shall ask your brother for your hand, but the way we've been at each other" — that wicked smile of his came out on those words — "we'd best do it soon because there will be bairns on the way."

"May we marry on the morrow?"

Heath shook his head. "Absolutely not. I'll not dishonor you that way. We'll post the banns and I shall marry you in front of all the kirk with your brothers in attendance."

Her brothers.

She'd failed them.

There would be no defeating Fenella . . . but in this moment of such happiness, Margaret didn't care. She was in love. And she knew they would be happy for her.

Heath didn't understand. One who hadn't felt the impact of the curse couldn't. She grasped that now as well.

He took her hand and led her upstairs to his bed. After hours of making love with an energy that surprised both of them, she drifted off to sleep, contented, sated . . . and with the reflection that this was what Rose Macnachtan had known when she'd handfasted herself to Charles Chattan. She *had* considered herself married. Margaret knew because that is how she felt with Heath.

When she woke up the next morning, she felt a tingling in her left arm. Both Lyon and Harry had experienced the same sensation. The tingling was a precursor to the curse's wasting death. And at last, she knew that she, too, was a victim of the curse . . . and she discovered she didn't care.

Yes, love was worth her life, and she didn't want to lose it.

And so she kept her pain in her left arm a secret.

CHAPTER EIGHTEEN

Rowlly and Dara were buried in two days' time. The service was held for them together.

Of course, it was not lost on many that Dara and Rowlly had been in the barn together in the middle of the night. Perhaps Janet had confided in a few of the women. Perhaps not. Either way, Heath had the sense from his clansmen that they understood more than they would speak aloud. Rowlly's sons would be protected from his sins, just as Heath had wished them to be. And Janet would be comforted. That, too, was good.

As for him and Maggie, love brought a host of surprises.

The frustration and low level of anger Heath had experienced since the day they'd told him his brother had died and he was now chieftain and laird of his motley collection of clansmen had evaporated. The best part of being in love was having a partner. He enjoyed discussing his plans with Maggie. He could not have made it through the funeral without her by his side. They alone knew the truth of Brodie's death and it made the bond between them stronger.

Laren and Anice were happy for them. Each sister approached him at a different time and told him that she approved of Margaret.

"I think she is good for you," Anice said with her usual candor. "The moment I met her, I thought, finally, here is a woman as stubborn as my brother. And she's wealthy as well. Brodie is taking care of us, isn't he?"

Heath had not thought of matters that way. "Yes," he said. "I suppose he is."

Laren was more practical. "I pray you will be a good husband to her."

"Why would you believe I wouldn't?" he answered, mildly offended.

"Because you are male."

Her comment intrigued him. They were walking side by side after the burial. The other mourners were lost in their own thoughts of mortality and the meaning of life. Anice and Margaret accompanied Janet and her sons. Janet had placed a hand on Margaret's arm as if valuing her presence at this moment.

"In what way are men not good to their wives?" he asked. In his mind, Dara had not been a good wife to his brother.

"Sometimes in little ways that they don't even notice," Laren answered. "I believe Brodie cared deeply for Dara but he didn't understand her."

Now she really had his attention. "Why do you say that?"

"He expected her to work hard. He expected all of us to work hard. *He* was working hard . . . but Dara wasn't happy and he never noticed. That is important, isn't it? Noticing those close to us and caring how they feel?"

"Do I notice you enough, Laren?"

His sister walked a moment in thought and then said, "I believe the time has come when I want my own household."

Dara had told him that, hadn't she?

"Do you have the man chosen?" he asked.

"Not yet. But I believe that I might have a liking for Reverend Allen, the new minister in Dalmally."

"The one who came to dinner last month?"

"The same. We've been meeting from time to time, depending on where our separate duties take us. Of course we will wait a respectful mourning period for Dara."

Heath would not mourn for Dara. Considering the robust way he and Maggie went after each other, the sooner he married her, the better. There would be bairns on the way.

"And Anice? Has she set her cap on anyone?" Heath had to ask, a bit stunned to realize that while he thought he was in control of everything, he knew nothing.

"No, but," Laren said, a smile coming to her lips, "she might prefer a visit to London. Since you are going to do us all a favor and marry well." She put her arm around his. "And I mean that, Heath. I like Margaret very much. I will be proud to call her sister . . . and it doesn't hurt that we shall have some room to breathe where money is concerned. Papa and Brodie both felt that Marybone could be a grand estate. They lacked the wealth to see their vision fulfilled. That has all changed now and it is good."

It is good.

His sister's blessing was all that he could wish.

During the supper following the burial, he spoke to the minister in the kirk about a marriage. The clergyman understood Heath's suggestions that he wanted to marry as soon as their mourning had passed, which would be in six weeks. He agreed that the banns would be announced at the next morning's service, a service both Heath and Margaret attended.

A week ago, there would have been many who would have resisted the idea of a marriage between a Chattan and a Macnachtan. But as Heath stood when called in front of the members of the kirk, he saw nothing but approval on the faces of his clansmen and neighbors.

The only person who had any cause to object would be Owen Campbell, and he never attended church.

That afternoon, when they returned from services, the messenger Heath had sent to London had finally returned.

"Lord Lyon is very ill," he reported, as he handed Margaret a letter from her brother, although it had not been written by him. "I did not have the chance for an audience with him, but he sent word that he prays his sister is well and . . ." The messenger paused as if wishing to repeat the words as he'd been instructed. ". . . And he assures Lady Margaret that he has no doubts that his was the right course. Those were his exact words he bade me give you."

Heath was intensely curious to know what Lord Lyon had to say. From his vantage point a few steps away, he could spy the dark, slashing handwriting. The note was no more than a few lines. Margaret read them, nodded as if confirming something to herself, and folded over the note.

She did not speak of it to Heath.

And he couldn't stand his curiosity.

He pulled the messenger over. "Douglas, I know it was a long trip and you wish to spend time with your wife but I need a message sent, this one to Glenfinnan."

"It was not that long a trip, Laird," Douglas answered. He was a redheaded man whose cheeks were always the same color as his hair, making it appear as if he put great energy into everything he did. He lowered his voice to confide, "In truth, I just reached London four days ago. On the way down, any disaster that could befall me did. My horse went lame, I ran into a storm that washed out a bridge, and I was chased by robbers who turned out not to be anything."

"What do you mean?"

Douglas shrugged as if thinking himself a fool. "I could have sworn I was under attack. I reached an inn and told my story. A group of lads having a drink came out with me and I felt the fool when we searched and searched and there was no sign of anyone. But I could swear I saw three men in dark capes chasing me on horses."

"Did you see their faces?"

"I didn't. I was too busy running. After that, the rest of the trip was easy. And I'm happy to go to Glenfinnan if you give me a bit of a rest."

"I can do that," Heath answered, his mind busy on the implications of what Douglas had said. As his kinsman started to walk off, he stopped him by asking, "Tell me, you didn't see a small white cat, did you? It is a strange, deformed animal. Her little ears are folded over. She has the air of an owl."

Douglas frowned as if he thought Heath asking after a cat an odd matter. "I saw plenty of cats. I didn't pay much attention to any of them. I don't like the creatures."

"You would remember this one," Heath assured him.

"I doubt that," Douglas promised, and bowed, a request for dismissal.

Heath waved him on, although the interview unsettled him. Travel was never easy. There were always hazards on the road, but Douglas's report was beyond the ordinary. Heath said as much to Margaret a bit later as they walked around the charred ruins of the stable.

"She was trying to stop him," Margaret said, nodding with understanding, and then she changed the subject to the stables. "I think you should build the new building twice as large as the old," she said.

"Who is *she*?" Heath pressed.

Margaret looked at him. She was so lovely, especially with her hair loosely gathered at her neck. "Fenella. I believe she wanted time."

"Time for what?" he said, letting his impatience be known. He was tired of this talk. He didn't like it.

"Time for us to fall in love. It makes for perfect justice, don't you think? My fortune helps restore yours. Maybe she'll let me live. Perhaps our child will be safe."

"Stop this," he ordered. "Don't give this —" He almost said "curse," a word he'd come to hate. "Don't give this nonsense power. Think on it, Maggie. You and your brothers believe, and because you believe, it has meaning. Stop it. Let it all go."

"I wish I could, Heath. And yet, this is not so terrible. Lyon's wife Thea wrote the letter for him. Her lying-in time will soon arrive and she is feeling strong."

"Even with her husband ill?"

"He's not just ill, Heath. He is dying," Margaret said gently.

"Then all the more reason for her to be alarmed," Heath snapped.

"You don't understand —" Margaret

started with that complacent tone to her voice, and Heath interrupted her.

"I *don't* understand. You act as if it is acceptable for your brother to be dying. And if I ask what is the cause, you refer to some legend." He took her by her shoulders, suddenly so filled with fear for her, it was hard for him to breathe. "Margaret, don't give in to this. *Don't accept it.*"

Her response was to lean in and rest her head on his chest. "I love you," she whispered. "I will always love you."

That wasn't the answer he wanted.

She refused to speak more on the matter. She refused to listen to him.

He felt as he did when he was at sea and saw a thunderhead forming. He could see it coming and knew it was unavoidable. Its presence gave him an edgy feeling.

But he could prepare for a storm.

How could he prepare for his wife's mistaken beliefs?

His wife. She'd been completely his from the moment they had handfasted. The church service would be a mere formality. His spirit was already wed to hers.

And he would go mad if he didn't change her thinking, but he didn't know how.

For that reason, he sought out the counsel of the strange Indian servant Rowan. The

361

bones in his body were healing nicely but keeping him confined to his bed.

While his sisters and Margaret enjoyed a game of chess after dinner, Heath sought out the servant in his quarters. The valet was able to sit up, although he still could not move without help.

"It is good to see you, my laird," Rowan said in his accented English.

"Laird," Heath corrected. "You don't have to say 'my laird.' "

"Yes, Laird," Rowan answered. "What may I do for you?" His golden brown eyes had an expectant look as if he already knew Heath's questions.

Heath sat in the chair by his bedside. He didn't dither with conversation but said outright, "Do you believe in this curse? I assume Colonel Chattan believed."

"He did, Laird. He believed very much."

"And yourself?"

"I believe." Rowan held out his arms wrapped in boards to brace the bones for healing. "I have proof."

Heath wanted to deny the man's words, and yet there was something in his quiet certainty that unnerved Heath more than Margaret's insistence.

"I can't lose her," Heath said at last.

"You love her very much," Rowan answered as if confirming the truth in his own mind.

"I was meant to love her," Heath confessed. "Does that sound daft?"

"Perhaps it is as it should be," Rowan suggested. "Perhaps the two of you were supposed to meet."

"And then what?"

"Only you can say, Laird."

Heath frowned and came to his feet. "This is ridiculous," he muttered. "There is nothing at work here. All of it is imagined in our minds."

"All of life is imagined in our minds," Rowan said.

Heath picked up the wooden chair. "Are you saying this is in my mind and not solid and real?"

"I am saying there are matters that are beyond man's small brain. In my country, we listen to what we do not see and cannot touch as well as that which is solid."

"That is backward," Heath announced.

"Is it?" Rowan challenged him. "Is it more forward to only believe in what you can touch? What of your beliefs in God? Is that backward?"

"It isn't the same."

"Is it not? You pray, and if your prayer is answered, do you not accept that as proof?"

Heath shook his head. "A prayer does not give credence to a heathen-being like a witch. The Chattans claim that one of my ancestors had unworldly powers. I cannot believe it. We are flesh and blood and mortal."

"Have you never thought there might more to the world than your eye beholds?"

Like a small white cat that disappeared when he touched it.

Heath was quiet a moment and then he asked, "Then how can I defeat this curse? How can I defeat what I can only sense?" Heath asked.

"There will be a way," Rowan said. "When you decide to fight, there will be a way."

"I want to fight now," Heath declared.

"Then you will find a way," Rowan answered in his calm, annoying manner.

"That would be easy if I knew my opponent."

"Then you must think like your opponent," Rowan said.

"Think like an imaginary witch who has cursed people for generations?" Heath snorted his thoughts.

"Nothing is forever," Rowan said, his eyes intense. "All is written in sand. There is always a way to change what is. But first, you must change your thinking."

Heath set down the chair. Change his thinking . . . change Margaret's thinking. "That would mean accepting there is an enemy who could be defeated."

"What would you do if there was?" Rowan asked.

"My first question would be what is she afraid of? And if I were she — ?" He thought a moment. "She cursed the Chattan because Charles did not honor her daughter, her family. She didn't want just Charles to suffer, she wanted all of them to pay." He gave his head a shake. "Now I'm beginning to sound like the rest of you."

"And I believe Colonel Chattan was right. His sister does hold the answer. She is the first female born of the line. Is there something there?"

Heath shrugged. "I don't know. I'm the last male of Fenella's line. The first, the last . . ."

Rowan's grim expression lightened. "Yes, yes. The first and the last. It must have meaning."

"If it does, I'm at a loss. Good night, Rowan." Heath raked his hands through his hair as he left the room.

The first and the last.

The thought stuck in his mind as he went downstairs to the sitting room, but before

365

he joined the women, he heard their laughter. For a moment, he lingered in the hall where he could see them. Anice, Laren and his Maggie. Laren and Margaret were playing chess while Anice chattered, suggesting moves that Laren waved away.

Margaret sat with her left hand in her lap, giggling over Anice's antics. When it was her turn to move, she concentrated on the board a moment, started to use her left hand but then pulled it back as if in pain. She moved with her right hand instead. Then she caught sight of him watching from the hall. She beckoned him with a smile to sit beside her.

He was happy to do so. However, when they went upstairs, he had to ask, "Is something the matter with your arm?"

Margaret's brows rose as if she was surprised he had noticed. "It's nothing. I must have strained it in some way."

"I've noticed you've favored it quite often recently."

"Do I?" She shrugged. And yet, he sensed a tension in her as well. "It will be better in the morning," she said as if to placate him. She started toward her room.

He spoke, wanting to keep her with him a moment more. "Douglas, the messenger that went to London, left for Glenfinnan. I wanted to be certain your other brother knew that you are safe and in good hands."

Her eyes saddened and her lips tightened into a smile that held back a well of sadness. "I pray Douglas finds Harry well."

"He will."

"I doubt it. The impact of the curse was almost immediate on Harry. It hits harder, we think, the closer we are to the heart of the curse."

The damn curse. He wanted to relieve her mind in any way he could. So he said, "I spoke to Rowan earlier. He has a different way of looking at the world."

She nodded.

"We were thinking of ways of defeating the curse."

"The curse you don't believe in."

Heath leaned against the door frame. "I'm here to protect you, Maggie."

"I know," she said softly in an infuriatingly placating manner, "and I love you for it." She started to open the door to her room again, but he placed his hand over hers on the door handle and pulled it shut.

He then kissed her, deeply, fully, passionately.

And she responded.

After a few minutes, she turned her head so she could say, "I thought we were going to put this off until our wedding night."

Heath kissed a line from the lobe of her ear down her neck to her shoulder. "We had the intention," he murmured.

"It was a silly promise," she whispered, her voice catching as he found that one spot at the base of her neck that she liked so well — and any thought of waiting for his wedding day fled Heath's mind.

He was the one who opened the door to her room and they practically fell through it. He gathered her in his arms and carried her to the bed to throw her onto the mattress and then jumped on top of her. They rolled in the covers a moment, laughing like children, before their intent grew serious.

Taking her face in his hands, Heath said, "I love you, Maggie Chattan."

Her smile was everything he could wish for. No one had a smile like his Maggie. She kissed the palm of his hand. "You are everything to me," she said. "Every day I find another reason to respect you and love you."

A man could ask for no more.

Heath made love to her. There was comfort in her arms, understanding, a sense of being and of having purpose.

"We are going to have brave and intelligent sons," he told her in the aftermath as they lay entwined beneath the warmth of the covers.

"Bold ones like their father," she said.

"And sensible but daring ones like their mother," he added.

She rested her head on his shoulder and held up her hand. He laced his fingers with hers. She pressed a kiss upon the back of his hand. "And as our son grows," she said, "always remind him of how much his mother loved him, even before he was born."

"Don't use the past tense, Maggie," he ordered.

Her response was to snuggle in closer to him, and fall asleep.

But it was a long time before Heath closed his eyes. Instead, he found himself vigilant, alert, watching the dark corners of the room and dying flames of the fire for the witch that would take the woman he loved from him.

The first and the last.

The words echoed in his mind.

They took on more meaning the following morning when he heard Anice screaming his name.

He was meeting with a crew of lads from Dalmally who wanted to work on the rebuilding of the stables. The oldest, a man almost twice Heath's age, had some good ideas for improvements. Heath was glad that they had come calling. He was negotiating the price for their services when he heard Anice.

She came tearing down the path from the house. *"It's Margaret,"* she shouted. "Something terrible has happened. You must come."

He was on his way to the house before she had finished speaking.

CHAPTER NINETEEN

Cora stood on the steps with the cook as if they anxiously waited for Heath's arrival.

"Where is she?" he demanded.

"In the front hall," Cook said. "Miss Laren is with her."

He found them where Cook had directed him. Margaret was sprawled on the floor, her legs at a strange angle as if she were a rag doll. Her arms were bent, her fingers curled.

"Heath," Laren said with relief at the sight of him, "I found her this way."

He knelt beside Margaret. Her eyes were wide with pain. "What is it?"

"She can't speak," Laren said.

"You don't need to," Heath quietly assured Margaret. "Just be easy —"

A spasm of pain ripped through her. Her arms curled more as she groaned with the force of it.

"I shall fetch help," Heath promised. "But

first let me take you to your bed." He picked her up in his arms. Anice had joined them and she looked as anxious and frightened as Laren. "Grab one of the lads and send him for Mr. Hawson in Dalmally," he ordered his youngest sister.

Anice ran from the hall as if happy to have something constructive to do.

Heath rose to his feet. It was difficult to hold Margaret when she was so stiff. Even as he watched, her fingers curled tighter. It had to be painful and she could not have control over it.

He carried her up to her room, Laren hovering around them. Sitting on the bed beside her, Heath said, "Be brave, my darling. The doctor will come and we shall find out what this is —"

Those expressive eyes of hers said louder than words that the doctor would fail.

She knew he understood. She forced her lips into a smile that lacked her natural grace and ease. It was more of a grimace and she looked away . . . a dismissal.

"I fear we don't have much time," Laren said. "This malady has gripped her and it is taking her over."

Yes, it was taking Margaret over. He could see the muscles tightening. And the arm that was bent so tight her hand rested on her shoulder was her left arm.

"You've been feeling this," he accused.

Her gaze turned wary, an admission.

"Why did you not tell me?" he demanded, and then realized she had been telling him. From the very beginning, she'd warned of the curse.

"How much time, Margaret?" he asked, a coldness stealing through him.

The blue in her eyes lightened with the bleakness of her situation.

He took her hand and tried to pry open her fingers. They would not give.

Heath pressed his lips to her fingertips, his brain frantically trying to reason this out. There must be a way to stop it. There had to be a way.

"Why now?" he asked. "Why is she attacking you so virulently but didn't do so yesterday or the day before? Does she have more power? Is there a reason?"

"Does *who* have more power?" Laren asked as if she feared the answer.

But Heath didn't have time for explanations. "Stay with her," he ordered, before racing from the room. He took the steps upstairs three at a time and didn't bother to knock on Rowan's door.

"Fenella has her," he said to the valet. "She's trying to claim her. This is not how it was with her brothers, is it? Why now? *Why?*"

"I do not know, Laird."

"Someone must know," Heath said, desperate for answers.

"You must find someone who thinks like a witch."

"And where will I find one?" Heath threw out at him, annoyed with such a paltry suggestion.

"I don't know. Do you know a magician?"

"Not one who has true power, or believes he does —" Heath started and then stopped. "Swepston."

"I beg your pardon, Laird."

"Swepston claims he has knowledge or power. He had Margaret's book, the one she claimed was from Fenella. He destroyed it."

"But did he read it?" Rowan asked.

"I shall find out," Heath vowed, hope welling up in him. "Thank God, I ignored the fact that the bastard hadn't left."

He charged down the stairs and out of the house. He didn't stop until he reached the stables, where a number of his clansmen were cleaning. He grabbed the first man he saw, Irwin. "Where is Swepston?"

Irwin's eyes grew large, a sign as always that he was afraid he was about to do something wrong.

"I know I banished him, Irwin, but I also know he is still here. I was angry with him and for good cause. However, now he has the opportunity to earn his place in my trust. I won't hurt him, but I must speak to him."

One of the stable lads, Madoc, said, "Go ahead and tell him, Irwin. I think he already knows."

"I *do* know he is here," Heath said. "I saw him helping the other day. Tell me, Irwin."

Irwin looked to the others. Some appeared cautious, unlike Madoc.

"Where is he?" Heath repeated, his temper growing.

And then Irwin's gaze went past Heath's shoulder. Heath released his hold and turned. Swepston stood ten feet from him.

The man had cut his beard and wore decent clothes instead of his robe. "You want me, Laird."

Right there was an improvement. Swepston had not recognized Heath's authority before. And Heath could meet him halfway. "I need you," he said. "Come with me."

Together the men walked up the path. Heath could feel the approval of the lads behind him. They liked Swepston.

Close to the house, Heath stopped. "We

are kinsmen. Cousins."

"Clansmen," Swepston agreed. "Distant relations."

Heath drew a deep breath and released it before saying, "I don't come to you as the chieftain. I searched you out as a man who loves a woman who is dying."

"The Chattan."

"Aye. You may have your wish —"

"I wished her no harm."

Heath didn't know if he believed him, but now was not the time to argue. "Is the curse real?"

"Aye, Laird, and placed on the Chattan by your great-great-great-grandmother."

"Did you read her book?"

"I looked through it."

"Was there anything in there about the first and the last?"

Swepston frowned. "Not that I read. Most of it was about soap and cheese making."

"But a few spells?"

"If one believes in that sort of thing."

"You don't?" Heath didn't hide the surprise in his voice.

"I'm no fool. There were love spells and other woman nonsense. I don't believe in that."

"Was there anything about coming back to life?" Heath asked. There was a time when he'd have felt foolish to ask such a question. No longer.

"What is this about?" Swepston asked.

"She's dying," Heath said. "Lady Margaret is losing her life to the curse. I must stop it. Do you understand? I meant what I said that day you and I had our confrontation when I spoke of how the curse has hurt us more than the Chattans. It has been a weight on our clan."

"And what would you do?"

"Whatever I must. You and I have had our differences. I don't expect those to vanish. At the same time, you know more about the history of our people than anyone else. I need your help now. I need to understand this curse."

Swepston took a step back. "I don't know if I can help."

Heath wasn't certain he heard him correctly. "What about this Druid and pagan nonsense? Isn't there something there?"

"I know stories my *seanamhair* told me, but that's all." He referred to his grandmother, a woman Heath faintly remembered as being someone everyone turned to for healing or advice.

"So you've been rousing the crofters and inciting them against me using something you don't know about?"

Swepston had the good sense to look sheepish. "I know a bit about it."

"Then tell me what you know," Heath demanded, "before I wrap my hands around your neck and choke it out of you."

"What of the man who said he needed me?" Swepston countered.

"He's about to be beaten. *Talk.* Give me *anything* you know."

Swepston's expression turned nervous, as it should have. Then he said, "I know the way of herbs. They hold remedies."

"Good," Heath said, trying to sound encouraging, even though his fists were clenched. "Perhaps they could help. She can't move or speak."

"I know of no herb for that."

Heath swore under his breath. He tried to be reasonable. "Margaret has had an attack. It's strong. Overpowering. Her brother in London is ill from the curse but his seems to be a long time coming. The Chattans suspect that the curse is stronger because they are here. Her other brother is also ill but I sense what Margaret has is different."

"That could be —"

"But you don't know."

"I don't know," Swepston said. "I do know that the moon is important. The full moon is powerful."

"Do we have a full moon now?" Heath didn't believe he had noticed the moon.

"Yes, but after tonight it will wane."

"How can I use that power? And don't tell me that you don't know."

"But I don't, Heath. My *seanamhair* used to keep mistletoe in water. She'd sprinkle it around to ward off spirits."

"Spirits! That is what I'm looking for — something to ward off dead spirits. Do you have this water?"

"It is easy enough to make. You take some mistletoe and place it in water —"

"Do you have mistletoe?" Heath said with impatience.

"Of course not," Swepston informed him. "But," he added, catching the militant gleam in Heath's eye, "I know where mistletoe is."

"And where is that?"

"It covers one side of the tree where Brodie was murdered," Swepston answered.

Heath's mind reeled. Was there a connection between his brother's death and the Chattan curse?

"Even if we do collect the mistletoe," Swepston continued, "where would we take it to be used against Fenella?"

A puzzle that had pestered him since that morning on Innis Craggah suddenly made sense. The cat, Owl, had taken him to the graves. She had led Margaret to the graves. That was where the power was. The grave was the source of what was left of Fenella.

He took Swepston by the arm. "Come with me, man."

"Where are we going?" Swepston asked.

"First, to the stables where we shall hitch up a cart. Then we shall collect mistletoe. And then we are going to battle a witch."

"Why do we need the cart?" Swepston asked.

"Because I'm not leaving Margaret behind."

Swepston wouldn't let Heath just chop down the mistletoe. It had to be "cut." Swepston chanted words from his grandmother under his breath as he did it.

They put the mistletoe leaves in the bottle filled with water brought for that purpose. Heath corked the bottle. He wore his naval cutlass and pistol from his belt. A dirk was tucked into his boot.

Margaret was buried in the cart beneath a stack of blankets. She seemed to grow smaller as the effects of the curse took hold of her body, curling her into a fetal position.

Swepston looked to Heath and said, "I

did not wish this on her. I'd wish it on no one."

"It makes a difference when we are faced with results of what we wish on others, doesn't it?" he answered.

"Aye," Swepston agreed soberly. "You are right, Laird. This has been a curse on us as well."

"Then let us end it here. Tonight."

Before leaving the great oak, Swepston sprinkled water with the mistletoe around Margaret. Heath did not see that any of Swepston's ministrations had an impact on her. He prayed that if this was the solution, he was not too late.

He could feel her watching him, sense the trust she placed in him.

Before he left the oak, Heath placed his hand upon his brother's bloodstains. After a moment's prayer that Brodie's spirit would help guide him, he returned to the horses and they were on their way.

The hour was growing late when they reached the part of Loch Awe's shore that was across from Innis Craggah. The full moon was rising and soon all would be bathed in a silvery light.

Once again, a bit of coin convinced Gibson to row them to the island. The fisherman was not pleased to be out on such a cold night. Fortunately, the loch was calm, but Heath knew that could be deceiving.

He held Margaret in his arms as Swepston and Gibson rowed. He didn't know what to anticipate. Considering the storm they'd experienced before, he feared what Fenella's power could do. But they had no trouble reaching the shore.

Once they'd landed the boat, Swepston asked, "What now?"

"Grab a torch, bring the water, and follow me," Heath answered, holding Margaret in his arms. "Gibson, we will return."

"Aye, Laird," the fisherman answered. He stood in the boat's remaining torchlight. "I'll be here, but don't tarry. My wife likes me in the bed."

Heath had no trouble picking up the path that led to the graves. It was darker here. Heath thought it was because of the forest and overhanging branches, even winter bare. But when he looked up, he realized clouds were gathering in the sky.

Clouds. A storm. *Fenella.*

Had she just started to realize what they were about? For whatever reason, they had made it this far without her detecting them. He needed to be faster. He picked up the pace, trusting his instinct.

Margaret weighed next to nothing in his

arms. It was as if she was disappearing. The muscles of her body were cramped and had to be painfully tight. "Please, hold on, Maggie," he whispered.

"That's odd that a storm seems to be brewing so quickly," Swepston observed. He was a good pace behind them now with the torch.

"All the more reason to move faster," Heath ordered.

At last, he came to the clearing where the graves were. He placed Margaret on the ground between them, right where he'd last seen Owl. "Be brave, my love." Her eyes were closed. There was hope but not time to spare.

He turned to look for Swepston. Thankfully the man was approaching with the torch and the water.

Heath walked to meet him at the forest's edge, anxious to start. "Hurry, man."

Swepston thrust the torch at Heath. "Hold this." He reached into the depths of his cloak to pull out the bottle, which he offered to Heath.

At that moment, there was a cracking sound overhead. Heath grabbed the bottle from Swepston and jumped back as one of the pines, the thickness of a man's body came crashing down upon them.

Heath escaped injury. Swepston was not so lucky. There was the sound of breaking bones.

Swepston groaned, dazed by what had happened, but he was alive.

Stunned by the suddenness of the tree falling, Heath started to set aside the water and the torch to help his clansman, but he heard another sound of splintering wood. Another tree came down, right where he had been standing a second ago. And then there were more sounds of wood splitting.

Heath ran for the clearing. He fell to the ground once he reached the graves as if they were touchstones that offered safety.

Margaret was awake, watching.

Her gaze in the torchlight was one of complete faith. He felt she should be more cautious. It had been Swepston who'd had some idea of what to do with the mistletoe water once they reached the graves. Heath didn't have an inkling, so he improvised. He started wetting his fingers and sprinkling the water around the perimeter of the clearing, staying away from the pines.

He assumed that there was some sort of chant or incantation that should be repeated. He didn't know of any so he relied on what he knew. "Dear God in heaven, help me." He repeated it over and over, but what played in his mind were Rowan's words about "the first and the last." He continued until he'd emptied the bottle of its contents. He returned to Margaret, placing his hand upon her, waiting to see if this old remedy would free them of Fenella. Maggie was still curled tightly.

The moon came out from behind the clouds.

All was quiet. Not even Swepston made a sound, and Heath prayed the man was all right.

The minutes ticked by, marked by the racing beat of his heart.

Nothing moved. Nothing changed.

And he felt frustration because what was he supposed to expect? How would he know if he'd helped Margaret?

"Fenella? Are you there?" His voice echoed in the night. "Are you done torturing us? Are you ready to return to your bloody grave?"

Silence.

The taunts helped him, though. They made him feel as if he was doing something . . . as if there *was* something he could do.

And what if there wasn't?

What if the illness that gripped Margaret was nothing more than some strange malady? Or a sickness that the physician at Dalmally could have cured *if* Heath had left her at Marybone? What if this was all just some elaborate trick of the mind as he'd suggested to Margaret many a time?

Then again, trees didn't fall without a reason. Cats didn't disappear. Storms on the loch didn't purposefully steer boats away from shores.

And that is when the hairs at the nape of Heath's neck started to tingle. He stood, holding his torch.

She was here.

He pushed the torch into the ground beside Margaret and pulled his cutlass from its scabbard.

The trees around the clearing began to waver as if his eyes were out of focus. The moonlight grew brighter. The torch flared, surprising Heath. He turned to it, sword in hand.

No one was there save Margaret. They were here, together. He took courage from her presence and faced the woods.

"Face me, you bloody witch. *Come meet me,"* he roared, done with waiting.

And his challenge was heard.

A shadow moved among the trees, its form human.

Heath waited as it took shape. This was

no crone . . . but a man. A man Heath could fight. Confidence surged through him. He would defeat this curse.

The man moved from the shadows and stepped into the moonlit clearing — and Heath found himself facing his brother, Brodie.

CHAPTER TWENTY

Brodie did not look like he came from the grave but exactly as Heath had seen him last almost three years ago. His hair was lighter than Heath's and his beard a bit heavier. He also had bluer eyes, more like their sisters'.

Heath's chest tightened. Tears threatened. He'd so longed to see his brother one last time, and here he was.

Brodie spoke. "Hello, brother. I imagine you are surprised."

Dear God, this sounded like Brodie. His brogue was heavier than Heath's. Richer.

A wind swept through the clearing. It ruffled Brodie's hair, a sign that he was no ghostly apparition but solid and whole.

Heath dropped his sword arm. He yearned to move toward his brother but caution held him back.

Still, he had to speak to him. "I've missed you."

"I know you have." Brodie shook his head sadly. "That was bad business with Dara."

"Aye, it was. And with Rowlly as well."

Brodie shrugged. "He was always a man led by his peter. You know Janet told him when he could stand up and when he could sit."

Heath remembered this conversation. Brodie had said these exact words to him one night before Heath had taken his leave to return to his ship and his career. "I never meant to come back here," he heard himself confess to his brother.

"I know you didn't. I didn't mean for Dara to murder me. Bad doings with the Macnachtans. I should have been wary."

"I miss you, Brodie," Heath said. "We all do. I'm not the man you were. Not the leader."

"You are a good laird," Brodie answered. "You are learning patience. I see that."

"Do you, Brodie? Where you are, do you see everything?"

Brodie's answer was a smile, and Heath felt blessed to be in his brother's presence once more. Fear left him. He began walking toward Brodie, outstretching his arms, wanting to welcome him with a hug.

And then Brodie said, "You are going to have to give up the Chattan, Heath. You can't have her."

Heath stopped in his tracks. "She's mine. My wife. I've handfasted to her, Brodie. I will not let her go without a fight."

"She's already gone, brother. Fenella's taken her. She's left you."

Heath turned in alarm.

Margaret lay where he'd placed her, her eyes closed, her skin deathly pale.

"No." The denial was pulled from the very bowels of his being. He started toward her. She could not have passed, not without him being aware.

And then he knew. That was not his brother but Fenella having her way. She knew his weakness.

If he was to save Margaret, he could not let the witch distract him.

He wheeled round, raised his sword and charged the apparition.

Brodie raised his arm as if to ward off the blow. Instead, a powerful force struck Heath in the chest, throwing him backward. He hit the ground, the wind knocked out of him.

"Don't fight this," Brodie said. "You can't. Fenella vowed the destruction of the Chattan and so it shall be for eternity."

Heath forced himself to breathe. He came to his feet, lifted his sword — and felt it fly from his hands. Brodie had orchestrated that with a wave of his hand through the air.

"You won't come close to me," Brodie explained. "You can try, but you will not defeat me."

"I don't want to defeat you," Heath answered. "I want Fenella gone. I want her out of our lives. She is not of me and my clansmen. She doesn't represent you."

"But I'm here," Brodie said, opening his arms like a magician to show he hid no tricks.

"This isn't you," Heath said. "You can't be here. You are gone, Brodie. You are not with us on this earth."

"Do you really believe that?" his brother asked. "Can you not believe your own eyes?"

There it was again, the challenge of belief.

"I can't," Heath said, his heart heavy. "I won't."

"You would deny me, your brother, for a woman?"

"A woman *I love,*" Heath said. He lunged for his brother. Again, Brodie easily deflected him. They did not touch and yet it was as if hands grasped Heath and threw him to the ground.

And he knew he was defeated. He could not fight this force that was Brodie. He couldn't even come close to the specter.

"There will be other women to love," Brodie said. "Look at me. I loved Dara. Love did not suit me well. Leave this place, Heath. Leave the Chattan to me."

Brodie's voice was that of the devil, of temptation, of evil.

There had to be a way to defeat him. There must be.

The first and the last. The phrase echoed in Heath's mind.

Margaret was the first female born of Charles Chattan's line.

Heath was the last male of Fenella's — and he knew then how to end the curse forever. He understood what kept Fenella alive. His blood was her blood, passed down through the ages.

He pulled his dirk from his boot. The blade was so sharp it could cut silk.

Brodie laughed. "Your weapons are useless against me," he said as if pitying Heath. "There is nothing you can do, especially on this spot where my power is so strong." Brodie lifted his face to the sky. "There is power in nature. These trees, this earth, they know our stories. They outlive all of us. They are our silent witnesses."

"Aye," Heath agreed. "But your time has come, Fenella. I cannot let you continue to destroy. It's done."

"It will *never* be done," Brodie said. His smile was slow and confident, a goading expression the good man his brother had been would have never used. It made what Heath was about to do easier.

Heath lifted the dirk into the air.

Brodie's eyes lit up in anticipation of another chance to prove his power.

But Heath was not going to waste the dirk upon an apparition. Instead, he plunged it into his own heart.

The pain was not immediate. It took several beats before his body recognized the attack. Heath felt his heart falter, miss its rhythm, tighten and then explode.

Brodie cried out, *"What have you done?"*

Heath smiled, a coldness starting to gather in him. "I've defeated you, Fenella. I'm the last. You are a parasite no more."

Before his eyes, Brodie wavered, the air around him shimmering slightly, and then he disappeared. He evaporated.

His beloved brother was gone.

And Heath was done.

He sank to the ground. The knife was still in his heart. It gave him time, time to gaze lovingly at Margaret. His beautiful, generous Maggie.

Then, to his amazement, she stretched out

an arm, spreading the fingers of her hand as if testing them. Her body unfolded and she had the sudden strength to sit up.

In that moment, he knew complete love.

He'd sacrificed all for her and he was well pleased. He'd protected her and he had saved generations into the future of not only the Chattans but the Macnachtans as well — and in that moment, he was surrounded by knowledge, by understanding.

He understood why Fenella had attacked Margaret so virulently. It had nothing to do with the full moon but with her own survival. She couldn't let him breed with Margaret. The curse would then destroy her line.

But now he'd resolved all, and a sense of peace and wonder filled him. Love had destroyed the curse. Love was the only force more powerful than revenge.

Margaret cried out his name and crawled to his side. She leaned over him.

"Heath, you shouldn't have done this. I'm not worth your life."

He smiled. She was wrong.

"Rose gave her life for her love," he managed to say. His legs were very cold. Her warmth felt good. "It's complete now."

"It isn't," Margaret said. Her tears fell upon his cheek. "This is not right."

"Pull the dirk out," he said, raising his

hand to touch one more time the softness of her hair. "It will help me go quick."

"I don't want to —"

He shushed her softly. "I love you, Maggie. And if there is an eternity, I shall love you for all of it. Now be brave."

"I love you," Margaret whispered. She leaned to rest her cheek against his. "I was always meant to love you." She pulled the knife from his chest.

It would be seconds now. What was left of his heart's strength would pump the blood free and he would die in his Maggie's arms. There was no better place on earth to be.

He closed his eyes, wanting to drink in with his last breaths the feel and the touch of her. His mind grew dizzy, his thinking confused.

As if from a great distance, he heard the sound of a cat purring.

He could almost feel the animal here beside him, feel her fur against his neck. Her purring calmed him and he drifted off to death's deep sleep —

"The bleeding has stopped, Heath. *It's done.* Can you hear me? You are safe. We are safe."

There was excitement in Margaret's voice. Her hands shook him.

Slowly, he opened his eyes.

395

The clearing was exactly as it had been moments before, cold and silvery in the moonlight. The torch still burned.

But the pain in his chest was gone.

Margaret leaned over him. Her hair was down the way he liked it and she was smiling. "You are whole," she whispered. "It's a miracle."

He reached up to touch her hair. "I heard purring," he confessed. "Just as you claimed you heard after the coach accident."

"You defeated Fenella," Margaret said, wonder in her voice. "You battled her and you won."

Heath dared to sit up then. He felt no twinge of pain. He was weak and bruised, but whole. There wasn't even blood around the slit material of his shirt.

"Did you see any of what happened?" he asked her.

She shook her head. "I could not. I heard you speaking but I was not able to make out the words."

"Brodie was —" he started and then stopped. The vision that had been here had not been his brother, and Heath would not desecrate his memory by linking him to Fenella.

Margaret wrapped her arms around him. Her body felt warm against his. "I did see you plunge your knife into your own chest. I was so afraid."

"But then the paralysis ended."

She nodded. "How did you know to do that?"

"It was something Rowan said that made me believe it might work. He is an odd character."

"Yes, he is. He's devoted to Harry."

"And to you. He urged me to think of all angles and mentioned you were the first female born of your line since Charles Chattan. I'm the last male to Fenella's direct line, and I started wondering what if we were keeping her alive. We, with our superstitions and fears."

"Fears you don't have," she said, nodding.

No, he didn't. Not any longer.

Heath rose to his feet. He offered Margaret his hand and helped her up. Her legs were strong and the color had returned to her cheeks. She was completely as she should be.

"Let's go home," he said.

Epilogue

Of course, no one challenged the union of Margaret Catherine Chattan and Heath Graham Davis Macnachtan, and so after the banns had been duly read and noted, they were married on the twenty-second of February, 1815, under a bough of mistletoe.

It was good winter day with fine sunshine and a wind that the pines surrounding the small church could hold at bay.

Everyone from the glen was there, with the exception of Owen Campbell — and it was just as well that he wasn't in attendance since he would not have wished them well. Even Swepston, who had miraculously survived his injuries, was present to bless the union in the old ways.

Margaret could not love Heath more than in the moment when she said her wedding vows. The formal words of the church sounded stilted compared to the promises they'd spoken in love that night in the library when they'd handfasted themselves. Still, it was a proud moment for her when they were introduced as man and wife to all present in the kirk.

Her joy was even more complete because both of her brothers, strong and healthy, stood beside her.

Her brother Neal, Lord Lyon had the most amazing transformation. The last time Margaret had seen him, he'd been too weak to even turn himself over in bed. They'd known he was dying and their prayer had been that he would live to see the birth of his son. Now he walked on his own and moved with grace and purpose. He'd even brought his two young stepsons with him. Margaret loved Jonathan and Christopher as nephews.

His wife, Thea, was confined to home due to the baby they expected at any moment.

"You should have stayed with her," Margaret said.

"I would not have missed your wedding," Neal vowed, adding, "As head of the family, I wish to witness your happiness. You deserve this, Margaret, and so much more. Thea wishes she was here as well."

Neal took her hand. "You gave me back my life. I knew the moment the curse was broken. I sat up with a strength I'd not had in months. It was necessary for me to be here, Margaret. I wanted to welcome the man you loved fully into the family."

Harry and his wife, Portia, were also in attendance. Portia told Margaret of how afraid she had been that she was going to lose her husband. "He was paralyzed," she confided. "It was frightening."

Margaret understood exactly what she meant.

Now Harry kept up with Jonathan and Christopher and a host of lads from the glen. Over the days preceding the wedding, they had all ridden, hunted and competed in games of sport on Marybone's front lawn, actions that bonded the Chattans and the Macnachtans.

Margaret also liked the quiet pride that Heath was developing. Her brothers had been complimentary of the Macnachtan horseflesh. Both Neal and Harry were avid horsemen, and Heath had shared with them his plans for the new stables. They were keen to be a part of the enterprise. If Heath had felt any intimidation over having her well-known brothers, with their reputations for being the best at everything they attempted, under his roof, those fears vanished in the good-humored camaraderie they offered him. He was their brother-in-marriage and they honored him with their acceptance.

After the wedding ceremony, there was a dance that included everyone far and wide. The Scots did not stint when it came to celebrating. Heath announced that he had buried a small keg of whisky to ensure the success of the day. It was an old custom, one designed to appease kelpies and sprites. However, by mid-afternoon, Heath was leading the party of men armed with shovels to dig that keg up. After all, what good was whisky in the ground?

And who knew if kelpies and sprites would even appreciate it? Better to drink a dram or two or three in honor of the happy couple.

The celebrating went long into the night and continued after the Macnachtan had chased the bridal couple to their bed with good-humored suggestions. Heath barred the door, not wanting any of that rowdy bunch to think about coming and joining them.

"They would," he predicted. "Anything to see you happy. They love you as much as I do."

"And I return that love," Margaret said. She took her husband's hand. They now shared the room that had been his alone. A wood fire burned in the hearth and she saw that Cook and Cora had prepared a table of food and drink to last them through the night and for days to come if they had a mind to never leave this haven.

She continued soberly, "I'm surprised at how many different facets there are to love. I thought I could only care about my family, but my heart has expanded to include so many others."

"And it shall keep expanding," he promised. "There will be no shortage of love between us or around us."

They made love then. Happy, joyous love.

The act of joining was no longer just a rite of nature. It was the communication of two souls who longed to be together.

And in that night, she knew his seed had taken hold. They would truly become one.

Later, as she lazed in his arms, she said, "My only regret is to lose Owl. We never saw her again after that night on Innis Craggah."

"If you are right and she was the spirit of Rose, then she'd accomplished what she wanted. Her intent, I believe, was to ensure that when the time was ripe, I would know to return to the site of those graves."

His arms around Margaret tightened. "She'll come back to us someday," he said.

"When she is ready."

The wedding feasting didn't end after a single week. Margaret found herself feted wherever she went.

Neal returned to London just in time to be present for the birth of his daughter. Grace Elizabeth Chattan was certain that the curse was truly broken. Their father had hoped that Margaret's birth had been a signal, but she now realized that she had just a part of the events that needed to be in place to destroy Fenella's power.

The first of May, when the hint of spring was in the air and the rebuilding of the stables well under way, Margaret announced her pregnancy. Heath had already known, or so he said. The entire clan was happy for her, and Margaret felt pleasure at being truly part of them.

Later that same day, she and Laren went for a walk. They chose a path that led down by the loch, and that was where they caught Irwin hunched over talking to himself by a group of bushes.

Or at least Margaret *thought* he was talking to himself. A moment's listening brought about the sound of meowing.

"Irwin, what are you doing?" Margaret asked.

The man practically jumped out of his skin. "Nothing, my lady," he said, using his big body to block her view of the kitten.

"You are doing something," she insisted. "You have a kitten? Why are you hiding her?"

His gaze dropped to the ground. Irwin could look so guilty.

"What is it?" she pressed.

"My ma didn't want the kitten. She said she's sickly."

"Sickly? How?" Margaret asked.

"She's not born right," Irwin answered, picking up the small white cat and showing her to them. The cat had wide blue eyes . . . and folded-over ears. Just like Owl's.

"She was fine in the beginning," Irwin said, "but after a few weeks her ears bent over. Ma said that's a sign the cat's not strong. She told me to bring her out here and let her go to fend for herself, but I like the wee creature. I don't want to leave her."

"Let me see," Laren said, taking the kitten from the big man. She held the kitten up for Margaret to see. "Her ears *are* funny."

"Her ears are a blessing," Margaret said as she reached to pet the kitten, who licked her gloved finger with a tiny rough tongue. She wasn't a copy of Owl. Her eyes were the blue of the sky and she had a patch of black under her chin and on one paw. "You see her, right?" she asked them.

"I see her," Irwin replied with his easy simplicity.

"I'm *holding* her," Laren said. "She has the most unusual eyes, even for a cat. They seem to swallow her little face."

"Yes, they do," Margaret agreed, feeling a mixture of happiness and sadness. They all saw the kitten. But this cat was not Owl . . . still Margaret understood that here was a sign from Rose. A gift on this day when she'd made such a happy announcement. And, perhaps, the confirmation Margaret had wanted that Rose now rested peacefully.

"I'd like the kitten," Margaret said to Irwin. "That is, if you will let me have her."

"You don't think she is sick?" he asked.

"I believe she is very healthy, and I like her ears."

"I do as well," Laren said. "We have been needing a cat in the house."

Irwin smiled his pleasure. "Then you can have her, my lady. I was having trouble keeping her safe. You know I always take care of the pigs, but she keeps finding trouble. Just now I found her caught in the wild rose bushes here. I scratched my hand rescuing her."

"You are very kind," Margaret said to Irwin, meaning the words. "And you have done a good job protecting her."

The big man blushed at her praise.

"And we shall call kitty Rosie after the rose bushes Irwin rescued her from," Laren said, taking complete command of the cat. "That is the perfect name."

"Yes, it is," Margaret agreed. "The perfect name indeed."

Heath was happy to see the cat as well, and as Rosie grew, her folded-over ears remained.

She proved herself to be a good and astute mouser, earning the approval of Cook. And there was no one in the house who wouldn't happily play with her or let her curl up in his lap.

However, once James Robert Macnachtan was born on a brisk morning in November, Rosie forgot about the rest of them. She purred her approval of this new member to their household and from that moment on became Jaime's self-appointed bodyguard, or as Heath said, Jaime's body*cat.*

And as time passed, Marybone became known as much for the barn cats with the folded-over ears, wide, comprehending eyes, and almost human intelligence, as they were for the horses the Macnachtans bred.

As for the laird and his lady, theirs was a mighty love story, the stuff of which legends are created.

Margaret took to keeping a journal, the sort chatelaines pass down from one to the other. On the first page, she wrote these words to her children: "Love well, love fully, love completely. Because in life, love is all that truly matters."